Let's Be Alone Together

Let's Be Alone Together

An anthology of new short stories

Edited by Declan Meade

The Stinging Fly

A Stinging Fly Press Book

2 4 6 8 10 9 7 5 3 1

Let's Be Alone Together is published in September 2008

Set in Palatino
Printed by Betaprint, Dublin

The Stinging Fly Press
PO Box 6016
Dublin 8
www.stingingfly.org

ISBN: 978-1-906539-02-3

The Stinging Fly gratefully acknowledges funding support from
The Arts Council / An Chomhairle Ealaíon and Dublin City Council.

Baby, let's get married,
we've been on our own too long.
Let's be alone together.
Let's see if we're that strong.

—Leonard Cohen & Sharon Robinson,
'Waiting for the Miracle'

Contents

by way of an introduction

Rumours of the short story's imminent demise have been in perpetual circulation in recent times. People don't want to read them, we hear; publishers don't want to publish them, we're told. Yet certain facts stack up against the doom-and-gloom merchants. Take, for example, the recent success of writers like Kevin Barry, Claire Keegan and Philip Ó Ceallaigh; or the arrival of new short story collections from writers such as Anne Enright and Colm Tóibín; or the ongoing exemplary output of contemporary masters of the form, Alice Munro and William Trevor.

The publication of this second anthology of stories from the Stinging Fly Press can be seen as further proof that the short story is, in fact, in robust good health. We received more than four hundred stories from around two hundred and eighty writers in response to our call for submissions late last year. Reading through all the submitted stories, it quickly became clear that a) we would have more than enough good stories to fill a second book and that b) there were enough good stories by new writers to allow us to choose an entirely new line-up of authors this time.

In *Let's Be Alone Together*, twenty different writers give us twenty very different short stories—reading them all together, we get a sense of just how versatile the form is. Yes, it makes serious demands on the writer, but equally it allows great freedoms. In the writing of a good short story, fortune favours the brave.

The greatest pleasure in working as editor of *The Stinging Fly* comes from the excitement of finding new work by new writers and being able to share that new work with our readers. I had already put the stories for the anthology in order when I discovered that Jim O'Donoghue and D. Gleeson, the authors of the first and the last story respectively, were having their fiction published for the first time. I was pleased to learn that a third writer, Helena Nolan, was making her fiction debut here as well.

In working with these newcomers and with all the other writers in preparing their stories for publication, it was heartening to see the level of commitment each one of them had. It's not the word count that matters, we said in our original call for submissions, it's making the words count. So long as so many fine writers are drawn to the challenges of writing short stories, and so long as they give such great care to getting it right, then readers, I'm sure, will willingly take up the invitation in this book's title.

Declan Meade
Editor

Dublin, August 2008

Let's Be Alone Together

Carson's Trail

Jim O'Donoghue

SHORTLY AFTER HIS SEVENTH BIRTHDAY, Carson had flown over to England with his father, but now his father was sick. Soon after they'd arrived, he spent two days in hospital; but on the third day they sent him away with a bottle of medicine. Now he hardly had the strength to get out of bed and eat breakfast; he dozed in an armchair with his head nodding forward on his chest, or he watched TV; he did nothing now but look out at Carson from behind a pane of glass.

Carson and his father were staying with Carson's grandmother in a bungalow in a village with a stream at one end, hills around two sides of it, and a shop on the main street that sold everything from Matchbox cars to envelopes to dog food. Beside the shop was a playground where Carson went to play whenever his grandmother could leave his father. She was nearly eighty and her small, lined face showed its feelings only in the rearrangement of its creases, but he could tell that it made her happy to see him swing himself or use the climbing frame or race about the edges of the playing field.

The older boys from the village were uninterested in playing with Carson but they came almost every morning to his grandmother's garden. She gave them apples and biscuits and asked about their parents—and afterwards they fought or rolled each other about in the little wilderness at the back of the bungalow or they played throw and catch with Carson's toys and teased him when he didn't understand their accents. He would have preferred to stay indoors, away from them, but his grandmother told him it was summer still and he ought to be outside. Carson only half-believed her; in the Nantucket summer he'd just flown in from, even walking or lifting an arm had made him break out in a sweat. Here the wind seemed to tear through the trees from morning to night and clouds swept constantly across the sun, throwing huge cold shadows.

'And when the summer's over,' his grandmother said, 'the radio says we'll get an Indian summer.'

'What's that?' he asked.

'It's a special kind of summer we get sometimes when the real one finishes,' she said. 'We don't always get it, but maybe this year we will.'

In the third week of his father's illness, the old lady helped Carson put a tent up in the garden. It was a windy day and while she wrestled with the ropes and the flysheet, Carson watched her with love. He hadn't known that he loved her before—before it was nothing more than a word to him—but seeing her struggle against the gusts of wind, catching the edge of the canvas again each time it flew from her hands, made him know he did. That week he spent a lot of time in the tent, sitting on the sheet of blue tarpaulin she'd laid inside, while the light from outside changed shade as the sun moved across the sky. During part of every day he had to share the tent with the boys from the village, but in the evenings it was his until bedtime. The day when it poured with rain from early morning right through and the boys didn't come, Carson sat in the tent, in the greenish light thrown by the walls, and listened to the water drip from the trees. That was his favourite day.

One night towards the end of that third week, Carson was woken by a shout. His father slept in a bedroom overlooking the large, tangled garden at the back of the bungalow, while Carson slept on a mattress on the floor of his grandmother's room across the corridor. He heard his father call out several times in a loud, strained voice; after some time, the old lady woke and put on her dressing gown and went to him, but even then he continued to moan loudly and to shout. Carson sat up and listened while his father shouted; he went on shouting as if he couldn't help himself, saying things that Carson had never heard him say before.

'Oh my God,' he shouted. 'Oh Jesus, Jesus Christ.'

When his grandmother came back into their bedroom, Carson could see she was crying. His father still called out, but for a while she only sat on the edge of her bed, scrabbling at the edge of her nightgown with her hands. To Carson it felt as if he was trapped in the semidarkness of the room, in a cage made of sound: the bed in the next room creaked constantly while his father called out to his mother, who sat above Carson on her bed, rubbing her hands against the hem of her gown. Between the rustling of the gown and his father's shouts, if Carson listened hard enough he could hear himself breathing—short, hard breaths as if he was running away from something or standing outside the principal's office waiting for punishment.

In the end the old lady went to the phone and rang the doctor. Carson heard her dialling in the hallway. She got no answer; she must have known that she would get no answer, but she called again anyway. The doctor would never answer the phone, however often she called; Carson somehow understood this, even at the age of seven. When his grandmother went to tell his father the news, his father groaned and began to sob. His sobbing was low and throaty and went on and on, like the sound of a wounded animal, like the horse with an arrow in his side that Carson had seen in a film about General Custer.

Carson didn't like lying there in the darkness being able to hear but not see and he got up and crossed the corridor to his father's room. His father's sheets were covered in raw-looking gobbets of blood, some of them already drying to a dirty brown. His father lay sideways in the bed, being sick into a bowl, his arms clasping his ribs while his mother bent over him, her head near his, holding the bowl steady. When she noticed Carson standing in the doorway, she let go of the bowl and rushed over, pushing him out of the room.

Later, when his father was quiet, she sat down on the edge of Carson's mattress and talked to him, told him stories about the village from when she was a girl, how she had played down by the stream with her brother and sisters, how they climbed over the wall into Miss Webb's orchard to steal the apples. She told him how once they trespassed on Gale's farm and her brother got on the back of an old horse without a saddle and she got on behind him. She talked to him like this for a long time, perhaps for hours; but neither of them felt drowsy, and that night he was allowed to sleep in the tent.

Carson woke with the dawn. He opened the flap of the tent and the sunlight poured in, as it hadn't for several days, with real brightness. Something had scraped the clouds from the sky, which stood above him blue and forthright, not brilliant, but clear and giving off warmth. Perhaps the summer was over, and this was the Indian summer that his grandmother had almost promised him.

It was warm but not warm enough just for dungarees, and he went into the bungalow to fetch a jacket. Inside it was quiet. Usually the old lady would be up making tea, but that morning he didn't see her; he found his jacket hanging on the back of the chair in the hall and went out, closing the door gently behind him. He put his jacket on and ran across the lawn, jumping over the flower bed onto the garden wall and down onto the gravel. At the gate he met the village boys; he was among them for a minute, and they pushed him between them like a pinball until he was dizzy. Then he fell over and cut his knee on the gravel and they left him and went into his grandmother's garden.

Carson got up without crying. He ran up the lane, the way he had often gone with his grandmother when they went out for a walk. The lane led up to the church and away from the playground with its one swing, which swung back and forth when he shifted his weight, squeaking because it was years since anyone had oiled it, away from the village shop with its popsicles and Feasts and model aeroplanes. Carson ran all the way to the top of the lane and then slowed as he jumped down the steps that went one side of the dip and up the steps again on the other side, where he entered the graveyard. This was where his grandfather was buried. He had been here several times since the beginning of his visit, and he knew where the old man's grave was. He ran across to it now and read his name and straightened the jar of flowers his grandmother had brought with them the last time they came.

Some of the flowers were dead, and Carson took the dead ones out and replaced them with fresh wild ones he found in the hedge. Then he ran out of the graveyard through the other gate and went down the lane that came out at the brook. It was a beautiful morning. He hadn't known until then what beautiful could mean, but when he saw the fresh blue light come back off the stream and shine in the grass thick with dew, he heard the word in his head. Taking off his shoes, he tied his laces and stuffed his socks inside and slung them around his neck and waded up the shallow brook until the banks became almost too steep to climb. He pulled himself up to the top of the bank, stinging his hands whenever he grasped the nettles by mistake and pricking his ankles on the thistles. Carson didn't mind the nettles or the thistles; somehow, they could sting him and prick him as much as they liked and he didn't mind.

At the top of the bank was an abandoned car, with only one door on the driver's side and the roof rusted through, the tyres long gone. He sat in the driver's seat and honked the horn, which made no sound except in his imagination. But in his imagination the sound of the horn joined the other sounds of the morning—the wood pigeons and the starlings and the blue tits and a dog barking somewhere and the engine of a tractor starting above him, on the hillside. And so he went on up the road, towards the army ranges.

Carson knew that he mustn't trespass on the army ranges so he turned off after the sign and walked on tiptoe down the gravel drive of someone's house. There were no cars in the driveway, but he clung to the wooded side in case anyone from the house called to him; he was ready to disappear into the trees. But no call came from the house, and Carson passed over the edge of the garden and through a broken fence, coming out as he knew he would at the watercress beds. He was proud of himself for finding a shortcut he had never taken, and finding it by instinct; his grandmother had always led him the long way round to the watercress beds, by the road that everyone took. Feeling tired from all his running, he wended his way to the middle of the beds along the narrow dry path and crouched down. He splashed his hands in the water and washed his face, which he remembered now he hadn't done this morning. But just as he closed his eyes and rubbed his wet hands over his cheeks, he heard a hissing sound, immediately to his right, right into his ear it seemed.

Carson stood quickly and confronted a black swan, which had approached him soundlessly out of nowhere on its webbed feet. Carson backed away and the swan stood its ground and extended its dark neck towards him, its red beak. He had heard that swans could break your arm or your leg with their wings. Carson turned and ran up the narrow path, falling from it now and then and getting his feet caught in the watercress, until he got to the stile. Even with his grandmother he had never passed this point before, but the swan stood blocking his path, and Carson climbed the stile and dropped over onto the other side, into the meadow. Looking back, he saw that the swan hadn't followed him but still stood on the path where he had found it.

Now he was in wild territory. Although he hadn't meant to come so far, he was glad. He would have something new to tell them when he got back home—something they might not have seen themselves, or not for a long time. His father had grown up in this village, but he had never seen his father go through a meadow or climb a fence. At home, his father only walked from their front door to the door of the car. Perhaps when his father was a boy he had gone this way, but if he had he would have forgotten it by now. So Carson put his shoes back on and went on up the meadow.

There was no path through the meadow, which headed straight up the hill that overhung the village. It was dotted with enormous rabbit holes, which were almost wide enough at the mouth for Carson to climb into, and huge bramble bushes. Sometimes there was no other way onward and he had to squeeze through the bramble bushes with the branches clutching at his jacket, pulling it off his shoulders, the thorns sticking in his hair and scratching his face. But eventually he came out at the top of the meadow, where the fields began. He pushed up the middle wire of a barbed wire fence and put one leg through, catching his trousers as he brought his second leg over so that he fell over in the grass, one barb snagging his calf. Carson lay in the grass, holding his leg and expecting to cry, but no tears came.

He felt a long way from home, but when he raised his head he could see past the meadow full of brambles to the village at the bottom of the valley, still where he had left it that morning, and he was reassured. He would have preferred to be back down there, in the village, in his grandmother's garden. At that moment he would have preferred to be there even if the other boys were there too, pushing him around. But he couldn't go back through the barbed wire fence, through the brambles. And so he went on, upwards, through the field—or rather he went around the edge of the field, not to tread down the stiff stalks of wheat. The sky was the same blue, enormous now that he was closer to it, and to protect himself against its vastness he let out a yell, his first word of the morning.

'Geronimo!'

The sky swallowed his word. The field was steep and the top of the hill seemed endlessly far away. Carson took off his jacket and slung it over his shoulder. He had come a long way without any breakfast and as he climbed he looked around for something to eat, but he doubted whether he should eat any of the things he saw in the field. There was the wheat, but it was hard and it had bugs on it and it belonged to the farmer. There was grass growing under the fence, but grass was what made cats sick. Now and then he came across a poppy and he stopped and considered it, but he remembered a film in which poppies made a girl fall asleep, and he knew he mustn't fall asleep. If he fell asleep now, he would never get to the top of the hill, he might never wake up, he might never get back home again.

But now even the word 'sleep', as it sprang to his mind and as it sounded on his lips, made him stagger in his climb. Carson went on, but he was blinded by the blueness of the sky and by the sweat that ran from his eyebrows into his eyes. He kept his eye on the brow of the hill, blinking through the sweat, his feet dragging now, tugged at by the wet grass. The top seemed to come no closer, the sun became too hot for him, the sky seemed to be swallowing him up as if he weren't climbing the hill but climbing a ladder and going further and further into the blue. He wanted to turn and look back at the village; he remembered someone from the village saying to him that from the top of the hill you could see his grandmother's house, plain as day. But he knew if he stopped climbing he would never start again.

Even when he ran out of strength and couldn't climb any further, even when he sank into the wheat and lay there panting and closed his eyes against the Indian summer sky, Carson didn't look. He lay there with his eyes closed and didn't look down, because what would he see if he looked? He knew what he would see; he saw it already in his mind's eye. The men arrived and carried his father's body through the garden on a stretcher, loaded him into the big black car and drove away. His grandmother knelt at the bottom of her wilderness; then she, too, was taken away. The boys from the village came and pulled out the tent pegs, the wind came and blew the tent away. The door was open but the sheets were stained with blood. The house was dark.

Thieves of the Dream

Emer Martin

I DON'T KNOW WHO FIRST SUGGESTED IT, but they both committed the crime. It was a family trip to Yosemite National Park and my little brother and I cringed in the car, while my parents heaved and groaned two big slate rocks into the trunk. They wanted to take the rocks home as ornaments for the front garden. The rocks were so hard to lift that one fell out of the trunk, scraped and bloodied my mom's hands and shattered into two pieces. On reaching our house in Sacramento, they shoved and rolled them towards the flower beds—where they have remained to this day. Three jagged pieces of multicoloured slate rock. Testament to my parent's foreignness and lack of regard for America and all it holds sacred.

Thieves of the dream.

Not only were my parents foreigners to my country, they were foreigners to each other. He was from Iran and she was Irish. Dad was swept up in the 1978 revolution and had spent six years in prison before escaping. While he was being transferred from one prison to the other, he bolted, chained to another man, a common murdering rapist. Together they ran through the streets of Tabriz and hid in the house of Armenian Christians. He had been smuggled over the mountains into Turkey, been arrested by the Turks, and spent six months in a prison in Turkey. From there he had gone to a brother in London, and finally on to America where he had successfully claimed asylum. My brother and I loved that part of the story: he had been saved. He was free. In our black and white way, we knew this was a happy ending.

Maybe Mom and he had been in love once, but not in my lifetime. I was conceived by mistake a few months after they had met in San Francisco. She was just twenty years old and he was thirty-five. They were working in the same restaurant on Fisherman's Wharf. Her past seemed more ordinary, and her country more familiar. She was from a family of five from Belfast. Usually we went back every summer to play on the Victorian redbricked streets with a multitude of cousins. There had been a war there (but not on the scale of my dad's), and now there was peace. We were considered very exotic; dark-eyed, long-nosed Californians. Our dad never travelled with us. He was a stateless citizen and his years of trying for American citizenship finally paid off when he got a green card through my mom. She had won her green card in a lottery. Dad resented this favourable treatment for the Irish. 'America is made for people like me,' he would say, 'people who need it! Not some cowboys who just get it to show off to their friends and use it as a fridge magnet.' This was his elaboration on a story Mom told him of a relative who won the green card and didn't use it. Instead he had it stuck to the fridge with a magnet.

If Dad's favourite story was one of escape, Mom loved to tell how she had been pregnant with my brother and heard the Morrison visas were offered. She filled out five hundred visa applications and mailed them. Not content that this would work, she filled out five hundred more, and drove from Sacramento to Washington. I was a toddler in the back seat. Dad came with us, knowing if she got a foot in the door then he could get a green card from their marriage. After a week of driving and sightseeing, we arrived at a small post office in Virginia. Already there were thousands gathered with trunk loads of envelopes. The police put canvas hampers outside the post office and yelled through bullhorns.

'AT 7PM YOU CAN START FILLING HAMPERS. ANY ENVELOPES IN THE HAMPERS BEFORE 7 P.M. WILL BE DISCARDED. WAIT FOR THE SIGNAL!'

And so it came to pass that at seven o'clock the stunned small-town police watched as thousands of desperate people tried to crush up to the canvas hampers. Many did not make it. They threw the envelopes from behind. The air was full of envelopes. When it was over and the crowd scattered, the post office windows were full of visa applications. There was a large oak tree that looked like it was in blossom. Not with flowers but with white envelopes.

That is my first memory—the tree.

Our lives revolved around the Palace of the Mediterranean, a Persian restaurant in Sacramento. Dad and Mom's pride and joy. My dad's sister Shirin, who owned a share, did all the cooking with the help of a couple of Mexicans. Mom worked alongside Dad and his family but she never learnt more than a smattering of Farsi. All the other Persian kids spoke it, but we were only half Persian, and there is a reason why they call it mother tongue. Persians constantly admonished my dad for not teaching us, we were a great shame to the community, but Dad said it was better we learn something useful like Spanish. Since no one spoke Spanish, we ended up like good Americans with only English to converse in.

'Palace of the Mediterranean!' Mom would joke. 'Iran is nowhere near the Mediterranean. That shower are always pretending to be something they're not.'

She never sat through the numerous visits from relatives. Much to Dad's chagrin she always made an excuse to avoid the crushing boredom of Persian gatherings: the tea sipping and pistachio eating; the obvious bitterness when one family member was doing well, only parallelled by the triumphant disgust when they were confirmed losers. After anyone left the house Aunt Shirin and Dad would burn some herb in an empty can of peas to ward off the evil eye. They would say the name of all the guests and wave the smoke over our faces and around our heads.

Mom said, 'It's a horrible assumption to believe that everyone who comes to your house wishes you ill.'

'They're Persian!' my father would retort. Aunt Shirin nodded in vigorous agreement.

In turn, my grandparents barely disguised their horror at my mom. She was not tall enough, she was not college educated, and she was not tidy. They had no English so we never understood each other. They tried to convince Dad to take us back to Teheran for growth injections in case we'd turn out short like her.

'They are Americans,' he would say proudly. 'What is Iran to them?'

His family knew he would be shot if he ever returned so they did not push too much. My brother and I went to every party Mom avoided, we loved to watch the Persians dance. Aunt Shirin taught us how. Those women were beautiful and glamorous: they always wore black sleek dresses, they had golden olive skin, they dripped with gold, their oval faces painted meticulously, their bleached blonde hair rigorously styled. I loved to watch their long thin arms curling and twisting to the music. The men were dark haired and swayed their hips and held their arms out wide. It was the only thing that saved my brother and me in the eyes of our Persian Sacramento family. We could dance.

Dad would disappear for days on end to Reno or the casinos in Lake Tahoe. Typically, he was quiet and moody and we attributed that to the years of torture and solitary confinement in prison. Iran had always been a sinister place to us. We had heard about SAVAK—the secret police created by the Shah with the help of the CIA. The Persians hated SAVAK; it was responsible for all the disappeared and tortured, for creating the atmosphere of fear under the Shah. In the pre-Islamic regime no one spoke of anything that mattered, for if there were three Persians together, you could count on it that one was the dreaded SAVAK.

When my brother and I looked at Dad we would be so relieved that he was here in America—he had made it. Now that he was safe he was still sad. We understood that, too. We thought we'd be all right. His sadness would not contaminate us because we were born here, born free. I thought, when I pledged allegiance to the flag every day in school, that I could stand taller (even without those growth injections). I felt confident that I could understand more than my classmates simply because I had something to contrast America with.

I remember trying to sleep as a child and hearing those two yell at each other. They should never have married, they had nothing in common. I never doubted that, but instinctively it troubled me. We should never have existed. Just before I slept there were disembodied faces that spun before me: like plucked alone planets, red as pomegranates, each face morphing into another face or object. Sometimes they were the faces of apes, big wide Orangutan faces with those sad, noble eyes. These visions were different from my dreams. My dreams were as heavy as the stolen rocks outside the house. Opaque dreams that did not float. Immovable dreams—unable to lift off.

Dad spent more and more time in Reno. He lost so much money that Aunt Shirin was forced to buy him out of the restaurant. Mom began to bring us home for the entire summer to Ireland. As much as we loved my grandparents and cousins and the long Irish summer days, we were eventually involved in stuff at home and did not want to be separated from our friends and activities. My brother was playing on a basketball team that was the focus of his whole life. In our suburban neighbourhood every garage had a basketball hoop on it but ours was the only one so used. I was on the gymnastics team and training for a big competition in the fall. This was an issue with the Persian side of the family.

'You should play basketball like your brother. Then you'll be tall. Gymnastics will make you short,' Aunt Shirin lamented every time I came home with a medal.

'It's not the sport that makes you short or tall,' I'd argue with her. 'Jockeys don't shrink because they ride horses. They're tiny to begin with.'

'Foolish child.' She'd shake her head while pulling open the restaurant blinds and turning on the many baroque plastic white fountains. 'Height is multi-factorial.' She'd smile to herself, proud of her command of English.

Aunt Shirin's daughter Afsi and her two grandkids had come to live with her from LA after a bitter divorce. The other Persians talked about this in hushed shocked tones.

'Poor Shirin. How is she expected to put up with them all? And those children are deaf. It's hard enough to put up with healthy children but the burden of defective children. That is too much. Did you know he was a plastic surgeon, the husband? Why would anybody leave a surgeon? Afsi got all her work done and then left him. Three nose jobs until she was happy, a boob job and a chin implant and off she flew!'

On and on the family would bemoan the defective children. Finally, we were elevated in their eyes despite our own handicaps of shortness and lack of Farsi. Suddenly, we were white skinned sporty Americans. Our hair even had tints of Irish red in the sun.

Summer was over but Mom didn't come back from Ireland. The low ranch-style wooden house had a bereft look to it. No one cut back the rose bushes when winter came. I ran down the garden path averting my eyes from the long, lonely grass, the chaotic tangle of weeds. As the months passed we missed her so much that the piles of dishes in the sink, the layer of grease on the oven, and the stacks of pizza boxes in the living room almost felt like grief. Mom called every day.

'I've got a good job, pet,' she said, 'I can support us all. Your Granny would love it.'

'We need you here, Mom. You have to come home.'

'Call me Mam. You know I hate Mom. You know life with your dad is unbearable, please, you know that. Can I talk to your brother a minute, love?'

'He's too angry to talk to you.'

'Still? For God's sake. Where is he?'

'Outside at the hoop.'

'Where else… God love him. I'll make this up to ye.'

'Just come home, Mom. Mam.'

My brother stayed out till late at night banging the ball into the hoop. Dad would come from the restaurant at midnight and my brother and I would have just gone to bed. Dad was a very handsome man. Aunt Shirin said that when he was young women would sometimes stop in their tracks on the street. Those nights he would stay up surfing through the soft porn on the cable channels, until I wondered if he missed having Mom to yell at.

After school our house was so empty my brother and I went to Aunt Shirin and Afsi to get fed Ghorme Sabzi, Ghemez, Fes en joon and Ash Reshteh, and to hang around with the deaf children who were both teenage boys now. Wires came out of their heads as if they were robots. I was told that it was not sound they were hearing, not like our version of true sound, but some shape of sound. It was not music they heard but the outline of the noise that built the song. They spoke a little funny but otherwise you could not tell they were deaf and once we got used to the wires sprouting from their skulls we liked them. They were older than us and wilder. They were both going through some tragic Goth stage. Comic books were their passion, they smoked pot and despised the kids who hung out at the mall. Afsi, their mom, was super glamorous even for a Persian. She always looked like she was going to a dinner party even when she was driving around doing errands. She became the hostess of the Palace of the Mediterranean, and my dad said the customers worshipped her.

Mom did not come home that summer. Then September 11th happened. 2001. Mom called from Ireland as we were getting ready for school.

'Turn on your TV.'

We turned it on in time to see the second plane hit the tower. By the time we dragged Dad out of bed he saw the tower fall. He wept. My brother and I held onto each other.

'This is the beginning of a really bad thing,' Dad kept saying.

For days we didn't know what was happening. America was in shock. We put flags up on our house and our car. We put a huge flag up on the Palace of the Mediterranean, in case anyone would question our patriotism. For days I dreamt of the people under the immense rubble, trapped and dying. Faces upon faces came to me in my night visions before I slept. Then Mayor Giuliani, whom we had all come to love and depend on, said they were probably all dead by now. At once, the faces stopped entering my dreams.

Inexplicably, Mom came back almost as soon as the first flights were allowed into the country. She claimed that she wanted to show support for America. Now, she felt like she belonged here. She and Dad told anyone who cared, and no one did, that they were citizens. Technically only Mom had citizenship and Dad had a green card and was in the long process of applying. This has made Dad and Mom American finally, I thought. All their ambivalence and complaining disappeared.

Mom even allowed us to call her Mom. We were so happy to have them back together and not fighting that my brother and I couldn't help guiltily thinking that maybe September 11th had some positive effects after all.

Mom even resumed working in the restaurant doing the book-keeping and ordering. Aunt Shirin was so pleased to see our family mended that all the bad will seemed to dissipate. Mom was forgiven for not being Persian or a tall, blonde American. Afsi took her under her silky, bejewelled wing and Mom bought comics for the deaf kids and included them in everything; she and Afsi went shopping together and Mom started dressing a lot better. Mom said that many older deaf people hated the machines that doctors put in their heads because it was a debasement, that deaf people had a beautiful language called American Sign Language, a language of flying curling hands not tongues. Dad said the world was harsh enough on minorities as it was. Better to always align yourself with the majority.

We went on vacation to Tahoe and skied with Mom, while Dad hit the tables. That night I got up in the hotel room at the casino and went to the bathroom. The light was on and the door ajar, I pushed it tentatively. Dad jumped in fright, caught by surprise in his boxers, counting out stacks of money. Giddy, he smiled at me and we both organised and counted the notes. Maybe, he confided, if his luck kept up, he could pay off his debts and buy back his share of the restaurant from Shirin. That would make Mom happy. We giggled and he gave me a hundred dollar note before I went back to bed.

I don't know why I never told my brother this. Usually I told him everything. When my deaf Goth cousins laughed at Dad, my brother and I would rise to his defence. They could only see him now. When we looked at Dad we saw a hero who had fought a revolution and been unjustly imprisoned.

Each evening, after school, I worked in the Palace of the Mediterranean. I had to agree with Mom about modern Persian tastes. She tried to get Aunt Shirin to revamp the place but my aunt said that's what Persians liked. The white faux Louis XIV furniture, the plastic plants in fake terra-cotta pots, the pastel pink and green carpet, the white plastic fountains, the faded posters of Persepolis and Isfahan. Even the belly dancers on Saturday night were always white girls who had taken classes at the local community centre—no respectable Persian would do such things.

By the time America had bombed Afghanistan and was threatening to invade Iraq, Mom was once more becoming miserable. She took down all the flags and stuck homemade peace signs in the garden which embarrassed my brother. Teased by his friends, he took them down and pretended it was neighbours that did it.

Mom drove to San Francisco to go on peace marches. The deaf kids and Afsi went with her. They marched in the morning and hit the boutiques and comic bookstores in the afternoon. I was winning medals in gymnastics and too busy to think of things that had nothing to do with me. My brother wore a Support the Troops badge just to drive Mom crazy. My apolitical dad told her that the flag outside the restaurant was for protection and she should leave it alone.

Aunt Shirin was frantic one evening at the restaurant as I started my shift. She and the Persians talked in Farsi, and then told me that the Department of Homeland Security had contacted her and wanted to speak to her and Dad. She'd told them to come to the restaurant but they insisted on meeting at the house.

Three men arrived. They were all white. One was older and spoke fluent Farsi. My aunt had hissed at my dad, it's all my mom's fault with her politics. Now they are blaming us. Even Mom thought there might be something to this and had taken her Support the Green Party placards from the garden. My brother, Mom and I listened from the bedroom. But it was nothing to do with Mom. They wanted Dad and Aunt Shirin to use the restaurant as a way to gauge the Persian community in Sacramento. Tell us what people are saying, tell us who is saying it, and tell us how the community feels about George Bush, about America. Aunt Shirin shook her head; we can't spy on our own customers. People who come to the restaurant aren't talking politics, Dad scoffed in disbelief, all they talk about is BMWs, Mercedes, Rolexes, who had bought what size house in what neighbourhood. Persians have done so well in America, why would they cause trouble?

The three men were scrupulously polite but firm. We expect you to report to us every month. Aunt Shirin refused, the men smiled and said, there could be trouble for you. You might be sent back to Iran. The Homelands Security men reminded Dad and Aunt Shirin that their citizenship applications were not yet through.

It was then that my mom, brother and I felt sick. It was then that our fragile little suburban family seemed different and not as before. Aunt Shirin protested, I am not SAVAK, he was, but I am not. The Homelands Security men seemed to know all of this. They didn't have to say anything.

After they left, politely shaking hands, and having left the sweet tea and pistachios untouched, Dad and Aunt Shirin shouted at each other in Farsi for half an hour. We three sat in the room. The room got dark and none of us rose to turn on the lights. The only sound you could hear from the outside world was the scraping of the huge banana tree leaves off the window.

My dad had been SAVAK—that was why he was in prison. Aunt Shirin left; for the first time in her life, without saying goodbye. Dad came into the dark room and sat on the floor. He told us he had not been a torturer, just a lowly operative, but had probably reported on people that would have ended up being tortured. Yes, he would have to report to the US Department of Homeland Security because if he was sent back to Iran he would be killed. They know all about me, he said. They trained us. They're all the same people. SAVAK in Farsi stands for department of homeland security. Then he got into his car and drove to Reno.

My first memory is of a tree blossoming with visa applications. That comes to me now as a vision before I sleep, the envelopes are luminous and glow in the dark, I can see every leaf in its greenness, every twist of each branch, all is comprehensible, every name and address inside every envelope, all clear and contained in a vision. In contrast, my dreams are immovable, slate markings jutting sharply from the suburban flower beds as something foreign hacked from mountains, dragged far, shattered but still huge. Our family could not rise, nor soar, nor find freedom in this hot flat valley, in this town where nothing happened until the Terminator came. Mexicans out in the fields with their white cowboy hats, and wide, dark, indigenous faces; the tiny historical downtown with scented candle shops for the few tourists to whom our home was not an ultimate destination but a stop-over; the sprawling ranch-style wooden houses, water hungry gardens; banana leaves scraping off my window; the white girls at the mall throwing back their blonde ponytails, sprinting long legged down the track at school; the palm trees swaying in front of the post office. Generic, bland, consumer culture, call it what you will, but it was mine and now it was all tainted. Tarnished like the old countries my parents came from. What Dad had escaped from, he had found waiting, tricked by the silence of decades, as if he had crawled in a long slow circle. He was not a torturer, but he was the one who led you to the chamber. Hero at the blackjack tables, in the cold stark alpine beauty of Lake Tahoe, stacking dollars in the hotel bathroom while his family slept. My world was contaminated by him and by the three men driving in the same government car to our suburban house, walking up our concrete path, past our slate rocks, not touching their lips to our glasses of tea.

Some of us never wake up, but I have woken. I was a deaf child. Now, at fifteen, I have heard the sounds of the real world. The song this new world was singing to me all along.

The Dog's Life
Ragnar Almqvist

TOBIAS WAS IN THE BATH. His whole emaciated frame, right up to his shaggily bearded neck, was soaking in a lukewarm mixture of bath salts, shower gel, and dirty water. He had been lying here for almost two hours now, ever since his father left for work that morning, and the tips of his fingers, the soles of his feet might have belonged to Methuselah so withered did they seem. Every fifteen minutes or so, whenever the water's temperature seemed in danger of sinking below his comfort zone, Tobias would fiddle the plug out of the bath using a graceful, perhaps slightly oversized foot, and drain a certain amount of water from it. Then, with these same elegant levers, he would, not without difficulty, twist the tap just far enough to the right to replace what cold, dirty water had been lost with its hot, clean equivalent. Tobias suffered from no degenerative muscular or skeletal disorders but, lying in the bath, often liked to imagine himself a Christy Brown character, incapable of movement from the waist up, and to consider how differently the world might view the stunning grace of his own right foot, were he so constrained.

Tobias was twenty-six and jobless. Five years ago he had completed a diploma in cookery at the local technological institute. Though a star student, graduating with first class honours and outstanding recommendations, he had found restaurant work tough. A prodigious sleeper and longtime stoner, Tobias was ill-suited to the early-morning, late-night nature of cheffing. Spectacularly unreliable, he had been sacked from each of the three junior positions he had held since graduation. Nine months he had been on the dole now, living back at home, during which time he had begun no fewer than three night courses, completing none. In April he had received thirty-four certificates, erroneously mailed along with the night school's winter programme, according to which he spoke fluent Mandarin, Polish and Java, was qualified to administer first aid, counselling, acupuncture, and, should the need ever arise, teach beginners' golf. He had not given the certificates back. They were blu-tacked to his bedroom walls, beside posters of the Incredible Hulk, Kurt Cobain and Metallica. Whether the administrative error was a sign of God's favour or derision, Tobias could not decide. It was an indication the big guy was thinking about him, though, and that, in itself, was pleasing.

It is not easy to live at home beyond the age of seventeen, but nor, it must be said, is it particularly difficult. While you cannot smoke weed, or drink whiskey, or casually masturbate in your bedroom without fear of your mother bursting in the door or your father shouting 'dinner' at you from below, at home you are privileged in not having to buy every slice of bread you eat, or worry about the next heating bill. Knowing too well what it was like, Tobias was keen to defer reentering reality as long as possible. He was not in much of a position to move out anyway, his bank balance being lower than the credit most six year olds have on their mobile phones, and his immediate job prospects, despite his innumerous accreditations, being even slimmer than him.

From downstairs Tobias heard the jangling of keys. 'Hey,' he shouted, as the front door whined open. There was no response, but, after a few seconds, he heard his brother's familiar footsteps pounding up the stairs, and the bathroom door swung open. Walt came in, unzipped his fly, and started, with limited accuracy, to piss into the toilet bowl.

'What the fuck?' said Tobias. 'I'm taking a bath here.'

Walt didn't respond until he had finished pissing, wiped whatever urine he had left along the seat rim off with toilet paper, and flushed. He looked down at his brother then and grinned guiltily.

'Sorry.'

'You could have waited.'

Walt shrugged. 'I was bursting. Anyway, it's about time you got out of there. You aren't a fucking merman.'

Walt was six years Tobias's junior and his superior in all things bar sleeping. In many ways the brothers were alike, save that whatever attributes they shared Walt seemed to have got the better of. They were both tall and thin, but while Tobias tended to be called lanky or spindly, Walt was always referred to as slim. Their faces were so alike that, placed in a cast of thousands, a stranger could have identified them as brothers with little trouble. Yet Walt was good looking and Tobias was not, and there was no escaping that fact.

Though not exactly jealous of his brother, Tobias was as aware of Walt's abilities as he was of his own defects. He could remember drawing a comic book sequence for art class as an eleven year old and getting a gold star for it, only to come home from school the next day and find that Walt had redrawn the thing from scratch, tightening the graphics immeasurably, and adding dialogue—a feature of comics which had escaped Tobias's attention entirely. His life was littered with such instances. They danced through his self-concept like pop-up adverts on a computer screen, an irritant that could be avoided only with concentrated effort. And concentrated effort, as Tobias was the first to acknowledge, was not among his more outstanding attributes.

Tobias got out of the bath, threw on a pair of boxers, a Spiderman tee shirt and a well-worn dressing gown and went downstairs to the kitchen where Walt was cooking beans and rolling the first spliff of the day. Stone, their dog, a great shaggy wolfhound of forgotten age, lay sprawled at his feet like a sheepskin rug. Tobias pulled a stool up to the counter.

'How'd the exam go?' he asked.

Walt, busy stirring beans, shrugged. 'It was okay.'

'Good,' said Tobias. 'What was it again?'

Walt was in the final weeks of a philosophy degree, where, having managed honours in each of his first two years, he was now struggling to secure a pass. He had failed three of his seven papers at Christmas and been issued two warnings for non-attendance at tutorials since. Tobias realised that the spliff and booze to which he had introduced his brother was likely a factor in this sudden shift, but he wasn't culpable for it. A man could make his own mistakes. He'd read that in a poem somewhere.

'I think it was existentialism.'

'You think?' said Tobias.

Walt turned from the beans and smiled sheepishly at his brother. He was in the habit of smiling sheepishly. 'You know how philosophy is,' he said. 'It's kind of hard to tell one subject from the next sometimes.'

Tobias pressed his lips together and made a sort of kissing noise. He rubbed the sole of his right foot along Stone's back, felt the hard edge of her spine beneath the great mess of fur. The dog growled contentedly. 'How many more have you got left then?'

His brother shrugged. 'A few.' Tobias frowned. 'To be honest man, I'm not sure I'll bother going in for them. I haven't really done any study or anything.'

The right thing to do at this point, Tobias knew, was to sit his brother down square and tell him to get his fucking act together, slap him a few times perhaps, the way hysterical women were slapped in movies. But he couldn't bring himself to, somehow. He had spent enough of the past nine months bumming around with Walt to know exactly how little work his brother had done. And, though he would hardly admit it, even to himself, there was a kind of satisfaction, a pleasure in fact, to be drawn from Walt's failure, if only that it softened his own.

'You gonna tell the folks?' he asked.

Walt shrugged. 'Sometime, I guess.'

Walt got two plates from the dishwasher, slapped some toast down on them, and covered them with beans. They ate in hungry, worried silence, using spoons instead of forks. When they had finished Walt opened the kitchen door and lit the spliff, careful not to let any smoke drift inside the house. After a few drags, he turned to Tobias.

'You want?'

Though the issue was hardly in doubt, Tobias rubbed the hair along his chin wisely, as if considering some great dilemma. Walt handed him the blint.

'Who you trying to kid, bro?' he said.

After they had finished smoking, they took some ice cream from the fridge, went into the living room and stuck on the TV. They watched a special edition of *The Antiques Roadshow*, a *Deal or No Deal*, half a *Home and Away*, and ate a tub of Ben and Jerry's and forty-eight wafers between them.

'Damn,' said Walt, looking at his watch during a break, 'Dad'll be back for lunch any minute.'

'Uh huh,' said Tobias, dreamily.

Walt frowned. 'I think I'll go hang upstairs till he's gone. Don't let him know I'm around, okay?'

'No worries. Roll another spliff while you're up there, will you?'

Easing off the lazyboy they had bought their mother for her fiftieth birthday—'I always wanted triplets,' she'd joked—Walt nodded. 'Sure thing, bro.' He hurried upstairs with the spliff in hand, leaving Tobias on his own in the sitting room, staring at the blank television screen.

For a long time he just sat there, sucking on his lower lip, wondering what he was going to do with his life. Beyond an episode of *Battlestar Galactica* that evening, he couldn't think much further ahead. Letting his gaze wander across the room, he noticed the ice cream tub upturned by the lazyboy; a large glob of ice cream had spilt over onto the floorboards, forming an oozing, butterscotch coloured scab. Tobias got down on his knees and started picking at the scab with his fingernails. Though the main part shifted easily enough, he soon realised he'd need some kind of cleaning product for the deeper stains. He went down to the kitchen and poked around under the sink, where all kinds of bottled good intentions—from shoe shiners to ceramic hob polishes— lay three quarters full, until he found some cleaning spray and a steel brush he thought suitable for administering it. So empowered, he returned to the sitting room. The cleaner, an odourless foaming gel called Stains Be Gone, lived up to its name and the job was done, as the advertisers promised, in next to no time.

Happy and tired—it did not take much to make him either—Tobias slumped down on the lazyboy and flipped on the TV. He'd put the cleaner and brush back in a minute, there was no rush. An old episode of *The Crystal Maze* was on, his favourite show as a kid. He watched a team of engineers from Surrey debate whether or not to spend a crystal buying back a trapped team-mate. The team-mate, a girl—quite hot, Tobias thought, in a nineteen eighties jumpsuit way—was pictured sitting in a dusty corner of an Aztec room. After some argument, the team decided against spending the crystal 'now'. 'We'll come back to her later,' the captain said. Tobias smiled. He'd seen enough episodes to know that such good intentions never came to anything. Not when a weekend's paragliding in the Hebrides was at stake.

Stone wandered through from the kitchen—she wasn't supposed to, because she shed hairs all over the good furniture, but Tobias didn't care particularly. Hairs had never bothered him.

She was a big dog, three feet tall, five long, with soft, dopey eyes that seemed always on the verge of tears, and ears shaped like butterfly wings. Her fur was the same dull grey as wet cement, her mouth lined with teeth big as Neolithic flints. Ambling through the suburbs, she elicited gasps of horror from middle-aged women, screams of delight from their eight-year-old sons. Dobermans and bulldogs had been known to cross the street to avoid her. But really she was as docile as a sloth and as interested in fighting as most teenagers are in calculus.

She had never been weighed, but Tobias, who, stoned, had tried lifting her a few times, reckoned she must be at least twice as heavy as he was, probably more. He was teasing out the logistical difficulties getting her on the bathroom scales would entail, when his dad shouted 'Boo' at him through the window, startling him into an undignified yelp.

'Get up off your ass and open the door for me, will you?' the old man barked, smiling through his neatly kept, greying beard. 'I left my keys back in work.'

Tobias went out into the hall and let him in.

'Hey,' said his father. 'Did you check any of those jobs websites your mother mentioned last night?'

Tobias nodded. 'I had a look at a few of them, yeah.'

The old man looked at him incredulously. 'You did in your hole,' he said. Tobias laughed, as his dad shook his head. 'God, you're one lazy son of a bitch.'

'Hey,' said Tobias, punching his father playfully in the shoulder, 'that's my mother you're talking about.'

The old man poked his head into the living room. 'What are you watching?' he asked, then answered his own question. 'Shite. Why doesn't that surprise me?' He looked at the bottle of Stains Be Gone, the steel brush beside it. 'Will you ever learn to clean up after yourself when you're done cleaning up after yourself?'

Tobias shrugged. 'I was just getting to that.'

'Oh sure,' said his father, 'clearly, I mean.'

He started down towards the kitchen, Stone behind him. The old man ruffled his hand along the dog's broad skull as he walked. 'And what's she doing in the sitting room?' he asked over his shoulder, but he didn't seem to expect an answer this time and Tobias didn't bother giving him one. The old man sat on one of the high stools at the counter and pulled a two-day-old copy of *The Guardian* out of his bag. 'Mix me up some pasta will you Toby,' he asked, 'and maybe a scrambled egg?'

Tobias nodded. 'You want spinach or anything on it?'

His father considered a moment. 'Maybe some onion. Do we have any onions?'

Tobias made enough for two and, after serving his father, sat down to eat. 'Nice scramble,' said the old man, looking up from an article on global warming.

'Thanks,' said Tobias. 'How's work?'

'Okay. You should try it some time, maybe you won't need to keep asking.' The old man smiled at his own wit, showing big yellow teeth and greying gums, then frowned suddenly. 'Your brother got away all right this morning?'

Tobias shrugged. 'He wasn't around when I got up.'

His father lifted his chunky, square framed glasses off the bridge of his nose and wiped them with the corner of his shirt. 'He has exams today, you know?'

'Yeah?'

The old man nodded. Tobias stood up and brought his plate over to the sink to rinse.

'You think he's happy?'

'Sure, I guess.'

Tobias's father shook his head. 'With the course, I mean.'

Tobias paused a second before answering, not because he was considering what he was about to say but because he wanted to give the impression that he was. 'I wouldn't say he loves it maybe, but I think he likes it well enough.'

The old man nodded, gazed down at the paper for a moment, then back at his son. He frowned. 'Toby,' he said. 'Piece-of-crap degree or not, it's important your brother finishes this thing. You realise that?'

'Sure.'

'Well and all as you kids get along,' said his father. He didn't finish the sentence. He looked confused, a little angry maybe, sharp creases replacing the faint ripples along his red and wind-chilled skin.

'Walt will do fine,' said Tobias. 'He's smart.'

The old man chewed a last mouthful of pasta, looked at his son, and swallowed meaningfully.

'People used to say you were smart too, Toby.'

After the old man had left, Walt came back downstairs. His eyes were wet and red as a fish's just pulled from the sea.

'Nice lunch?' he asked.

'Not really. Dad bugging me to get a job, worrying about your exams, usual stuff.'

Walt nodded. His lower lip was a deep, resinous brown. 'You want to go for a walk maybe? I could do with some fresh air after all that sitting.'

'Sitting?' said Tobias. 'Yeah, I'll bet you could.'

They went as far as the harbour. Though it was only early May, the first sight of sun had brought out girls in string tops and mini-skirts, joggers sporting wraparound shades, bands of boys wearing Celtic replica kits, carrying slowly deflating footballs, neon ice pops sucked to their mouths like soothers. Tobias rolled cigarettes as they walked, talked about the screenplay he had been writing, mostly in his head, for seven months now. A biopic of Elliot Smith, he had produced fifteen pages of script, all stage directions for the first scene, in which Elliot stares at himself in the mirror, unblinking, for two minutes. He knew how the rest of the thing would pan out, he explained, but wanted to get those first few images spot on before proceeding.

Walt smoked and nodded and let his brother waffle on unchecked until they had reached the far end of the pier. The sea was like an army jacket, patched in green and grey and black. Wind rose off it carrying salt and freshness into their cancer-harbouring lungs. When the sun fell behind a cloud, the waves seemed to groan.

'They're going to be pretty fucking angry when I tell them,' said Walt.

They sat at the pier's edge, legs dangling above the waves.

'I guess,' said Tobias. 'Nothing they haven't heard before though.'

Walt nodded. 'Still.'

Silence for a few moments.

'And, I mean, you haven't even failed yet. You might not have done much work, but you could still have passed.'

Walt pulled hard on his lip. 'I didn't sit the test this morning,' he said. 'I'm meant to have started another one,' he glanced at his watch, 'twenty-five minutes ago.'

Tobias looked at his brother in profile, jaw clean and square as a US Marine's, eyes grey and vacant. 'Well, I guess that probably means you failed,' he said.

Walt nodded. 'Probably.'

Tobias scratched his beard, caressed the hook of his nose. The moment called on him to offer consolation, but nothing sprang to mind. That was one of the problems with spliff—things seldom sprang to mind when you needed them, though when you didn't there was often an abundant supply. He gazed out across the sea. For a thing that people were always calling beautiful, he thought, it could look pretty damn ugly sometimes.

When they arrived back home, they found the dog dead in the living room. The bottle of Stains Be Gone lay upended beside her, a puddle of clear liquid, flecked with blood and spittle, spread like a giant's footprint across the varnished panels of the floor.

'Jesus,' said Tobias, falling to his knees.

Walt stood behind him, rigid as sheet metal. 'No fucking way. No fucking, fucking way.'

Her eyes were like marbles. Tobias felt for a pulse, put his trembling hands to her mouth, forced open her jaw. She was warm, hot almost. 'I think she's breathing,' he said. He pushed her flank heavily. A great belch escaped, as from a whoopee cushion. 'She must be breathing,' he said. He pushed again, again, again, until he felt his brother's arms clasp his from behind.

'She's dead, you stupid prick.'

Tobias squirmed. 'Let me go,' he demanded. He was released. Then a closed fist cuffed him round the back of his head. He yowled, fell clumsily to the floor. Kicks to the stomach, hard and clean, followed; twice; three times; he lost count. He was shrinking, organs turning to mulch inside him. It was not exactly pain, more the absence of feeling, though it hurt too, in its own way.

'You killed her, you dumb fuck,' he heard, sort of. The words were echoes in his ear, slow motioned, dreamlike. They might have been his conscience, he couldn't be sure, though retrospect suggested they were Walt's. Then footsteps, the slamming of a door, and the throb of his abdomen, solar plexus, lungs, heart, head, a stinging worse than a thousand nettles breaking out across his body.

He lay there for less than five minutes. But it was long enough. As the pain dulled, reality grew. And that was worse really.

He rolled over. Stone's body was there still. From upstairs, periodically, came smashing sounds, breaking glass, shatterings, screams. He got up, doubled over, winced, looked at the dead dog beside him, fell again to his knees. His head, throbbing like a misfiring heart, slumped onto his pigeon chest. He stumbled as far as the lazyboy, lay down and began to cry.

His bedroom looked like Dresden in 1945. The certificates—all thirty-whatever of them—had been ripped from the walls; the contents of two boxes of comics spilled over the floor; his novelty ashtrays broken into fragments. Tobias stood there a minute, wondering what the fuck he was going to do now. He could see things going a number of ways, none well. A lump the size and shape of a golf ball was growing along the crown of his head. It made it hard to think.

Walt stood in the doorway. His face was red with tears. He looked about nine years old. 'You killed her,' he said, his voice hoarse.

Tobias nodded. There was no denying it. 'I didn't mean to.' He meant that as the beginning of an explanation, but found ultimately it was all he had.

Later, when their parents had come home, Tobias, Walt and their father dug a hole out back, beside the doghouse. The earth was dry and stony and the labour hard. They dug as deep as they could manage, but what they could manage was not very deep, barely three feet.

'It'll have to do,' said the old man, staring into the worm lined hole.

The evening had come and, though the sun shone still, the air had cooled around them. The boys had not been to Church since their confirmations, nor indeed had their parents—they believed in God no more than the tooth fairy—yet each spoke prayers over the graveside, thanked a Lord who did not exist for the friendship of a dog now gone. Tobias mumbled penance under his breath, promised in future to be more vigilant, to care more for others, to tear his life from the great mess it had become or had, perhaps, always been.

They lifted Stone's great bulk, the four remaining members of the family, and placed her in the three-foot hole, covering her in the rubble of day. The brothers stayed by the graveside awhile, after their parents had gone in, feeling the evening chill rise electrically along their skin.

'I think I'll head off for a bit, maybe,' said Tobias. 'Travel or something, see the world.'

Walt nodded, continued staring at the heap of displaced clay before them. Both understood this was not an option but a necessity. Though their parents had said nothing, the violence in their father's eyes, the shame in their mother's, was enough. They would not force Tobias out, but he could not stay.

He pulled his cigarettes from his jeans' pocket, took one himself and handed Walt the pack.

'Thanks,' said Walt.

Tobias looked at his brother, trying to commit this image to what little memory he had left. The handsome lines of Walt's face had smudged, the sockets of his eyes grown deep and dark. He seemed at once older and younger, midges hanging above his head, a fuzzed and itchy halo.

'You should finish those exams, I think,' said Tobias. 'For what it's worth.'

'Yeah,' said Walt. 'I guess I should.'

They lit their smokes and sat there then in silence, Walt biting his nails, Tobias rubbing the rough hairs along his lower neck, watching the light die around him.

Looking for America
Tom Tierney

I LIKED THE TOWN. I liked the idea of myself in this town. I liked the wooden homes with green lawns and white railings, the High School flanked by playing fields and car parks, the diner with its Formica and stainless steel furniture and waitresses who poured endless cups of coffee and called me honey. I saw myself as a character in a nineteen-fifties movie in this nineteen-fifties town. I took to wearing my jeans turned up at the bottoms and having my hair cut in a short back and sides so that I would look the part.

I was staying in a motel and I walked from bar to bar and from restaurant to restaurant looking for work. A few said maybe but nobody said yes. I was close to giving up when I thought to ask in the motel itself. The woman working in reception had her hair dyed blonde and worn up at a height that was unfashionable at that time, and its elaborate detailing contrasted strongly with the ill-fitting pink tracksuit she was wearing, but she smiled and she said that maybe I could have a job if I called back when her husband was there.

Her husband's name was Almos. When I came back he shook my hand and said that maybe it was true that there was a job and that maybe I could have it. He asked me where I was from and why was I in America and if I liked it here. While I tried to find a way of answering that would get me the job, he told me that he was from Hungary and that he loved George Bush but had loved Ronald Reagan more. He asked me what I thought. Who had been better? I said I wasn't too sure. They were maybe both a little too right-wing, I said. Almos brushed this away with the back of his hand.

'There is no right wing and left wing,' he said, 'I have been through the second world war and revolution and occupation and all these things. There is communism and there is democracy. And democracy is better.' He asked me again where I was from and I told him Ireland and he said that was good, and did I like America. I said I supposed I did.

That was apparently enough. He told me the job was to do a little painting and a little maintenance and to try to get the motel ready for the height of the summer. He showed me a windowless room at the back and said I could sleep there and start work the next day and that I'd be working with Michael. He told me that Michael talked to himself a lot and sometimes to God, but that he was a good boy.

I moved my bags and walked down to a bar to have a beer and wished I had somebody with whom I could celebrate.

Almos would sometimes come and work with me in the afternoon when Michael wasn't around. He would paint for an hour or so and then step back and stretch his back and admire his work and say that I was lucky to be a young man and to have a young back. He would wander off to find new jobs that needed to be done: a bathroom where the tiles were cracked, a bit of carpet that needed to be replaced.

'We will do that tomorrow,' he would say when he reported back, and then he would produce a cold drink and we would sit on two of the plastic seats that were left in front of the rooms. His English was always understandable, but every word was carefully formed in a manner that suggested years of struggle with the language.

'Michael is a good boy,' he told me then, 'but he is not well.'

He looked at me and seemed to wait for a response of some sort. I shrugged my shoulders and said that he seemed all right to me. Almos frowned and said that no, Michael was not all right, that he talked to himself all the time and sometimes to God and that this was not all right.

'I did not know this when I hired him,' he said, as if he owed me an explanation. 'I thought he was just a kid needing some work. But then after I hired him, his brother came to me and thanked me for doing this and I wondered why he was thanking me. And then I heard Michael talking to himself all day and talking to God and I understood.' And then he smiled. 'I would have fired him then,' he said,' but I couldn't because his brother had thanked me for hiring him. He thought I was being a good citizen. So damn it now I have to be one.'

He laughed at his own misfortune and said that he supposed there was nothing wrong with talking to God. 'We should all talk to God,' he said, 'do you talk to God? Do you go to church?'

I shook my head and he sighed and said that it was always the same with young people and that his boys were the same. 'Nobody goes to Church anymore. Not even Michael I think, and he talks to God all the time. He just works two days a week. I think he is harmless.'

I thought he was harmless too, but I wasn't certain and I was uncomfortable with some of the conversations I overheard. Sometimes he became quite argumentative and the anger in his voice was clear.

'That's just one opinion. I have *another* opinion,' he shouted out one time when we were painting one of the bedrooms. 'My opinion is *just* as good as your opinion. I don't want to do that. I *won't* do that. No, No, No!'

I didn't know what it was he wasn't going to do but I quickly checked that I was closer to the door than he was in case he yielded to pressure and decided to do it after all.

'That's *enough*!' he said then, with some emphasis. 'That's enough now! I don't want to *hear* any more of that. You got me?'

It was never necessary to make an escape. His anger would always abate and soon he would speak to me with warmth and friendship as if nothing unusual had happened.

'We're doing some good work here,' he would say. 'We're doing *good* work.' I was never certain if the 'we' included just the two of us or extended to all the characters in his head but I was pleased that he was pleased.

Taking a break one time he told me about his conversations with God.

'He talks to me,' he said, 'He likes to talk to me a *lot*.'

I took a drag on my cigarette and watched the cars pass by and followed the progress of those people who parked in front of the motel and walked through the gap in the dunes to the beach beyond. I watched them and did not turn towards Michael because I was uncomfortable. But despite my discomfort, I was curious.

'What does he say to you?' I asked.

'I guess he's just a guy like any other guy,' he said. 'I guess he just likes to talk just like you or me. He bears the weight of the world, you know. All the drugs and the shootings and the wars and the terrorists and stuff. He's got a lot of worries. He nodded his head slowly, and said 'Oh yeah.'

I finished my cigarette and said I should get back to work. 'Oh yeah,' Michael said again, and lingered outside and mumbled to himself or possibly to God.

I came to like Michael in a way. He always greeted me with a warm smile and asked me how I was and how I liked it here in America. But he was not someone with whom I wanted to become friends. He was not the cure for my loneliness. And I was lonely.

I ate each evening in the diner and the waitresses had got to know me and they'd ask me how I was and when I'd say I was good, they'd say how they loved my accent. But they were all middle-aged women and they gave the impression that they had done some hard living in their time and I knew that they, too, were no cure for my loneliness.

After the diner I'd step into one of the bars for a beer and watch some sport on TV and try to figure out what was happening. All I really understood was the fighting. I would drink a few beers and pretend an understanding of the games and fall into conversation with the bartender or another drinker. But the bartenders and the other drinkers were all men and all older than me and they were not the cure for loneliness that I was hoping for.

One weekend, a bunch of students were in town and came to the bar. They were loud and drunk and spent the evening laughing and flirting. The girls wore tee-shirts and shorts and pulled their hair through the backs of their baseball caps into a ponytail. I sat at the bar longing to belong to such a group, or to any group, and wondering how I could connect with them and knowing that I could not. When the bar began to fill up and I felt self-conscious sitting by myself, I left and went to walk home but walked past the motel and onto the beach where I sat for a while listening to the ocean.

I liked the idea of myself sitting there and thought I must cut a handsome enough figure against the dramatic background. In the movie in my head, I pictured myself in the role of a loner passing through town, a loner who during the movie would connect with somebody and change their life, and then move on to another town and to new experiences. I liked the idea of myself in this role. I thought the shot of me sitting on the beach late at night and staring out to sea would be a good shot. But the truth was that there was nobody there to see it, so I left and walked across the road and into my dark room at the back of the motel.

I had been there a few months when Almos told me he was retiring. He had signed a deal with a big hotel chain. They would take it over in the summer and they would demolish it and rebuild a bigger, multi-storey hotel on the site, with an underground car park and a restaurant and a bar. I thought about that. I wondered about its effect on a small beach town with few tall buildings and no big hotels.

'It's a good deal for me,' he said, proudly. 'We can buy a good home and work less.'

We were standing on the balcony, drinking a coke and facing the beach.

'I suppose we'll stop the painting and all that,' I said to him, wondering had I just lost my job, and was this why he was telling me.

'Oh no!' he said, 'We will continue.'

I thought about this and tried to see how it could make sense. 'It's all going to be pulled down,' I pointed out.

He took a long drink and watched some people who had taken one of his parking spots but were pulling chairs and coolers and towels from the back of their car and clearly had no intention of renting one of his rooms. He frowned and looked at me to share his indignation. I tried to do so and raised my hands in a gesture that I hoped would ask what could you ever hope to do about such people. That they simply didn't understand.

'When I bought this place I bought it from an old man,' Almos said then, and I took it that he had moved on from his indignation. 'And when I bought it from this old man, every room in it was fresh painted and was very clean. It was *super* clean. And when I sell it, it will be super clean too. I don't care what they do with it then.'

I nodded. I enjoyed the work and I was getting paid. It mattered little to me how purposeless it all was. And when I thought about it, the idea of painting a building so that it would look good when it was knocked down quite appealed to me.

I gave up on the idea of making friends in the town and becoming part of a gang and decided that I should try to make as much money as I could instead. I checked the rooms that we had already cleaned up and counted how many were left and did some figuring. I caught Almos at a busy time and pointed out that we'd be lucky to get finished by the height of the summer. I could work longer days, I told him, and he nodded absentmindedly and said that maybe I should.

I started to rise early and walk down to the diner for breakfast where a handful of construction workers would be meeting for a quick coffee and a bagel before climbing into their pick-up trucks and heading on to work. I ate with them and felt camaraderie of sorts and had a second coffee and walked back to the motel. By the time Michael arrived I would already have an hour's work done.

I noticed then that that the harder I worked, the harder he would work and that when he was working hard he was less inclined to talk to God. We began to make good progress. Almos stood at a doorway watching one morning and said he didn't know what had happened to us, but that we were doing great work and that he should maybe leave us alone.

When Michael was done in the evening he would search his pockets for a cigarette and fail to find one. I would dig out a pack and offer him one and he would smile and thank me.

'We're doing good work here,' he said again as he had said before and I found myself sharing in his pride in our work. After he left it was my job to cover up the paint and to wash out brushes, but instead I thought I'd do just a little more. Almos would pay me for whatever I worked. So I started on a new wall and found that I soon had it finished. I had a look around and decided I might as well finish the room. I found myself working until well after dark, and then in the evening I had no time to feel lonely. I decided to do the same again the next day.

Soon, it had somehow developed that I would race each day against how much I had got done the day before and try to set new records for myself. If I could paint a wall in an hour, I reckoned, surely I could get it done in fifty minutes, and if I can get it done in fifty minutes, I should be able to push myself just a little bit harder and get it done in forty five. When Michael was working I would leave him behind, working one or even two rooms ahead of him, occasionally hearing him shout out to God through the walls. When he wasn't working, I would go back over some of what he had done to reach the new standards I was setting for myself. In the evenings I had barely the energy to walk down to the bar to eat a burger and drink a beer and hope that there'd be a fight in the baseball.

But after a few weeks of this, when there were only a few weeks left before the motel was sold, I began to doubt that that it was possible to finish the whole job. I said again to Almos that I should maybe work even more, maybe that I should work through the weekend. He said that work was important but that so was rest.

I said that I wasn't sure if it was going to be possible to finish the job. I told him my figures and explained how much work we were getting through in a week and how much there was left and how it looked to me that there would definitely be at least two or three rooms and maybe more that we wouldn't get to paint. And that this was before we started on the shampooing of the carpets.

He considered my figures and said that he doubted it was as bad as I said. I argued with him, wondering at the anxiety I heard in my own voice, and pointed out how much we had done in the previous week and the week before. It was impossible to finish, I said. Not at the rate we were going. He had to understand.

He looked at me with what might have been concern and nodded and said that maybe I was right but that it didn't really matter. The whole thing was going to be pulled down anyway.

I said nothing, silenced by his abandonment of his plan to hand over the motel in pristine condition, wondering why it was that I had come to care so much myself.

And then he went on fill the silence and to tell me about the Second World War. In the last years of the war, he told me, he had been drafted to fight on the side of the Germans. He had not wanted to go. Nobody in his village had wanted to go. But they had had no choice.

There had been no training beyond the rudiments of how to fire a rifle and being told that if they disobeyed an order they would be shot. And then they had been sent from town to town, sometimes spending days on end on trains that would run slowly all night and then sit unmoving for hours during the day. They could occasionally climb down to stretch their legs but they had to stay right beside the train because at any moment it might move again. They never knew where they were or where they were going. They were told not to talk to any civilians but that that hardly mattered because they never had a language in common with any of the civilians they encountered.

One day they were told that the war was over. He had never seen the enemy or been involved in any fighting. They were told they should wait where they were, in the temporary barracks on the edge of a small town, which they now learned was in the east of Germany, and that soon they would be taken prisoner and held by the Americans or maybe the Russians and eventually they would be sent home.

They waited for a few days but nobody came. There was little to eat and they had no money but anyway money was no good because there was nothing to buy. He decided that he would not wait and that he would instead go home. So one morning he said goodbye to his companions and he set out on a walk across Europe with only a vague recollection of school geography in his head for a map. He slept rough and ate what he could find in the fields. For day after day he became increasingly lost and desperate. He wondered should he rejoin his unit, but he realised he had as little hope of finding them as he had of finding home. He came to a main road and followed it south for a few days and slowly came to realise that he was in Austria. He followed the map in his head and turned left and tried to keep to a generally straight line. He came at last to a border and returned into the countryside for a few miles and slept for the day and waited for night and at night he walked through fields until he hoped he was back in Hungary and slept again. The next day he could speak to people and they could understand him.

Some allowed him sleep in their outhouses. Some offered him a small share of what little they had.

And eventually one day, he saw the steeple of the church in his town on the horizon and he knew he was home. A familiar figure was walking out of the town towards him and she recognised him and he recognised her. She ran to him and welcomed him home and she was the most beautiful sight he had ever seen, and that was the woman that he married soon after in the church whose spire he had seen from the distance.

I thought of the woman with the tall blonde hair and the ill-fitting pink tracksuit. And now they lived in America, he said, and their children were Americans and didn't go to church any more, but they owned a small motel there and now they were going to sell it. Things had worked out for them.

I don't know why he told me the story just then, but I supposed that if I had such a story to tell that I would tell it whenever I had the chance, and sometimes I would tell it just because I hadn't told it in a while.

On my last day, I looked through the rooms we had failed to clean up. I had slept in worse, I thought, but I was saddened still by their tawdriness, by the dusty carpet and the scratches and marks on the paintwork. I collected my bag and sat beside Michael where he was sitting on a plastic chair waiting for Almos to find some more work for him to do. I wanted to say goodbye to him and to shake his hand but he was muttering to himself and seemed unhappy and I don't know if he even noticed I was there. I said goodbye anyway and clapped him on the shoulder and he looked up with a warm smile and said hi.

I told him I was going and he nodded and said that that was good and that I should take care. There were a lot of drugs and shootings and stuff out there, he told me, and I should be careful. His smile faded and his face clouded over as he listed all his concerns. He muttered something to himself that I couldn't hear and looked away from me and answered.

I said goodbye again but he was too distracted to hear. I pulled my bag onto my back and walked towards the bus station.

A Wonderful Indifference

Damien Doorley

'IT'S MAGGOTY DIRTY, THIS PLACE,' said the old woman as she led Emma into a dark room. The curtains were drawn, though it was the middle of the afternoon, and on a table in a corner a brown woollen lampshade smothered the glow of a weak bulb.

She coaxed Emma inside on a leash of words. She wore thick stockings, slippers and an old-fashioned garment, part apron and part dress, tied at the waist. Her hair was thinning and of a faded purple colour; blotches of dye stained her scalp, like the marks left by some now-eradicated disease.

'You're a good soul,' said the old woman. She was wringing her hands; her fingers were plump and looked like a litter of small puppies crawling in agitation around each other. She wore bowl-thick spectacles that made her eyes seem slow and uncomprehending. 'There's a giant great fly in there. It must be the size of a bird. Will you get rid of it for us, darling? Come all the way through now. You're a kind soul. What are you, dear, a schoolteacher? You keep those hours.'

Emma was surprised she did not recognise the old woman, and, as an observer of others, was unsettled to discover that she herself had been observed and pinned down.

The room reeked of old teabags and cigarettes. Unemptied ashtrays overflowed on the mantelpiece, the coffee table, and the breakfast bar that separated the kitchen from the living space. At the back of the room long brown curtains were pulled across a French window.

'The weather's stinking, stinking hot,' said the old woman. 'It brings out the flies in droves, swarms of the things.'

'Let's open the curtains and the window,' said Emma.

'Oh, Jesus, no, there'd be wasps, bees, daddy-long-legs and God knows what all. They'd be straight in here like another Armada, fast as rats.'

Across the floor stood dismaying, mad stacks of old newspapers. Emma shook out a few leaves of a Sunday something and rolled them up like a baton and squinted around at the walls. The old woman shuffled to the door. They both stood still and listened. The old woman retched and put her hand across her mouth.

Emma heard a small tired grumble and saw the fly, like a glistening blue bead, hovering in the middle of the room. She caught it with a wild swipe and it hit the wall with a tap.

Once the fly was dealt with they both felt calmer.

'Fancy a cup of tea and a fag?' said the old woman. 'A smoke always settles me stomach. Do they not make you feel sick, flies?'

'No, I don't mind them. No milk in my tea, thanks.'

'We're the same about milk anyway.'

While the old woman made the tea Emma looked around the dark room. She went to look closely at three black and white photographs stuck on the wall. They showed a girl squinting and grinning as she sat on the sand in a shapeless bathing suit. Sunlight in old pictures looks like dust. The dust of sunlight lay on the girl's forehead, and sheathed her arms and her legs. In the background Emma made out a blurred blooming of waves, and people busy in their patch of sand. Beside the girl sat a smiling man biting on a pipe. The father, supposed Emma. The mother was implied, absent from the frame, as the photographer.

'That's me,' said the old woman from the kitchen.

'You look very young.'

'Nineteen.'

'It's a nice age.'

'Only happens once.'

'Like every age.'

'No, all other ages last longer. That one is short and it never comes back. You only get that one once.'

'You look very happy.'

'Nnhh.'

The old woman went on making the tea and Emma squinted at some other pictures, mainly postcards, stuck on the walls. The old woman must be a Catholic, she supposed, as there were pictures of saints whose names Emma did not know showing their wounds: pierced hands, torn breasts, eyes that shed tears of blood.

Emma had attended her local village church in Suffolk as a child. It was a place to think of history rather than worship the infinite, a place to be with parents and the past, a tranquil, chilly, barn-like interior decorated with a tatty regimental banner and the names of dead soldiers chiselled on a marble slab the size of a bed. Everywhere were words, words, words.

She looked at a familiar image of Christ, in a postcard of the Titian painting stuck to the old woman's wall, as he draws delicately away from Mary Magdalene in the 'noli me tangere' recoil. Emma had not noticed before how Mary, as she kneels before Christ, seems to lift up her hand to touch and kiss his penis; but she is gently and utterly rebuffed.

Emma turned her attention once more to the photos. The girl in them was not beautiful, just young and well-looking. Emma was the same type, but she was uncomfortable with her body; the result, when she was with a man, was a clumsy, accident-creating stiffness. She had long fingers, and green eyes, and hoped that one day she would be able to let someone simply like her for them and not become anxious.

The girl in the photo looked happy. Her bathing outfit was homemade, probably knitted. It hung in folds around her body.

The old woman came back and poured the tea and started to murmur. 'That was my baby-bearing year, that one in the snaps there. Before they knew. A weekend in Clare. Before it showed. They took her away. Then after. They rolled her down the strand.'

Emma frowned.

'I was in a clinic a while. Lots like me. Not allowed to talk. We whiled away the days. Miles away. Some county, some other county. They brought us home after. And then my mother. My mother rolled her down the strand. He ran off, to America, my fella. Long before, when he knew. Saw I was expecting. She went out with her. One night my mother went out. My father locked the door. He held me. Sat on me.

Didn't cry. No we did. No there was a lot of it. In those days. By the sea in those towns. And if not in the fields. And if not in the woods. I wasn't alone. That was before things changed. The country's different now, they say.'

Emma could not easily follow what the old woman was saying. Her eyes felt heavy. She sensed she was falling back towards the hinterland of her dream life and as sleep tried to draw her away she felt how delicious it would be to give in.

After a pause the old woman went on. 'I went out next day. To the sea. Found her. Alive still. Still alive. She opened her mouth. Opened her mouth and looked at me. A fish my father caught one time, its eye went glazed and it gave me a stare I'll not forget when the fight went out of it. I think she blamed me. She was covered in flies. Flies in her mouth and in her eyes.

'I came to London then. People leave you alone. There's a great indifference here. It's wonderful, wonderful altogether, when you have a thing to put behind you.'

Oh, thought Emma, the flies, that explains the flies. A cot of sand, a quilt of flies, she thought, and charmed away the disgust she was beginning to feel.

'I'm so sorry,' said Emma. 'So sorry.'

The old woman nodded. 'Well, it happened a lot,' she said.

Emma's sleepiness faded. They said nothing for some minutes.

'Why are you not away on holiday, anyway?' asked the old woman.

'Bit strapped this year. Not sure where to go. Friends are off somewhere,' Emma said. 'I'm trying to—' she stopped herself and swallowed the word 'write'.

Emma was alone that summer, and believed the risk of solitude in the city was bringing rewards, rather than driving her loopy. She was writing and she had a routine. After turning out, in longhand, three hundred words in the morning, she had breakfast and went for a walk. She did not head for the open spaces of Hampstead Heath, Primrose Hill or Regent's Park, but tried to lose herself in the wide streets, abandoned to the stayers-on like her. She had not known she adored London. It crept up on her, like a difficult friend who declares his love and becomes kinder, deeper, and entirely available. As she walked she daydreamed, or made observations that she stored in her mind or in a small notebook. She typed, corrected, and read in the evenings. She imagined she could truly sense the hemispheres of her brain crackling with life as new thoughts climbed up from the unconscious. Sometimes she felt a trickle of sheer joy leak from her heart. She touched with her middle finger the place where it was happening beneath her blouse.

Emma had finished a story that afternoon. She printed it off and wrote a covering letter by hand. She felt an editor should see what a writer's handwriting was like. She slid her letter and the story into a manila envelope and sealed it carefully. She walked up the road, leaving behind that morning's word count in a paper tray, snug and neat as a box of eggs.

But as she slipped the envelope into the postbox all the faults of the story occurred to her, flew out in her face like disturbed moths. She was trudging home again, morose in the startling brightness of the day, when she saw the old woman standing outside the front door of a house on the same long street as her own. She called out as Emma passed on the other side of the road, 'Would you ever help us a minute, dear?'

The street was summer-bare. Emma was now feeling alone and stranded in August. She wanted to forget herself. She walked up the old woman's steps and said 'What's up?' There was no one else in the flat. When the old woman said 'us', she meant only herself.

The old woman did not seem to mind that Emma did not finish what she was saying; she too was lost in her thoughts. They sipped the thick black tea.

Emma had read that brutalised people freeze the shock that has disturbed them and go on until one day they just fall to pieces. But it seemed the opposite had happened to the old woman, the shock had taken centre stage, playing and replaying, like a dream that had escaped from the world of sleep, and it was the rest of her that was frozen.

Emma determined not to take herself seriously ever again. But how? What mattered to you just mattered to you; that was the way things were. Your concerns could not be deleted, just relativised. She did not know where she had picked up this word, but she didn't trust it. You could decide to do good, decide to help people, but you knew you wouldn't get around to any of it. You could only feel something for other people; was that important?

The doorbell rang.

'It's the Persians,' said the old woman and hurried to the front door.

She let the Persians in and introduced them to Emma, who recognised them as the owners of a junk shop at the end of the road. Emma remembered that the older one often sat outside the shop on a plastic chair, smoking, or eating rice from a plate with a spoon like a child, while the younger brother prowled inside among the stock, scowling as though it had all been delivered by mistake.

The older brother had a friend who sat with him sometimes on another chair and listened while he read aloud from a notebook in which he had written poetry in Farsi. Emma glanced at the open pages as she passed and she recognised the sweeping loops and fussy dots and severe verticals of the script from her stints of teaching at language summer schools. She also recognised that he spoke with the accent of Tehran, as distinct as the tones of Dublin or the Bronx. His friend sat beside him on a chair on the pavement and smiled at the poetry and nodded at the explanations the writer interrupted his own readings to offer.

'I'm on my way home next month, darling,' cried the old woman. 'These kind gentlemen have promised to give me a good price for my earthly goods and chattels. And then I'll fly away.'

'You're really going back there?' Emma felt angry for the old woman but she did not want to show it.

'Home, darling, home. Where else would you go to see out your days? It's a different place now. You get a fair hearing. And there's compensation, they say.'

She turned to the Persians, who were still standing calmly at the door. She introduced Emma to them, not by name, but with a strange personal claim. 'This is my best girl, the best girl in the whole world,' she cackled.

The Persians smiled and stepped into the room and each in turn shook Emma's hand. They looked at her with kind, limpid eyes. They were both heavy, and carried their paunches before them with pride, like awards.

'It is a good thing to visit your mother,' said the younger brother to Emma. 'Unfortunately we cannot visit ours as often as we would like. She has moved to an apartment in Shiraz. She is alone there. Our father came here with us. But she did not want to leave Iran and went back, like your mother wants to, to the city of her birth. She says she is happy there, but I don't know. Still, we have bought her a really good apartment.' Emma said nothing about the man's mistake. She could hardly hold up the flow of events to disown the old woman. She just smiled and nodded, and gave a little bow as formal as his speech.

'So, you are returning to Eire,' said the other brother, the poet, to the old woman. 'You know, don't you, that Eire and Iran come from the same root in Sanskrit? That is the language that they speak in parts of India from time immemorial. I am sure if you travel there you will still find many who employ it in certain provinces. The old word means just area. You can hear the similarity. Area. Eire. Iran. We all come from one place, don't we? And return there. Is that not true? All the poets say the same thing. In the meantime, where are we? In a space, an area, a place of one sort or another. Does it matter for how long?'

Emma thought she detected not only a fellow writer but a fellow teacher in the older man: along with his compulsive scribbling in notebooks, and his need for a smiling audience, there was his pleasure in offering illumination to others who had not asked for it. Today Emma could not illuminate anything. She felt a deep and unsettling need for someone to explain to her what to think and feel, a need she had not felt since she was a child.

The Persians began to move around the room with their large notepads, stepping among the stacks of newspapers, and valuing each item and jotting prices down in pencil. They argued in hushed tones about the old woman's dresser. As they walked about they already seemed to own the place. One of them had a torch. He must have visited before since he knew the old woman would not let any daylight into her room. He flashed his torch on the pictures, the chairs, and the carpet, which was moth-eaten.

Emma and the old woman sat together on the sofa out of the way.

The old woman's thigh touched Emma's carelessly. Emma could smell the warm sweat from the grimy blouse she wore under her charwoman's apron.

She imagined the old woman spending hours in empty family homes, the kids and parents out at school and work, as she wiped and swept, washed and rinsed, ironed and folded. She would have left before any of them got back and down the years she would have plumped up and patted down, and smoothed and arranged the places of several families, glad all the while to be alone in her work in strange houses of which over time she would have taken silent, unnoticed possession, like a ghost.

The Persians finished their task. They talked quietly in the middle of the room. They refused tea. They frowned and shook their heads and sucked their teeth, like mechanics emerging from under the bonnet of a clapped out car. They whispered, cleared their throats, and turned to the old woman.

'Two hundred and thirty-one pounds,' the older one said.

The old woman opened her mouth but it was too dry for her to speak and she closed it again and swallowed.

'I am sorry. We would like to give you more,' said the younger brother. 'But to be honest, it is not even worth that.'

The old woman nodded, as though her shoulders and head were dangling from strings and a breeze were passing by.

'For everything?' she asked.

'Except the photos,' he said.

'The photos?' asked the old woman, her eyes brightening.

'Yes, we do not take photos,' he said. 'They are too personal. You can never get rid of the things.'

Emma winced in embarrassment for him. He could not know what he was doing to the old woman. If he had known he would have behaved differently, she was sure.

The older brother, still standing up, wrote out an inventory and estimate and tore it off with a loud rip and handed it to the old woman. The brothers smiled, nodded and left, hurrying and sweaty.

Emma stayed with the old woman for an hour. They heard thunder far away. Heavy splats of rain hit the window. Lightning flicked on and off nimbly ahead of a clap of thunder right over the house. The storm rumbled past. A shower settled in, sedative as a lullaby. The old woman and Emma kept looking towards the window because the curtain moved in a draught.

'I don't suppose I'll be going anywhere for a while yet then,' said the old woman. 'Sometimes,' she went on 'the things that happen make you want to do something to yourself. But what's the hurry, I say.' Her big eyes creased as she looked to Emma for agreement.

'Yes,' said Emma. 'There is no hurry. I'm sure there isn't.' She thought and thought, but she could not see anything else she could say that would not come across as some kind of insult, or diminish her for saying it.

When the rain stopped Emma said goodbye to the old woman and went out into the damp air, fading-bright. She turned her face away from the smells that rose off the wet pavement. She did not want to cross the road, twist her key in the lock and step into the sharp unhappiness of that evening in her flat. She began to walk. A big black car flew past her in a burst of music, paused at the end of the road, and fell silent like a baffled parade. It slid around the corner and was gone.

She walked for what felt like a long time without seeing a soul; so many people had left London for August it was like scouring a sunlit town after a war.

Scenes from an empty attic

Rosemary Jenkinson

ANGELINA PUT ON HER COAT and presented both profiles to the mirror, deciding that the left one was best. The late nights were telling on her skin. The scar on her forehead appeared whiter than usual against the shadows. All these nights spent with people who longed to be everywhere at once, restless and impassioned, inflamed and burnt-out, rubbing coke onto their pale gums, showing their teeth in the candlelight like vampires... Every morning she turned up at work exhausted.

The room rocked slightly as a train shuddered along the siding that passed by the back of the house.

'Annie, Annie,' called a voice anxiously from the landing.

'Christ,' went Angelina, going out.

It was Stuart, the boy who rented the box room. He stood awkwardly, head hunched forward, the door jammed tight behind his body, so that she couldn't see past. On one occasion she'd had a glimpse of walls lined with clear plastic packing boxes. It had reminded her of the locker room of a train station.

Stuart suddenly unleashed a torrent of words.

'I've been speaking to Coleman and he says it's up to us what we do about buying the oil...'

'Look, can we talk about it again, Stuart,' she interrupted. She was already running late. She zipped her coat up to the neck to confirm that the conversation was now closed. She ran down the stairs and leapt out into the open air, as if released.

*

The lights on the walls of 'Kelly's Cellars' were the shade of malt whiskey and the yeasty smells from the beer pumps added to the warmth. The bar was full and the air buzzed with Belfast accents, honed into harshness through generations of roaring at peelers and Protestants. Angelina joined her friend, Maria, who was sitting with a group of professional drinkers who were always good for the craic.

'Sure us Irish blew up all the buildings,' one man was saying, 'but then we got all the jobs building them back up. Oh, we knew what we were doing alright.'

A large group of tourists came in, armed with cameras, and looked up at the cracked ceilings and black-lacquered beams, hushed and wide-eyed as though they'd just entered a chapel. They started clicking away at the bar and in particular at an elderly man in a outsize tweed jacket sucking on a pint of Guinness.

'Most photographed man in Belfast,' someone commented.

There was a wistful silence, a sudden unspoken communion as everyone thought of the past, sensing that all things local and Irish had been driven underground to the last few pubs, as if it was quaint history, finished with the bloodshed, swept away entirely.

The tour group filed out without even taking a drink.

'Would you look at that,' muttered one of the men, offended, and he snapped them with his mobile phone in mockery as they left.

Two strangers kept looking over. Angelina had already noticed the beautiful brown eyes and fine bones of one. His skin glowed next to Irish faces the shade of pink-grey limestone scored by years of drink and cigarettes. Maria pulled over two stools and gestured for the men to join them. They were Spanish and barely spoke English. Cosme was the name of the man Angelina liked and he managed to communicate to her that he was a student on holiday and was leaving for Dublin the next morning. She tried to explain that she worked in the foreign currency section of a bank but he seemed to think she was describing her own rich jet-setting lifestyle and they laughed and shrugged and gave up.

'A cigarette?' Cosme offered. In his accent it sounded to her like 'a secret.'

They went outside and the smoke poured deep into her lungs and surged up into her brain and he smiled to see the pleasure of the cigarette and the smile filled her too, like the smoke. He looked at the ruby-coloured stone on her necklace which sat above her chest and said it was beautiful.

Then he spoke to Maria and Angelina was jealous, until she saw his eyes move for a second away from Maria's and in that second was a gulf and Maria had lost him. Angelina noticed the muscles on him from carrying his backpack and the energy and curiosity in his eyes. He was like an animal rippling under its pelt.

It had been four years since she'd come back to Belfast after years teaching abroad. During her time away, she would haunt anyone who had an Ulster accent, anyone who said, a wee drink, a wee walk, feeling the pang of the loss. She'd been so happy to come back but the feeling had faded. She was travelling once more, only not across huge spaces, but within her own mind, falling and surging on drugs and joy and pain.

Last orders had been called when one of the group suggested a house party and everyone started throwing money into the centre of the table to get a carry-out of beer and cider.

'Are you two coming?' Angelina asked Cosme. She looked at him in his tight-fitting coat and wanted him. He checked quickly with his friend.

'Yes, we come,' he smiled.

Outside, they had a long wait for taxis. Cosme was chatting to his friend. It was as though the frosty air was blowing through the earlier dream. His eyes under the cold streetlights were black and not warm. His body was covered up and shivering and hunched. Maria decided to bale out of the party and Angelina wondered if she should go too, if it was pointless to hang around, but then a taxi rolled up and she got in next to Cosme and he slapped his hands against his legs to warm them up and laughed, still half in shivery convulsions, delighted to be out of the cold.

Just as they were arriving outside the party house which was in a street off the Falls, Maria rang.

'You know where you're going,' said Maria, 'well, I've been there before at a party with Eamonn and do you see the stairs straight through the door? There's a pink carpet and walls.'

Angelina could see the stairs through the frosted glass of the front door. They radiated a kind of womb-like warmth.

'Horrible, isn't it?' laughed Maria. 'Well, if you go straight up the next flight, there's an attic room which is very nice. Take Cosme there.'

Angelina laughed. 'You're crazy,' she said, but her imagination leapt up the stairs.

The party was in full swing in the open-planned front room and kitchen. It wasn't too packed and Angelina and Cosme got beers. They stood silently, the one question standing between them; she immediately felt frail and vulnerable under the receding of the night's alcohol.

Cosme took her hand.

'We go...?' He pointed upstairs.

They went out into the pink stairway. She followed Maria's advice about going up the next flight of stairs. It led to the attic room, without a door. The bedside lamp was on. A bare-mattressed bed was covered in bundles of essays which Cosme with one sweep of his arm sent flying onto the floor. Used teabags sat lumped greenly in an old pint glass. Another glass was full of cigarette stubs.

They quickly took off their clothes, shaky-fingered, interrupting the rush only for a clumsy, yet needy kiss and they laughed a little at their own recklessness and hunger, then fell onto the bed. She noticed an old injection mark on his arm, white against the tan of his skin; she found it beautiful, this small, white flaw. There were no bedclothes to cling to or hide under and the open doorway made them nervous. They began to fuck hard out of panic and need. A cross hanging from his necklace swung violently against his skin and hers.

After coming, he brushed the side of her cheek gently with his knuckles, out of awareness that tenderness was missing, and they both smiled, looking at each other with the same unsated hunger as before.

They hurried back down to the party. Cosme began to look around anxiously for his friend. Oh, he's just left, someone said, and, without a word, Cosme turned and ran straight out the front door.

'I have that effect on men,' Angelina joked.

She kept looking at the door. She was hurt that he'd bolted without a goodbye but she understood. A traveller. Leaving Belfast in the morning. Travelling. Sometimes in the bank she put the foreign banknotes to her nose, just to breathe in the palms of hands, the earth, the food, the sun; all she did all day was imagine…

'That was a beautiful man, alright.'

An older man, clutching a can of Guinness to his chest, was nodding, like he had just delivered a eulogy at a wake. A feeling of pride came over her.

'Yes, that was a man,' she smiled.

She joined the party, the epicentre of which was rocking the kitchen with its music and laughter. A man with blue hexagonal glasses was whipping it up. She chased away her thoughts with red wine. The man was chopping up china-white coke on a kitchen tray, flicking it expertly into lines like a chef preparing a delicacy. He was a party professional, hiding his carry-out in the washing machine from the hangers-on.

She wasn't going into work the next day. She couldn't focus on the banknotes at the best of times… Russia, Senegal, Cambodia, the Emirates… she put on the man's blue glasses—icy blue tracers began to shoot from the light bulbs.

'I wear them to hide me bloodshot eyes,' he said.

Cold, such a cold blue world at five a.m.

She woke up. There were pins and needles in her nose. The man next to her on the sofa shifted and snuffled, fingers like creepers slowly moving up his face. It was Blue-glasses.

One of her legs was caught under his and she extricated it painfully. It looked as though their bodies had been smashed up and thrown onto the sofa. She could see through to the pink hall, spilling with sunlight.

She got up and stumbled around, looking for her coat. It was nine a.m. and she called a taxi. Outside, the duck-egg blue of the sky cracked goldenly. It was a beautiful day. She wondered if she would ever go back to work again.

Back at the house, she could hear the isk-isk-isk of the brush as Stuart swept out his room. He pulled his door open as soon as he heard her on the stairs and sidled out from behind it, then started his monologue on the need to purchase oil. Angelina stood and listened and agreed, then went to her room. A train rattled past, shaking up through the floorboards and into her feet. She thought back to the pink staircase and started laughing louder and louder to herself and then she realised that Stuart probably told people he lived with a mad girl who kept laughing to herself alone in her room and suddenly tears sprang to her eyes and she was crying and laughing and crying and laughing and she pulled off her clothes, touching her skin with her fingers, like she could feel the heat, the food, the voice of a sun-filled land, a beautiful language written on her body.

The Bride is Crying in a Toilet Cubicle
Colm Liddy

THE BRIDE IS CRYING IN A TOILET CUBICLE. She is crying for two reasons, the second of which is she desperately needs to pee and can't. The problem is her wedding dress. It's so large that it takes up the entire space. One minute ago, she walked in quickly, as voices approached, girls from work just looking for a mirror to fix lipstick and hair. Once in the cubicle, the Bride managed to twist around sufficiently to close and bolt the door but then found herself stuck.

There are, stitched deep within the fabric of the dress, a series of three wooden hoops which maintain its magnificent volume and bloom. Somewhere behind her, one or more of those hoops has hooked onto or into the toilet roll holder. She has tried several times already and found that she can't take a step back, nor a step forward. She has tried shaking it loose but the problem is directly behind her so she can't see how.

She closes her eyes and leans her head against the wall for support. She is not at all noisy but her chest makes jerky little spasms and she is crying again. Her professionally made-up face is being ruined. In a moment of inspiration she tries to wriggle out from underneath but the back of the dress is an elaborate lattice of pearl buttons and knots that only a bridesmaid could open.

In the neighbouring cubicle sits her First Bridesmaid and best friend since they met in the Gaeltacht in the summer of '93. In normal circumstances she should surely have heard something of the Bride's distress and rushed to her aid. Hers however, are not normal circumstances. She is sitting on the closed toilet seat with her left breast exposed. Clamped upon it is an electric breast pump and it is making a loud rhythmic humming noise as it extracts the milk. Loud enough so that she hears nothing of the goings-on next door.

She has recently had a baby boy and is breast-feeding. At the moment he's being minded up in the hotel room by a baby-sitter, who can give him formula if he wakes up starving and it's absolutely necessary. The First Bridesmaid left a bottle of boiled cooled water and a plastic canister containing six scoops of powder. But all the same she'd really rather he was exclusively fed breast milk. There is an absolute ton of research about the benefits in terms of intelligence, physical development and most especially susceptibility to disease and disorder. It's simply not worth it. Once the other breast is emptied she'll drop the contents up to the room and be back on the dancefloor before anyone knows she was gone. She looks down along her cerise gown and notes that her belly looks bloated again. Jesus! But then it's been only five weeks since the birth and also the meal portions were gi-normous! That girl taking the orders was spot on when she recommended the braised lamb.

In the third toilet cubicle sits a member of the hotel staff, again sitting on a closed seat. Employed as a waitress, she should be working, clearing tables at this exact moment, but instead she is reading a copy of OK magazine. And from time to time, breaking off to just stare into space. Because she is angry, she is fuming, she is (between scanning articles about Becks and Posh Spice) seriously considering a one-way ticket back to Warsaw.

The waitress arrived in Ireland just four months ago. She was hoping for a new life of opportunity and a higher standard of living. The reality, so far, has fallen well short. She is living in a box room, in accommodation sharing, with three Latvians. None of whom she particularly likes. None of whom ever trouble themselves to wash the grill after cooking meat. She has two jobs, this one as a casual waitress for weddings on the weekends and another stacking shelves in a supermarket by night. Both are for minimum wage.

Back in Warsaw she went to college and qualified as a pharmacist.

However, her degree counts for nothing over here. She applies for all sorts of pharmacy jobs but they simply throw her CV in the bin. The problem, as an official from the HSE told her, is that as yet the EU has failed to agree on the harmonisation of professional qualifications from the newer accession states.

In both her jobs, she meets many other Poles. That is the particular source of her anger this evening. The new Duty Manager is from the very same street in Warsaw. They were in the same school, even the same class together. The waitress was always studious, this other girl disruptive and bold. Back in Poland, it was always clear which girl would come to something. But here in Ireland? Here, she must take orders from a fucking *Prostytutka!*

In the fourth toilet cubicle sits an elderly lady. She is a dear neighbour of the bridegroom's family. She is partly thinking what a nice surprise it was to find Fr. Pat Murnane seated at her table. Using two walking sticks, but mentally still perfectly agile. He must be what…94, 95 at least. She'd just assumed he was dead long since. But mostly she is thinking about the task in hand, that for which the toilet was invented and intended. As she waits impatiently for the second instalment another thought occurs. 'When I get back to the table, I really must ask Fr. Pat what ever became of Fr. Michael?'

In the fifth and last cubicle there is a man sitting on the closed toilet seat. He is the bridegroom and his trousers are down around his ankles. Sitting straddled across him is a woman with a cerise dress hitched above her hips. Their nether regions are conjoined and his face is buried between her bosoms. They are rocking very slightly and trying to be oh so very quiet.

They were discovered by the Bride, one minute ago, when she barged into the Ladies and happened to notice something out of the corner of her eye. A glint of belt buckle was visible from under the cubicle door. Standing back away from the door and tilting her head sideways, the Bride saw the label inside the waistband of the trousers, recognised all too well the design of black leather shoe. Hadn't she gone for the fitting months ago, when choosing what suit he would hire? Hadn't she picked up the shoes herself in Fitzpatrick's when her husband-to-be could not find the time?

As to what he was doing? She pressed her ear to the door and detected just enough rhythm to know that his 'mistake' with the stripper on his stag night was being repeated only inches away from her. As to with whom, she doesn't have to see to know it is the Second Bridesmaid. The one with the big tits and nothing else to recommend her. The one who is a total bitch. The one who is her cousin. The one who she never wanted as a bridesmaid in the first place only her mother guilt-tripped her into it.

Since they were born on the same day twenty-nine years ago, their mothers have always maintained the fantasy that they're the best of friends. They're not. And now this...

The Bride's first instinct was to pound on the door, to scream at her loutish husband and scrape fingernails across the Second Bridesmaid's face. But she didn't. At some level she was not 100% surprised and had already rehearsed such a situation in her mind. She had realised that to face them down in this sort of public scenario would only invite humiliation and mortification upon herself. Everyone would see. And then those who didn't see would be told by those who had. And then they'd all stand around in whispering huddles saying he's an awful man. Really awful. And the Bride? God, she's a poor thing. On her wedding day that should have been the best day of her life. Yes, she's a poor poor pathetic little thing.

When she heard voices of the girls from work approach she bolted into the first cubicle and closed the door.

In the fifth cubicle they begin to rock a little faster. Then faster still. They allow themselves the odd gasp and moan, moving now in a determined fashion towards the finish line.

But all is not entirely well. The Second Bridesmaid is a substantial girl and as her feet leave the floor, her weight falls fully on the bridegroom. In the heat of things, his body slips slightly sideways. As a consequence he feels the silver toilet flushing lever pressing into one of his back ribs. It's uncomfortable. As their combined weights shift further it feels downright painful. Momentarily, he removes a hand from her buttock and pushes against the cubicle wall to get back straight. But he can't. And now the toilet lever is boring a hole in his back. He stops rocking but the Second Bridesmaid continues heedlessly. It matters not. His potential orgasm is draining away and will not be resurrected. On a brighter note, it sounds like the Second Bridesmaid is coming.

Sounds like.

The Bride is still crying in a toilet cubicle, though not quite as intensely as before. The wooden hoops in her dress are now broken but that is of little account. She is sitting down on the toilet and one of her reasons for crying has disappeared.

She tears off two squares of toilet tissue and blows her nose. Then she flushes the toilet and the four neighbouring toilets also flush, in unison. It's time for the Bride—it's time for all of them—to go back out to the wedding party.

An Attempted Resurrection

Danny Denton

IT WAS SUNDAY MORNING, cold and grey and on the verge of rainfall. Isaac Donovan, a tallish biology teacher of almost thirty years, arrived at the team dressing rooms a few minutes early. Isaac was freshly shaven, and though hollowed out by a certain fatigue and the strain of not wearing his glasses, his eyes were fresh and wide. The unlocked metal door signified that Noel Regan and Boris were already there. The manager and team captain usually arrived together in Boris's muddy van, talking tactics and results while most of the other members of the team still dozed or ate their Sunday breakfast. Isaac slipped in quietly.

'Howya, 'Saac,' Boris said, looking up from his place on the bench. Using his car key, he scraped mud from the sole of a football boot.

'Howya Boris, howya Noel.'

Noel turned from the thin strip of window, a large, charismatic man, a county footballer in his day. 'Morning, Isaac. 'Tis dry at least.'

Isaac dropped his gear bag onto the bench and sat next to it, leaning back slowly on the cold block wall. 'You're Mr. Reliable, Isaac,' the manager continued, 'always here first.'

'The pitch is after drying up since Thursday anyway,' Boris said, rubbing dirt now from the studs of the boot, 'we walked up around it earlier.' They'd been unable to train on the pitch on Thursday, but the days since had been chilly and dry.

'Still a bit soft around the bottom goal,' Noel said. 'But that'll suit us if we know it and they don't.'

Isaac started to take things out of his bag: his boots, socks and shorts, a stale vest, footballing gloves. It was an important game. They were facing relegation from the league and if they could beat St. Finbarr's their season might yet be saved. People often mistook Isaac for a nervous person, because he was quiet, but he wasn't in any way of an anxious disposition and certainly wasn't nervous today. He knew how to play the game and was confident in his ability.

Boris and Noel went back to their previous conversation about results so far and fixtures left, and how strong the chance of survival was. Isaac listened quietly as he unfolded his football socks. A car pulled into the car park and doors began to slam. After the sound of footsteps on the slate-gravel, Shammy's young head popped around the door.

'Howye lads!' He grinned widely and bounced across the room, flinging his bag on the bench in the usual spot. Johnny and Daniel Lynch followed him in, all three wearing the club tracksuit.

'It's fuckin' freezing,' Johnny moaned, rubbing his hands rapidly.

'Fuckin' fuck,' Shammy shivered, 'will it be played?'

'Pitch is good,' Boris replied.

Isaac knew that Shammy would prefer not to play; it was clear from his red-rimmed eyes that he'd been on the tear the night before, though he wouldn't admit to it because he might lose his place on the team.

'Are you fit?' Boris asked him, a challenge of sorts.

'I am,' Shammy laughed. 'Sure I've been warming up all morning with aul' Mrs. Lynch, haven't I lads?' He winked at Isaac. 'While I was waiting for them to get outa bed, like!' He rubbed his hands briskly.

Smirking, Daniel squirted water from a bottle in his direction, and Shammy yelped. Noel watched the goings-on with a wry smile, and said that he'd be lucky if they were as lively on the pitch.

With the bit of banter came the sound of more engines along the country road, slowing and turning on to the narrow lane that led to the dressing rooms, and over the next twenty or so minutes players arrived in dribs and drabs. They took their usual spots on the painted green bench that ran the length of the inside walls of the dressing room.

It was a dim room, the bulb not strong enough to illuminate the space, natural light coming only through the thin, grilled window on the east wall. Brian Breen and Paddy Whelan, two of Noel's selectors, arrived and offered their tactical suggestions to Noel in the privacy of the shower room. The dressing room dinned like a pub, was probably in fact a continuation or resumption of conversations begun in the pub the previous night. Men were shouting back and forth, goading and slagging one another, and laughter regularly erupted. Michael Ferry, who lived on the same estate as Isaac and was the team goalkeeper, arrived and squeezed in next to his neighbour.

'How's it going, Isaac?' he said with a mild sigh. Michael had helped Isaac out when he and his wife Judy had first moved in, recommending a good landscaper and inviting them over for dinner and drinks. Their wives struck up a friendship then, and spoke to each other now almost every day.

'The missus told me your good news,' Michael said, once he had unloaded his gear. 'Congratulations.' They shook hands.

O'Brien was sitting on the other side of Michael. 'What's the good news?' he asked, cocking his head and turning sideways to Michael. Isaac wished that Michael had kept quiet.

'Isaac and Judy have a young 'un on the way,' Michael answered.

'Hah!' O'Brien grinned. 'Congratulations! We thought it'd never happen. Listen to this lads!'

The room hushed a little and O'Brien announced to them all Isaac's good fortune.

'Judy Donovan is up the pole!' he roared, pointing to Isaac. 'Shake the man's hand! The guilty party here!'

There was a big cheer, and to his great shame Isaac was the centre of attention. The other players shook him and shook his hand and made remarks about his wife and his cock, until Noel finally hushed them, shouting that he was delighted for Isaac that he was in working order but that there was an important game to be played and focus was needed.

~

Noel Regan was a large, doughty man with a swollen nose and a thick neck. Like a lot of figures central to a social circle, he could be loud and funny or quiet and respectful, philosophical or pig-headed, depending on the given circumstances. Trained as a steel worker, he'd emigrated to Boston when recession had undermined life in Cork. In America, he continued to play football and hurling and when people spoke of him in the town's pubs now they said that, in his heyday, Noel Regan would have gone through a brick wall for the winning of a ball. On his return to Ireland, he became a prominent figure in the club. His involvement and dedication to the GAA in the town went a long way in painting over the fact that he had left three children and a wife in Roxbury, the reasons for the split never divulged.

His powerful chest had, at this stage, sagged to a broad belly. Because of his great reputation and dedication as a player, he quickly came to be the manager of the football team. Many of the younger players complained about him at the first opportunity. He was stuck in an older time, they said, his training methods were dated. The time was past for long distance piggy-back races, for sprinting up hills and dragging yourself through December muck on your belly like a soldier. They complained at the lack of ball work done and said that he knew nothing of tactics or of strategy. But come the important games, Noel Regan knew how to intimidate them towards inspiration, giving rousing, militant speeches. What they lacked in skill and style, they made up for in spirit and ignorant determination.

'A few changes from last week lads,' Noel began. There was absolute silence. He read the names from a crumpled sheet of yellow paper; no doubt there were tea and food stains on it from the morning's breakfast and the previous evening's deliberations. 'Same full-back line. Michael Ferry in goal, Tommy Rush at full-back, Hughie in the left corner and Paul Holly in the right. Ye're playing well together lads, keep it tight back there and use the wings when you're clearing the ball. Michael, call the shots as usual.'

On the bench the players stared straight ahead or at the ground between their boots, most with their elbows perched on their knees. Sometimes after a player had been named in the team, he'd rise and quietly begin to stretch. 'Martin King at centre-back. Gally right half-back and Shammy Scanlon at left half-back.' Isaac recognised immediately that he'd been left out of the team. Either that, or Noel had switched him to another position, which had never happened: he'd been a half-back since underage and he was sure now that he was dropped from the team. Quietly alarmed, he failed to hear who was playing in midfield. Did I not play well last week? he asked himself. Has my effort in training dropped? Didn't Noel call me 'Mr. Reliable' not half an hour ago?

Isaac was jolted out of his internal crisis by the little cheer Daniel and Shammy raised when Johnny Lynch was named at left half-forward. Noel paused briefly, raising an eyebrow at them, and they dodged his look like school children. 'Paul Lyons and Daniel Lynch in the corner forward positions, swapping back and forth lads, and Boris at full-forward.'

A gentle clamour began, players being handed their jerseys by the selectors and repeating aspects of the team to each other. Shammy and Daniel stood briefly and made a joke about something. Isaac couldn't think why he'd been dropped, but suddenly he felt that he was somehow incapable of playing football, that if he was brought into the game at some point he'd fumble his first attempts to catch the ball, that his passes would go straight to the opposition. He couldn't remember the last time he'd been left out of the team without being injured or ill. Looking around as the other men prepared to do battle, he realised that maybe he had never deserved to play in the first place, that he had been a pretender, filling the position until a more capable individual arrived.

The jerseys were pulled on and the bootlaces were tied and quiet fell again in the dim room. Dust particles swam slowly through the strip of light at the window. Noel had worked himself up now and grimaced as he turned to face everyone in the room.

'Lads, we all know how important this game is today. Ye don't need to be told.' He paced the room as he spoke, gesticulating with his hands as he went around in circles. 'I've made these changes because we've been flat in recent weeks and I'm trying to jizz things up a bit. Let's give Gally, Johnny and Paul our support. Gally, you're young and you've pace, so work your socks off and don't be afraid to get forward and attack the ball.'

As Noel continued, advising Johnny and Paul, a few players muttered words of encouragement to Gally. Isaac crumpled feebly into himself, the thought of being deemed inadequate and replaced by a youth who'd never before played a junior football game.

'Brendan and Harri in midfield will get up and down the pitch as they always do, so use them as outlets in both defence and attack. If we can get the early ball directly into Boris and play off him then there'll be plenty of scores in it for us. And remember lads, from defence play the wings, and going forward let's use the space.

'Now,' Noel said in a low voice, almost a whisper. People leaned in. Muffled shouts came through the wall from the other dressing room. 'We've not been up to scratch in recent weeks. We've not worked hard enough at all, and that's why I've freshened up the team.' As Noel spoke, Isaac retraced everything he could remember about his role in those recent games. 'Today is a chance for some of the fringe players. Take it lads. Work your socks off out there. If you have to crawl from the pitch afterwards I don't care. I want one hundred and ten percent. We're playing for the town today, and if we lose we're in danger of relegation from the division. The town relegated? It hasn't happened in our history and it fucking well won't happen today!' He growled loudly, pointing accusingly at each player he faced. He was red in the face and a ropy vein began to pronounce itself to one side of his forehead. 'Ye're men! And ye'll go out onto that pitch and hit the opposition fair and hard, like men. Go right through them if you have to. And if you have to put your head through a boot to stop them kicking a ball, then that's what you do.' He paused. 'Help each other out there lads, back each other up.' He clutched his elbow, as if he'd been stung, grunting and pausing again briefly. 'If any man isn't up for it, now's the time to say it. Because I want to see ye give everything today. I want to see ye working and scrapping for every ball, jumping higher than them, running faster than them, hitting harder than them. From the very first minute!' There were beads of sweat on his forehead and cheeks, and his voice strained at the point of cracking. 'The first whistle! Up on your feet!'

Everybody rose and the silence that had huddled around Noel's voice shrank away. Stud on concrete, like the hooves of horses on a road, like the movement of armies.

'Give me five lads!'

They marched on the spot and sounded each stomp of the boot: '*ONE! TWO! THREE! FOUR! FIVE!*' The shouts of enthusiasm and encouragement sounded like gunfire. Noel continued to incant his violent mantras: 'From the first whistle! Hit them hard! Everything! Everything!'

'Give me seven!' he shouted, his face so laboured that he looked in pain.

'ONE! TWO! THREE! FOUR! FIVE! SIX! SEVEN!'

Isaac was lost in the stampede, weak in the legs, feeling right then that if a wind had blown through the room he'd have collapsed under it. Noel opened the dressing room door and as light rushed in the players rushed out, each in a world of his own intensity. Boris glared like some crazed murderer, his eyes bulging; Shammy passed by Isaac with a delirious grin smeared across his face. Only Michael seemed calm still, mildly distracted.

When the last player had passed, Isaac joined the other substitutes in putting on an extra top so that they'd be warm on the sideline. As they left the dressing room, someone remarked that he felt Isaac shouldn't have been dropped. Isaac, embarrassed by the attention and not knowing what to say, hummed a non-committal response and started to jog up to the pitch.

~

On the pitch they did a long, thorough warm-up, led by Boris. Then, they began to pass the balls back and forth amongst themselves. The referee called for captains. Brian and Paddy, the token selectors, stood on the sideline with their hands in the pocket of their coats and quietly speculated.

Noel was walking over to join them when he collapsed, tumbling to his knees first and slowly pitching backwards till he was stretched out flat.

Boris ran over, followed by others on the team. It took a long time before everybody noticed the commotion on the sideline. When Isaac arrived, Boris was knelt over Noel. It was like they were looking into each other's eyes. Boris shook the body roughly, his knuckles white and big as stones. He bent his ear to Noel's mouth, which was opened slightly.

'Shit,' he said. He shook Noel again. 'Noel? Noel?' he said. Noel did not respond. Boris felt for a pulse and paused.

'Does anyone know CPR?' he asked the gathering crowd of men. Isaac hung back. Boris focused, put one fist on top of the other, and started to push down on Noel's heart. One, two, three, four, five. 'Christ,' Michael Ferry said. Isaac had been teaching first aid to secondary school students for years; he could see that Boris was doing it wrong but something stopped him from saying it and he stayed at the edge of the crowd. People were looking around at each other and back at Noel. Come on Noel, they were muttering, almost as if he was embarrassing them. Was there not a doctor among them? They asked players on the opposition but none came forward. Paddy called an ambulance and they listened to him explain the situation. His words made it clear for them what was actually happening, and they would be repeated many times afterward, borrowed for the telling of the story.

'Someone should call a priest,' the referee said from the edge of the circle. He was weaving through the crowd, getting closer to the centre.

'Try mouth-to-mouth,' Shammy said, as if in response. He was white as a bed sheet.

Noel's hands were still at his sides. Boris put his mouth onto Noel's mouth. He wasn't holding the nose closed. After a few moments, he ceased blowing and started to thump Noel's chest. 'Come on, Noel. Come on now.' He again begged the crowd for someone who knew what to do.

Isaac stole in beside him.

'Move over, Boris,' he muttered. 'You're doing it wrong.' Isaac resented Noel for bringing this on him, resented Boris and the crowd for being incompetent, resented himself for not stepping in sooner.

'Do you know what you're doing?' Boris asked, straightening and looking up at him.

Isaac knelt. 'Yes, move over,' he muttered again, not looking into Boris' pleading eyes. 'I need some space.' Reluctantly, Boris got to his feet. Isaac immediately began CPR.

~

'Does he know what he's doing?' Isaac heard Boris say again and again. Somebody told Boris that he'd done all he could. People issued words of encouragement to Isaac and continued to appeal to Noel as if he could hear them. Isaac felt his knees getting stiff from the cold mud of the field. He continued for five beats. A pause. He put his hand behind Noel's head, stroking his hair as he tilted the head right back to straighten the course of the windpipe. Mouth-to-mouth, holding the large, cold nose, breathing gently. The nose was like putty between his thumb and forefinger. Five heavy beats on the sternum again. He checked for a pulse. Men were tutting and huffing above and around him, and Isaac didn't want to raise his eyes to them. No pulse; he knew he wasn't mistaken. He repeated these acts four times. There was nothing he could do. People would tell him that later, he knew. At the same time, he knew that he couldn't be seen to stop until the ambulance arrived. Where was the ambulance? It had been more than twenty minutes. He released Noel's wrist from his gentle grip and started to pump the sternum again. 'Can I help?' Boris choked, kneeling again beside him. He continued to leave and return the whole time. The referee began, finally, to clear people away, and they were glad to be released from the situation, cleared of the duty of standing there and watching. Isaac, too, was glad to be free of their attention.

~

Half an hour passed before the ambulance appeared in the car park, like something waking late, disorientated and rushing. Isaac had tried to revive Noel all that time. The driver picked his way from the gravel to the grass and through the double-gates in the bottom corner of the pitch, and drove right up to the small crowd that was left. The paramedics seemed almost reluctant to get out. They looked alike, with day-old beards and tired faces, although one was much older than the other.

'Clear back now,' they said as they tramped over to Isaac and his dead coach.

'How long since he collapsed?' the younger asked, ignoring Boris's loud questions in the background.

'About half an hour, I think,' Isaac replied in a low voice. 'There's been no pulse from the start.'

He regarded the paramedics for a moment, and it seemed that both he and they thought the same thing. The paramedics were incredibly grey-faced and sober, moving slowly and methodically as they checked Noel's vital signs. They could have been production line-workers at a factory. Isaac had expected them to be more animated, to be almost chirpy in their efforts to save a man's life. He looked around and saw that everybody had that same look, gazing tiredly over the whole scene. It was, in fact, as if they were all on the same assembly line— Isaac, Boris, the paramedics, the referee, the remaining players—all standing in a long procession, making tiny adjustments to some nebulous object and passing it forward to the next person. Each man was vacant, tired, hopeless, the mind fixed on inane, recycled thoughts, skirting the horror of the present predicament.

Boris's agitation had withered and now he only stood hand on hip and stared out over the paramedics and Noel.

'Half an hour you said?' the older of the paramedics asked.

'Yes,' Isaac replied.

'Will we call it, John?' said the younger, his hand pressed on Noel's shoulder.

'Might as well.'

'Half an hour is a long time,' the younger concluded, shrugging.

Isaac expected Boris to make a remark about half an hour being a long time all right, especially if you'd been waiting for an ambulance, but he said nothing.

And that was it. They lifted Noel's cooling corpse onto a stretcher and into the back of the ambulance. The remaining people quickly scattered. After a few moments, the paramedics emerged from the rear of the ambulance and returned.

Speaking to Isaac, 'We'll need someone to come with us?'

'I'll go,' Boris said, drawing their eyes from Isaac as he spoke. He was fulfilling his duty as captain of the team and leader of the men and Isaac was relieved.

The three of them shuffled in the direction of the ambulance. The referee slapped a hand on Isaac's shoulder. They were the last two.

'You done all you could, player. Well done.'

'Yeah,' Isaac said. 'Thanks.'

~

There were a few left in the dressing room when they returned. Shammy said well done to Isaac as well. 'You couldn't have done anymore, like.'

Several times, players repeated their disbelief at what had happened, analysing the incident as if it had been a match in itself. Who did what? When? Where? Who had seen it coming? Some felt they had seen signs of it in the preceding moments, days and weeks. Some speculated that Noel took the whole thing too seriously and stress had got the better of him. It was only a game, after all. Others pointed out that at least he died where he'd have wanted to, out on the field.

Isaac listened to them as he showered, comments that would play over and over in his mind as he drove home. He knew he had done all he could, but he resented the predicament that he had been put in. He didn't know who to blame, or if blame could be apportioned at all, but nevertheless he felt aggrieved and bitter. He lathered shower gel and rubbed viciously at his stiff, dirty knees. Michael leaned in the doorway.

'Do you want me to drive you home? You must be fairly shaken.'

'No, Mike, it's fine thanks.'

'Are you sure?'

'Yeah. Sure I'd only have to come back for the car anyway. It'd be hassle. Thanks anyway.'

'Fair enough. Take it handy now.'

Isaac turned away and continued to shower, steam billowing around him and drawing his silhouette further into ambiguity. Michael paused, as if he had something else to say, but after the moment's hesitation he turned and left. 'See you then, Isaac,' he called after him. Isaac embraced the heat of the water, washing himself several times.

~

When Isaac left, Shammy, Hughie, Martin and Pat were still there. He felt their eyes on his back as he put his bag in the boot of the car. He imagined them muttering to each other. Could he have done more? Why didn't he come forward sooner? Did he know what he was doing? After every event came the fallout and the analysis. And after all that had happened that morning, Isaac began to dread for the first time the idea of his child coming into the world, what a terrible place it was. And people were helpless to stop it, chained to experience in this way. How could Isaac protect his child from all this when he couldn't even protect himself? Would his son or daughter one day find themselves kneeling over some dead body, face-to-face, having to touch its cold, slimy lips with their own quivering mouths? These thoughts poured over him like a wave, pounding and disorientating him. What could he do? He was powerless now to stop all of these terrible things from happening, powerless to protect himself or his loved ones.

As he started the car, he realised how badly he was shaking and took deep breaths. He couldn't go home. Judy would wonder why he wasn't still playing the match. She would soon find out what he had done, and inevitably draw every detail out of him. She wouldn't stop until she felt she had psychologically cleansed him. And he couldn't go to the pub, because word would already have spread, and because people only ever wanted to talk there.

He drove for a few hours. He drove the back roads in silence, came to the suburbs and inevitably the city. When he had crossed the river and passed through the northside, he found himself suddenly in the country again, the pleasing sense of unfamiliarity on a wide, flat road that cut through a valley. For a few minutes heavy rain blasted the windscreen and the landscape beyond it. Just as suddenly it stopped. He'd keep going another while, he thought, and in a daze, Isaac drove on.

Soul Mate

Viv McDade

HAD IT NOT BEEN FOR MY NEW BEDROOM CURTAINS, a lovely design of cornflowers on cream cotton, none of this might have happened. Having gathered the rufflette and spaced the hooks evenly, I stood on my dressing table stool to reach the rail and, quite by chance, glanced across to the green. I watched a child sweep her butterfly net to the ground and crouch beside it to examine what she'd caught. As I turned back to the curtain rail, a movement in a window of the apartment on the edge of the green caught my eye.

The movement had occurred in the bathroom. Although the build up of steam behind frosted glass made it impossible to distinguish the figure clearly, I recognised the movements of a body drying itself; first the head with short rapid movements, then the slower movement of a blue towel moving across the blurred shape. I got down from the stool and remained as still and attentive as a cat focused on the scuttle of a mouse.

The bathroom door opened and a naked man stepped into the bedroom, a towel in his hand. He was of medium height and slightly stout, belly and backside soft without being flabby. Right from the start I've liked the fact that his body isn't perfect. He half-turned towards the window and tossed the towel onto the bed. The hair on his chest and stomach was brown. A thin darker line ran from the navel down to the pubic hair, the penis pale against its darkness.

He went to the cupboard and opened both doors at once. With his back towards me and his arms stretched out, he looked vulnerable. It made me think of a crucifix and I had the immediate sense that he was a man who had suffered. A drawer was opened and he took out a pair of white underpants. He pulled them on, bending his knees a little, his thumbs moving around the inside of the waistband to get them comfortable. The shirt he chose was long-sleeved and looked as if it was made from thick, white cotton; he buttoned it in front of what must have been a mirror on the bedroom wall. He put on beige cotton trousers and tucked the shirt into them. I've seen those trousers in shop windows, teamed with tee shirts and casual sweaters. They're called chinos and the men who wear them are the kind who take care of their appearance. I liked the fact that he had gone for a white shirt rather than a tee shirt; it's the right choice for a man of his age. He's about forty, much the same age as me. He reached into the cupboard for a sweater and switched off the light as he left the room.

I sat for a couple of hours shaken by what had happened. The experience had a kind of purity I could not put my finger on. It was as if I had seen someone properly for the first time and a deep connection had formed between us. How could it be otherwise when I had been so close to the way he prepared himself to go into the world that night? Who else knew how he had showered, the way he put on his clothes, what underpants he was wearing? He had revealed to me a very private part of himself and it took away some of the feeling I've always had that people aren't able to connect with me.

It's no easy task to make a friend, much less find a soul mate. In my experience, even the nicest people turn out to be strange. It's the main reason I change jobs a lot. The jobs always start well: I'm a hard worker, able to understand new tasks quickly and easily and, at the beginning, people are friendly and helpful. They go out of their way to explain company policies and give me tips for dealing with various mangers. They share bits of office gossip and invite me to join them for lunch. I've never been able to work out why things go wrong, but I always know the precise point at which it starts happening. In fact, it's perfectly true to say that I can sense it will happen before they know themselves; it's a kind of sixth sense I have.

What happens is that people start going out of their way to avoid me. There was one occasion when a woman who sat near me moved to a desk on the other side of the office. She'd been behaving in an odd way for some time, avoiding eye contact with me and sometimes looking flustered and red in the face when she had to speak to me about work matters. It was hurtful because she was one of the people I'd especially chosen to befriend. I had imagined that we could be friends in the way many women seem to be: going shopping together, meeting for coffee, sharing confidences. On my second day in the job I'd invited her to join me for lunch. She was under the impression we were going to the staff coffee shop and became quite awkward and reserved when she realised I'd arranged a taxi and booked a table at a restaurant. She kept saying, 'I feel uncomfortable about this; I thought you meant the staff canteen.' I think it's very attractive when people are shy about someone making a fuss of them. After that I started bringing in little gifts for her; at first a chocolate bar, or the nougat I overheard her saying she liked, and then CDs and books.

After a couple of weeks, I picked up the familiar pattern of people avoiding me and whispering to each other. They would simply disappear for lunch without a word, or stop speaking when I was around. Whenever this happens I know that it will be only a few days before I get an email or a telephone call from the manager asking for a word with me.

I'm not saying I like these occasions but there is some comfort in knowing exactly how the managers will behave. They generally stand up to offer me a chair and their greetings are awkward. After a short pause they puff themselves up a little and get straight to the point as if to remove any opportunity for dissent.

'As you know…' is the popular way to start. They go on to remind me that either party is entitled to terminate the contract during the probation period. They feel it would be in the best interests of both parties if I left. It's always described as thoughtful, but never necessary, for me to continue to the end of the day. I am invariably paid for it in any event. They wish me well for the future. There has never been any criticism of my work so it is hard to see how it could be in a company's best interests for me to leave. It is, however, in my best interests: I have no desire to work in places where people whisper behind your back and avoid you.

*

At the time when I first connected with the man in the apartment I'd already given up on permanent jobs and enrolled with an agency that places people on short-term assignments. Although this meant I did not always have a job, it was a price I was more than willing to pay in exchange for seldom being anywhere long enough to become the victim of people's personal fears and inadequacies. It also, as fate would have it, gave me the opportunity to arrange my morning routine around my new friend's activities.

At six every morning he opened his bedroom curtains. The light in the room was low and soft and he sat cross-legged on the bed. An orange shawl was wrapped loosely around his shoulders and his open hands, one on top of the other, rested in his lap. His head was slightly bowed, as if he were focusing on some point a short distance in front of him. From time to time he stretched his neck lightly, or moved his shoulders but most of the time he was very still.

I sat in the armchair I'd moved into my bedroom, and his stillness entered and comforted me. Sometimes, at the edge of my vision, I was aware of a car reversing out of a driveway or the boy who delivers newspapers, but I had no desire to turn any attention towards them. Nothing intruded on the space we shared each morning.

After twenty minutes he would raise his head and arch his back, curling his arms so that his fists were against each side of his neck. He stretched each arm in turn then smoothed his hands over his face. He would unwrap the shawl from his shoulders and get up slowly, take off his sleeping shorts and go into the bathroom.

His body and activities were blurred while he was in the bathroom; it was his private time and I would go into the kitchen and make myself a cup of coffee. By the time I returned he had dried himself and was ready to get dressed. I would warm my hands around the coffee mug and watch him select clothes from the cupboard and put them on. It was like a poem, a beautiful refrain, this daily repetition of the simple activity that had brought us together.

After two weeks of our mornings together, I wanted to know more about the rest of his day. I waited until he reached the point of knotting his tie, then hurried out of my apartment and walked to the corner of the next street. In a few seconds the heavy doors of his apartment block swung open and he stepped onto the pavement. He was not as tall as I'd thought, perhaps because he leaned forward a little as he walked.

He stopped beside an old Citroën with rust on its bonnet, unlocked the door and got in. His head tilted slightly and he looked into the rear-view mirror. The car started on the second attempt and he pulled away from the pavement. He actually glanced at me as he drove past, and then turned in the direction of the motorway into the city.

The experience deepened our connection. He might have looked anywhere, but he chose to look at me, the only person on the street. There was also the fact of his car; although we are both professional people, neither of us has ever felt it necessary to impress others with fancy cars. I knew that the right thing to do was to see him off to work every morning.

Two days later he gave me a very small nod and drove past before I could respond. The following morning I made sure I was better prepared. I wore my pretty pink blouse and a pair of midnight blue slacks. As soon as he'd changed into second gear, I gave him a bright smile and a discreet little wave with my fingers. He frowned, nodded quickly and looked away. I liked that about him; shyness and restraint are so much more attractive than the big show of friendliness most people put on in new relationships.

I'd just got back to my apartment and was making another cup of coffee when a woman from the agency rang. It had begun to annoy me that they never give the slightest consideration to whether or not I might be busy. Would I be available to work for a week at an accounting firm in the city? A member of staff had been rushed to hospital and someone was needed urgently to help with the month end accounts.

Whatever the failings of individual staff members, the agency has definitely grasped my preference for very short assignments. I have become the person they turn to when companies need to be rescued. I find that I carry myself differently, am a little aloof, mysterious even. This is partly because of the urgency of my roles but it is also to make sure people sense that my private life is not something I intend to discuss with them. My approach is to take the task in hand immediately and use the pressure of work to protect myself from engaging with other staff. I have probably become less tolerant of others, which is not a bad thing; having a life of one's own frees one from the need to make friends at work.

The assignment hours were very disruptive to our routine. I didn't like the idea of having to leave before he was dressed and ready to go to work; it would unsettle the flow of our mornings. I had a chat with the manager and explained that personal commitments made it difficult for me to be in by nine. I suggested starting at ten and working through until six.

I saw immediately that she was the sort of person who gave no consideration to small personal requests from staff. She reminded me that the work required the co-operation of other departments, said she felt it would slow things down if there was an hour at each end of the day when not all staff were available to each other. She explained that she already had someone who was pregnant coming in late, but this was a short-term exception she had made for a permanent worker.

I was not prepared to take this lying down. I spoke up immediately and in a clear and formal manner so that she would be left in no doubt that I understood her veiled implications. 'I have two serious concerns with what you have told me. Firstly, you do not trust me to be alone in the office. Secondly, you are discriminating against me because I am not pregnant.'

She looked at me in silence for a moment, her eyes slightly narrowed, almost as if some sort of troubling realisation had just occurred to her. She spoke slowly, with the feigned deliberation they use when you've seen through them and they're forced to resort to their authority, choosing their words as if the smallest mistake such an important person might make could have enormous consequences. 'That is not what I was saying. I was not saying either of those things.'

I returned to the office and made a short announcement to the staff. I explained that distrust and discrimination were rife, and, in spite of the fact that I would only be there for a week, it was not my intention to let things pass. I pointed out that a labour lawyer would immediately identify the situation as one of blatant discrimination. A few of them, the weak and fearful type, looked bewildered; the others kept their heads down, pretending not to hear. At lunch time the manager called me in again. She'd phoned the agency and told them my services were no longer required.

I gathered my belongings and left. A few blocks from the office I saw two of the staff emerging from a coffee shop, chatting and laughing. One of them spotted me and her face immediately became serious. Without looking at her companion she said something. The companion looked at me, replied to her colleague and both turned abruptly into the next shop. I hesitated, unsure whether or not to pursue them into the shop and demand an explanation.

At precisely that moment I saw him walking down the pavement towards me. He glanced at his watch, stepped around three women dawdling in front of him, and hurried along the edge of the pavement. He did not see me until we were in front of each other.

'Thank God you've come.'

He stopped immediately, his eyes wide and his face tense.

I was crying and reaching out to him and his hands were in front of his chest, palms towards me as if cautioning me against a public display of emotion. He stepped backwards, lost his balance on the edge of the pavement and staggered onto the road. The car hit him with a soft thud and he fell like a rag doll onto the tarmac.

I ran to him and knelt over him, cradling my arms around his head and shoulders. People surrounded us and the driver, white faced and trembling, ran from his car. 'Is he okay? He fell off the pavement in front of me. There was nothing I could do.'

A woman crouched beside me and put her hand on my shoulder. 'For God's sake don't move him. He may have hurt his spine. Hold his hand, but don't move him.'

'He's still breathing,' said a man. 'Keep calm; an ambulance is on its way.'

The ambulance arrived. Two men got out, placed a stretcher on the ground and eased it under him. I stayed close, talking to him gently, telling him I was there. After they'd loaded the stretcher one of the men looked at me kindly. 'You can come with us,' he said and helped me into the back next to the stretcher. The doors swung closed and the siren wailed as we raced to the hospital.

The stretcher was wheeled into Accident and Emergency with me by his side. A nurse took my arm. 'Are you all right?'

I nodded.

'There's tea in the waiting room. The doctor will be here in a minute.' She moved her head in the direction of the admissions desk. 'If you feel able please go over and give them his details.'

I was in the waiting room for over an hour before the doctor arrived, a taut little man with a clipboard in his hand and a stethoscope round his neck. He pulled up a chair and looked at me.

'How badly is he hurt? Will he be all right?'

'What is your relationship to the patient?'

'I have to know if he's all right.'

His eyes searched my face. 'Perhaps you'll give me the admission details,' he said, resting the clipboard on his lap and taking a pen from his breast pocket.

I pressed my hands into my lap to steady their shaking. 'Does any of that matter? Please just tell me if he'll be all right?'

'The patient says he does not know you. He may have suffered more concussion than his injuries would suggest. You can help by answering my questions.'

I was frightened, then angered, by the way in which he simply looked at me and waited, refusing all my pleas for information, his face expressionless. After a while he suggested I should leave and there was something about the way he said it that made me feel there might be some kind of trouble if I didn't.

It was appalling to leave without any information, with the doctor's cold eyes escorting me to the exit. The only comfort was the knowledge that he was alive. If he did not return to his apartment the next day I would visit him at the hospital. No one could stop me from doing that.

I only visited once and it was not a success. An older man and woman sat in chairs beside his bed. I was conscious of the importance of creating a good impression as I walked towards them. He was propped up against pillows, the fluorescent light above the bed darkening the shadows under his eyes. The moment he saw me, he reached for the cord resting on his bed and pushed the button at the end. A nurse came to the bedside while I was greeting his visitors and he spoke to her in a low, urgent voice. I assumed he was asking her to bring a chair for me so it was a surprise when she took hold of my arm and asked me to step into the office at the entrance to the ward.

'The patient does not wish to see you. I insist that you leave immediately and do not return.'

It was hurtful but I left without making any kind of fuss. The combination of his concussion and my anxiety may have made me a little insensitive in terms of the timing of my visit. It was the first time he had been angry with me. I wanted him to know I understood and forgave him, and the best way to do that seemed to be to keep away from the hospital and wait for his return, to keep the home fires burning, so to speak.

During the following two weeks I watched his window as usual but he did not return. If he was recuperating elsewhere there was no telling how long he might be away. My anxiety increased until sleep was impossible and I was too nervous and distracted to take on any work.

I went to a new doctor, who was brisk but supportive in the few minutes we had together. She was clearly shocked that I had been there when the accident occurred; urged me to take it easy until he was out of hospital and we could get back to our normal routine. She prescribed sleeping pills and a light tranquilliser, which I take three times a day. 'All you need is a little support to steady yourself until the crisis is over.' She stood up and touched my arm. 'In the meantime, try to remember that what you are experiencing is perfectly normal. Anyone in your situation would feel exactly the same.'

Polyfilla

Mia Gallagher

THIS WAS GOING TO BE A BAD ONE. Sean felt it in his bones the minute he walked into the room. For a second he wished Lola had come, to buffer with her chitchat and smiles whatever discomfort was heading his way. Then he remembered, and the wish was gone as quickly as it had arrived.

The party had been thrown by a woman he'd met in college and who now worked in publishing. They'd kept in contact over the years; he'd done a few jobs for her, she'd regularly plugged his business and eighteen months ago, she'd drafted him in to oversee the renovations of her new house. She and her telly executive husband were childless and famous for hosting lavish dinner parties. Although Sean had been to a lot of these parties he'd never met more than a sprinkling of the same people twice. He wondered if his hosts did this deliberately, blending their guests like paint colours, trying out different combinations until they hit on the perfect mix. Maybe the choice was arbitrary, down to who was available and who had the flu. Up to now, it hadn't bothered him. He'd enjoyed the parties, the drink and the food and the mingling with whoever he happened to meet.

Tonight, though, was different.

He wasn't sure when he first noticed the woman in the blue dress. It would have been soon after he arrived. An ice-sweaty glass cooling the raging heart of his right palm. Bubbles of conversation rising around him, made meaningless by the thick membrane of his jangling nerves. His hostess dropping bits of him like breadcrumbs across the room as she ferried him through the crowd. He caught a glimpse of something in a corner—a swirling blue dress, a sparkling butterfly perched on a mane of red hair, a young bell-like laugh—and his hostess, reading the involuntary twitch under his skin, steered him in that direction.

'Sean,' she said, 'let me introduce you to Poppet.'

Poppet. Christ. What a stupid name. But maybe—

Her dress was made of some floaty stuff that seemed to change colour under the lights; one minute the virulent cobalt of grotto Virgins, the next the soft turquoise of the Greek sea. It reminded him of the things Lola used to wear, in the early days when she was shy and sweet, before he'd got his hands on her. She was wearing costume jewellery, the sort a girl would wear: bangles, beads, long silver earrings that brushed the white skin of her shoulders. Then she turned her head and Sean's maybes soured in a wash of irritation. Crow's feet. Flabby upper arms. Polyfilla make-up. Late forties, if she was a day.

'Sean's our architect, Poppet,' said his hostess, pressing her fingers into his upper arm. 'Very artistic. The two of you should get on famously.' She winked, released her grip and left.

A moment of awkwardness. The woman smiled. Then they both began to speak at the same time.

'Sorry,' said Sean and waved his whiskey glass. 'Go on.'

She laughed. 'Oh, nothing, just... You're an architect?'

Sean swished his whiskey, longing for the satisfying clink of contact; ice on ice. 'Mmm.'

'Wow.' Her lips curled, blow-job soft, around an invisible straw. She had drawn a line around the upper one to make it look fuller. 'I used to be a dancer.'

'Oh.' He wondered if he should make his boredom more obvious, let his eyes roam over the room, yawn loudly, glance at his watch. Maybe he should go the courteous route instead; offer to get her a refill and never come back.

'Aren't you going to ask me my real name?'

She was gazing at him intently. Her eyebrows were drawn-on, manufactured like the rest of her face.

'Most people do,' she said. 'They don't like to think of a grown woman being called Poppet. They think it's silly.'

'Oh, I…'

'Sometimes they even throw names at me. Right in the middle of a conversation. Like a, you know, ambush.'

'Really?' His curiosity surprised him. 'What kind of names?'

She smiled. 'Why don't I leave that to your imagination?'

His own mouth, he realised, had begun to curve in a smile. His pirate's smile, Lola used to call it. Casually, he swished his whiskey again, brought it to his lips.

'Hey, Josephine—' he said suddenly.

The moment suspended between them. Then she laughed. 'Nice try.'

'Not Josephine, then?'

She shook her head.

'How about… Phyllis?'

Her clumpy lashes flickered.

'No—I've got it. Bridget. Bridget.'

She laughed again. Her earrings tinkled. The skin of her shoulders was very white. Still laughing, she let her hands flutter up to pat her hair, as if it was a live animal she had enticed onto her head in the belief that it would be safe there.

He grabbed a refill from the tray and swallowed, willing the drink to do its warm work. Poppet had started to chatter away, punctuating her words with sideways glances, mischievous smiles, dramatic twists of her fine-boned wrists. Only half-listening, he smiled, laughed, making the right murmurings at the right time.

Everything about her was in motion. Her neck was full of little creases that opened and closed as she spoke. Her cleavage quivered, sand dunes fringed by a living sea of blue frills. She was constantly flicking her hair, touching it. Its bottle red jarred with the changing colours of her dress, playing tricks on Sean's eyes, making the space around her shudder. When she lifted her hands, the flesh on her upper arms wobbled. Sean imagined how it would feel, that flesh; soft and melting as a blancmange. He imagined touching it, gently at first, then roughly, grabbing and pinching and twisting so hard that in the morning she would find bruises. She moved and a sudden panic overwhelmed him. Was she leaving? Then she moved back. He grabbed another drink.

A bell sounded.

Dinner.

They had been placed several seats from each other; too far away to continue talking. Maybe, thought Sean, his head already mushy from the drink, that wasn't such a bad thing. Nonetheless, every so often he would find himself glancing over at Poppet, or feel the weight of her glance on him and, if their eyes met, would catch himself smiling before looking away, as if he had just caught sight of an old, distant acquaintance on a busy street.

The food was excellent, as it always was, accompanied by a constant stream of talk. Sean listened to himself explaining cantilevers to a budding fashion designer and wondered if anybody had brought cocaine.

Dessert arrived. Chocolate tart and a sweet yellow wine from France. Sean left most of the tart on his plate. He was pouring out his second glass of dessert wine when he became aware of a change in the room's temperature. The stream of talk had begun to falter, breaking into lesser tributaries around an intense group on the other side of the table. Poppet's laugh faded into silence. Sean caught sighs, murmurs of resignation, a sorrowful shaking of heads. Somebody had raised a serious topic.

'No, no, no!' said a thin bald man at the centre of the intense group. His voice was loud, heavy with authority. Sean remembered being introduced to him earlier. He was a cancer specialist from the Blackrock Clinic. The last few tributaries of talk trickled into a hush.

'Of course, it's an awful mess. But it's important not to think about it in simplistic terms. As Isaiah Berlin once said…'

The budding fashion designer was nodding gravely. Sean dropped his mouth to her ear. 'What's he talking about?'

'Iraq.'

Sean felt a grinding pain begin to throb in his lower jaw.

'With hindsight, it's very easy to be judgmental. But it was an extremely complicated issue at the time.'

Somebody laughed and Sean realised it was him. 'Complicated?' he said.

The specialist glanced over.

'There was nothing remotely complicated about it.' Sean's voice seemed far away and at the same time louder than he had intended. 'It's patently obvious that the whole thing was driven by economics. I mean, just look at the—'

A low murmur began at the far end of the table. The specialist lifted his hand.

'No, that's not what I—'

'Just look at the figures,' said Sean, louder. 'The death rates are—'

'That's not what I—'

'They're incredible. I mean, we call ourselves a civilised society. But what kind of civilised society kills eighty-five thousand—'

Sean observed himself, as if from a height. He was leaning forward, teeth bared, index finger jabbing at the specialist, statistics flying from his tongue like bullets. Aggressive ape behaviour, Lola called it. The specialist kept shaking his head, trying to interrupt. *That's not what I'm saying*, he kept trying to say. *No, no, no. That's not what I*—Two dots of red glowed painfully on his cheeks.

Sean heard his own voice, resonant with indignation. He was talking about morality. Double standards. Greed, capitalism, cynicism. Blah blah fucking blah.

Shut me up someone, please.

'Excuse me,' said a third voice, loudly.

The specialist, now cowering, his hands spread in defeat, glanced at the doorway. Sean finished what he was saying and looked over. The man who'd interrupted them was leaning against the surround. There was something boneless about the way he stood there; he looked as if he'd been flung at the wall, a piece of pasta thrown by a chef to see if it had been cooked enough. He had an expensive haircut and was wearing a Boss suit and an open-necked white shirt. Silver glimmered at his wrist.

Sean leaned back in his chair and eyeballed the newcomer. 'Yeah?'

'Well, what I was wondering…' The man stopped. His voice was slightly slurred, messy, at odds with his expensive appearance.

Sean sighed. The table's attention began to drift. Sean lifted his glass.

'What I was wondering was,' said the man in the suit, louder and clearer, 'was if you've actually met any Iraqis?'

Sean froze. The table prickled with unease.

'Yourself, I mean. Personally. It's just you seem to know so much about it...' The man at the doorway slitted his eyes. They were glittering at Sean, vicious little raindrops in a slack face. His mouth was a shark's; a wide thin-lipped triangle stained black from wine.

'All those numbers you keep saying. Very impressive.' He waved his hand. 'But you don't mind... you don't me asking where you got them from?'

Glasses clinked. Somebody laughed nervously.

'I mean, it wouldn't be the internet, would it?'

Sean swallowed his wine.

The shark's mouth smiled, revealing a row of pointed teeth. 'I knew it.'

Everything in the room sharpened.

Keep the head.

'I don't know,' said Sean carefully, 'what exactly your problem is, but—'

The suit laughed. 'My problem?'

Voices rose; some aimed at the suit, some at Sean, others trying to resuscitate safer threads of conversation.

'Leave it, Sean. He's had too much to—'

'Let's just—'

'Has anybody seen the latest—'

'You're the one with the fucking problem!' shouted the man at the door. 'You're the sort of liberal shit thinks we should sit on our arses and do nothing. Fuck Rwanda, fuck the Iraqis. You know how many people died in—'

'Oh yeah?' shouted Sean. 'As opposed to—'

And they were off.

A dim part of Sean wanted to stop, but he couldn't. They had engaged; once in, there was no easy way out. They had armed themselves, cherry-picking atrocities from opposing arsenals. Rwanda. Bosnia. Mugabe. Hitler. Pakistan. Belfast. Kabul. No point having weapons if you don't use them. Their words flew, landed, exploded, maimed. Sean felt the back of his neck sear violent red, saw flakes of spit collect on his opponent's lips. Once or twice, their host, perched nervously near the kitchen door, tried to intervene, but they ignored him, blinded by the frenzy of battle to everything but the need to bully the other into submission, to obliterate, to prove *I am right, listen to me.*

In the distance, the silence of the other guests crystallised around the peaks of the conflict like a frozen lake.

'Okay,' said the hostess, standing up. 'Brandy.' It wasn't a question.

The combatants eyed each other. Sean's breath was ragged. The other man's eyes had become glazed, unfocused. They could probably have taken it further but—

The suit slumped back against the door, spaghetti-soft again. Sean's shoulders drooped.

Truce. Nil all.

The hostess smiled a tight smile and laid the cognac on the table.

'Well,' said the host, 'that was lively.'

Timid attempts at conversation began to blossom, discharging the static. Avoiding eye contact with the other guests, Sean sipped his brandy and let his gaze drift around the table. His eyes landed on Poppet. During the argument he had completely forgotten her. She had vanished, ice melting in hot water. Now she seemed all too visible, her imperfections stark in the candlelight, her garish colours hurting his eyes. He wondered how he could have ever found her, even momentarily, attractive. She was gazing at her plate, where her finger was chasing a last piece of chocolate around the gold rim. Sensing him, she looked up, catching him before he could glance away.

The unexpected force of her hate struck matches on his skin. Sickened, he looked away. His glass was empty.

An hour later, the party broke up, the night's mix too flimsy to survive the brutality of the argument. The guests made their apologies, shuffled into their coats and left in their cars, swooping out of the driveway like participants at a secret wartime conference, their headlamps sweeping long beams of diamond-paned light across the dining-room wallpaper. The man in the Boss suit had been one of the first to go. Sean had stayed till the end.

He began to make his way to the door, his car keys flopping through his fingers like seaweed.

'Oh Sean, you're not driving,' said his hostess.

He turned and the room turned with him. 'I'm fine,' he tried to say.

'No, you're not—'

She was adamant. He had to call a cab. Eventually he agreed, sinking back into the leather sofa and letting her make the call because he couldn't get his fingers to push the right buttons on his mobile; couldn't get his mouth to form any sound except a grunt. The drink had soldered his jaws together. His tongue was flapping around his mouth like a beached fish; it felt disconnected, as if it had been severed from its root.

His hostess put down the phone and made her way to the sofa.

'I'm so sorry, Sean, but they're booked solid for the next two hours. Can you believe it?'

He nodded blearily. 'Fucking country we live in.'

Through the blear he saw the other guests—the ones who'd had the foresight to book their cabs in advance—look on, smirking.

'Fucking country—' he said, louder.

'Maybe you could stay here?' suggested his hostess. There was a pained look in her eyes.

'Yes, do,' said the host. He didn't look quite so pained but still...

'No,' mumbled Sean, having sense enough to do the decent thing. 'I'll hail one down on the street.'

Outside it was cold and murky, no moon. The wind blew chilling little gusts up under Sean's lightweight mac, a bad choice he'd made earlier, deceived by the evening's golden sunlight.

He staggered down the driveway. Objects jerked into sharp focus, melted into a fuzz. It was hard to tell what was real.

The footpath was a cold light blue, the colour of Picasso's dejected harlequins. Wavering through the gate, Sean stumbled over a loose brick, straightened up, stumbled again. In the corner of his eye he saw his car, long and white and useless. He thought of going over to pat its bonnet goodbye—or maybe even crawl in and sleep there till dawn—but sense arrived, a delayed, incomplete cavalry. He had a home to go to. Lola would be waiting.

Sean had been walking for about five minutes when he first heard it. An odd clacking sound, around a hundred feet ahead of him. Something wooden hitting off the ground. The sound was disjointed and uneven and reminded him of something. A children's story book, a—

Blind Pew from *Treasure Island*. The thought glided into Sean's soggy mind, dark and sinister as a U-boat.

He paused. The sound stopped. Instinctively he glanced around; an animal fearing ambush. Nothing. His eyes took in the empty avenue, the gaping driveways, the sparse streetlamps. He squinted up the road, in the direction the sound had come from. The path was drowned in shadows, cast by a dense bank of beech trees overhanging a rotten granite wall. Nothing there either, as far as he could see.

He took a step.

click CLACK

Another.

click—

Was that—

Yes. There was something moving under the shadows of the trees; a smudge of black against the lighter black of the wall.

Sean stopped. Silence ballooned into the night. He became aware of the stink of his sweat, sharp and mushroomy. Maybe, he thought, I should turn around.

That was possible. He could turn now, go back to his hosts' comfortable house and their equally comfortable sofa and lie down and sleep the drink off and leave in the morning after honourably refusing coffee and battle through the traffic and get back in one piece and—

His hostess's pained face resurfaced in his memory.

Okay. Maybe not.

Well… he tried to gather his thoughts. Well, it was only a matter of minutes till he reached the main junction and then, Christ, surely he'd be able to hail a cab. Once he walked slowly enough, there'd be no danger of catching up with whatever was in front of him.

*What*ever?

Whoever. Christ! What kind of fucking idiot was he, jumping at shadows?

He started forwards, trying to walk as slowly as possible, trying to ignore the clacking that started up again as soon as he did, the fact that it had slowed down too, that with every step he took it sounded nearer, taunting him. Ahead of him, through the shadows, he could see movement. He still couldn't make out any details. Whatever it was seemed to be one mass of black; no limbs. Maybe it was wearing a cloak.

A cloak? Who would wear a cloak—

A sliver of light knifed through the branches, glinting at the place where a head should have been—

Should have been?

Sean froze. The thing stopped. Now there was only a few yards between them.

Slowly, the thing began to turn, disengaging itself from the shadows. Sean's breath quickened. He made out a grey oval—

A face. Thank God. A head after all—

A white hand, reaching. Sean jerked back.

His foot lost contact with the pavement, his spine whiplashed. Arms flailing, he crashed towards the ground. His arse smashed into the gutter, landing him spread-eagled on a pile of sodden leaves. He groaned. His ankle throbbed.

Broken? Jesus, no—

He looked up. The figure in the cloak was standing above him, silhouetted against the streetlight. Sean twisted around, tried to scrabble away, but it was useless. Pain shot through his leg. He sank back, groaning.

The figure stepped back and tilted its head to the light. A pale face emerged, the same colour as the moon. A hand lifted, making an abrupt, almost absent-minded movement. Like it was stroking a small household pet that had got trapped on its head.

'Cat got your tongue?' said Poppet, and laughed.

Even afterwards he couldn't decide whether she'd meant it as a joke.

She sighed, the sparkly veil over her head slipping forward as she leant towards him and lifted one foot off the ground. For an instant

Sean thought that she was going to step over him, lift her skirt and piss on his face.

Instead she gripped her raised ankle and drew off her shoe. Her balance was perfect, the supporting calf strong, bunched with muscles. Cogs in Sean's memory whirred. *I used to be a dancer.*

She dropped her foot and held up her shoe to the lamplight. It had ankle straps, a stiletto heel and was some dark colour that looked black under the dull light. She pushed at the heel, and it gave way, bending inwards at a painful angle.

Blind Pew equals broken shoe.

Sean giggled.

Hissing, she dropped the shoe. Sean twisted his head. The fractured stiletto sped past his ear, landing spike down in the gutter. Sean's nose filled with snot.

Poppet stepped forward. Her feet, inches from his eyes, looked like something from a macabre fairytale. The bare foot was arched, her weight pushed onto its toes. The toenails, he saw, had been painted; the same noxious indigo as her shoes. The muscles in her leg twitched, rippling darts of black through her bone-white skin.

'You remind me of my husband.' Her voice sounded chisel-sharp in the cold air. 'I didn't see the resemblance at first, of course, but... Did I tell you I once had a husband?'

Sean said nothing.

'Did I?' she repeated, her voice harder.

Sean looked up and, not wanting to make eye contact, gazed at the top of her head. Her shod foot lashed out, landing in his ribs. He grunted.

Poppet laughed, a sound with no joy in it. 'No. I don't suppose I did. Then again, you didn't give me an opportunity.'

Her voice was soiled with bitterness, the same bitterness that had marred Lola's voice in the early days, before she'd learnt sense. 'I lived with him for twenty years, you see. My husband...'

Oh God, thought Sean. Now it's all coming out.

'He used to hit me.' She grabbed a curtain of her hair and pulled it away from her forehead, lifting up her face to the light. 'See.'

Sean wasn't sure what he was supposed to be seeing. A tiny fault line where her nose had been broken? A slight wander in her left eye? A chipped front tooth? From where he was lying, she looked intact.

She twisted her neck and pointed to her left temple. 'There. That's where he used the glass.'

Sean saw cracks in polyfilla. Marks he had half-glimpsed earlier through the strands of hair; craters and bumps he had taken for the leftovers of acne. 'I was always fast on my feet but the dancing wasn't much good to me when he got into his moods.' She smiled. The black lips stretched. The cracks widened. 'Maybe I should have learnt to box instead.'

Sean shifted his weight onto his other elbow. 'Look—' His teeth had begun to chatter. 'I don't want to—but—my ankle is—'

'You name it, I did it.' Her voice had become girlish again. 'Black glasses. Headscarves. High necked jumpers. Long sleeves. Excuses. I had them all. Walls, stairs, doors. Clumsy Poppet. Silly Poppet. Awkward Poppet. Poor Poppet.'

'Look, Poppet, I need to get to—'

Her foot lashed out again, the spiked heel connecting with his breastbone. Sean groaned and crumpled away from her, retching.

'I knew what you thought, the minute you saw me. Look at the silly bitch, you thought. Who does she think she is, the auld eejit, going overboard with the hippy dresses, pushing fifty if she's a day. She's not fooling herself, is she? That she's got a second chance, the stupid—'

The stiletto jabbed again. Sean curved away in time and her foot hit air. He grabbed it. The muscles bunched under his grip, racehorse-strong.

'Let go.' She pulled at her foot. Sean, sickened, clung on. 'Let me go, you prick.'

Her face was twisted, eyes and mouth the black holes of a Scream mask.

'I need a doctor,' said Sean. His words were coming out in clumps. Cold was racing up and down his body. His mouth was full of salt. 'I need to get—'

Her held foot jerked. Sean reached with his other hand, tried to grab her ankle. She pushed back on her heel and shook her leg. The power of the shake rattled through him, jerking his neck backwards. He released her. She tottered. The stiletto waved, inches from his face. If she loses her balance now, he thought, she'll send that thing into my eye.

The muscles in her standing leg strained. The gaping hem of her dress billowed, revealing the white shapes of her thighs, a flash of darkness. Energy surged through Sean's body, hardening his cock. Involuntarily he glanced down. The erection was pushing at his trousers; tent-pole obvious. He heard a laugh and looked up. Poppet had stopped tottering and was staring at his crotch. There were cracks all over her face now, raking down the sides of her mouth, driving trenches across her forehead, hatching fault-lines around her thin lips.

She lifted her eyes to his. Her smile faded. His throat tightened.

Then, with infinite slowness, her eyes locked on his, Poppet began to move. The movement was so small that Sean couldn't tell where it started. A twisting somewhere in her hips, a curling of her raised foot, a slow bend of her knee. Controlled, focused, her legs turned into flickering marble as she lowered her spiked heel, letting it drift towards his erection.

The tip of her heel brushed his zip. The contact was gentle; fingernail-light. Sean made a small ragged sound.

The stiletto moved down, still gentle, tracing the length of his cock until it came to a rest on the ridge between his balls.

Their breathing was harsh. Little white puffs of air. Their chests moved. Up, down. Up, down.

The stiletto quivered. One jab, thought Sean. One jab and—

She lifted her foot and swung it, whiplash-fast, away.

Bile filled Sean's mouth. His erection collapsed. He twisted onto his side and retched. The sound tore into the silence, ripping it like soggy paper.

When he turned back, wiping his mouth, she was hobbling away, a broken peg-leg ballerina sinking into the darkness. Pad click pad click. A few yards on he thought he saw her stop and bend. Then she continued, but now her footsteps were noiseless.

She disappeared.

Sean leaned over and puked into the gutter again, just missing her abandoned shoe.

*

He was woken by the growl of an engine and a blast of searing sunlight. A car, coming towards him. Groaning, he tried to push his torso up off the ground. Pain shot through him. He gritted his teeth and tried to call.

'Stop, please, help—'

His arm waved feebly.

The car stopped. Sean sank back and watched two feet shod in dirty grey runners walk towards him. Denim legs bent. A stubbled face with red-rimmed eyes peered at him. 'Jesus, pal. You been in the wars.'

Sean caught the smell of a mouth that had been awake all night.

'I've broken my—can you—I've got—' Weakly, Sean patted his coat pocket.

'Okay, no probs.'

Two hands wrapped themselves around his torso, lifted him, and he screamed.

'It's alright pal, I'm not far.'

The world bounced past, red with pain. A car door opened. The hands slid him inside.

'There you go.'

The front door opened, slammed. The key turned in the ignition.

'Vincents Hospital alright? It's the nearest.'

Sean nodded, his face pressed against the cool glass of the window.

As they pulled away, something on the ground caught Sean's eye. Standing upright in the gutter was Poppet's shoe. In the daylight it was red. He couldn't see the cracked heel. The cab swerved around a corner, and the shoe vanished.

A sprain, they said in the hospital, after making him wait for four hours. A few days' rest and you'll be right as rain.

When he got home, clinging to his crutch, Lola was sitting in the chrome and marble kitchen he had built for her, sipping coffee and leafing through the *Weekend* magazine.

He leant against the door and watched her. Shame crept red fingers up his throat.

'I'm sorry,' he said at last. 'I didn't mean...'

Lola sighed.

'Jesus,' he said. He hobbled towards her and dropped onto his good knee, ignoring his screaming ankle.

'Stop,' she said.

His head paused, an inch from her lap. He could smell her scent; coffee and Chanel.

'I'm sorry,' he said again. 'I never—'

She sighed again, silencing him. Her hand lifted.

He closed his eyes, longing for contact. In the blackness he saw steam rise from her coffee cup, draw circles in the air, reflect silver on the dark Jackie O glasses that she always wore to shield the cracked and bleeding traces of their bond from the unseeing, meddlesome eyes of strangers.

Cuts

Gina Moxley

FAT ACTRESS FUCKS FEDEX MAN. That's what went through her mind in place of a post-coital fug. She didn't normally think in headlines. In fact, she was trying not to think at all. And she'd never before used the word fuck for having sex. He had tried to deliver the fat pants parcel from her sister in Connecticut three times already but it wouldn't fit through the letterbox. She'd rung on Tuesday and made an appointment for it to be delivered today. It had to be today. This was three days ago when it was still important. Tonight was opening night of the play—that's what the pants were for. Americans were better at plus sizes. And her sister was better at shopping. She happened to be passing the door as the bell went and had to answer it because her shadow could be seen through the mottled glass. She'd clean forgotten about the arrangement—not surprising given the events of the last few days. Off came the paltry security chain. There, against piercing daylight, was a silhouette of a lovely fresh man in an ochre uniform. Like a cardboard cut-out outside a filling station.

'At last,' he said, smiling, and handed her the package.

At last, she thought, someone being nice. She tightened her jaded crêpe de Chine dressing gown—stolen from a film set—around her, then signed her name on his gadget. Their hands touched as she handed it back. She noticed his nails. Almost circular. So clean.

'Would you like a cup of tea?'

And already he was in the hall. She went straight upstairs ahead of him. The bedroom curtains had been closed for days. He arrived in the room behind her. It smelled of tired perfume.

'Queer place to keep the kettle,' he said, with a huh huh in his voice.

She shrugged and took off her top, then her pyjama bottoms. Taking his cue from her, he undressed and laid his clothes neatly in a pile on the floor—like a little campfire. Oh, she thought, a scout. Her bed was a bazaar of throws and shawls that had seen better days. They squirreled beneath them and fucked. She'd expected a sound from herself, like ripping cobwebs, or, at least a cloud of dust to expel itself—it had been seven years since she'd had sex—but mercifully, it was just the normal slather of wetness and flesh. Initially, she felt rusty, so she let him do most of the work, but then she got into the swing of it and nearly devoured him.

And after, she lay on top of him, covering him utterly. A passing bird wouldn't have known he was there, except, maybe, for his van outside the door. In a week of surprises this was a pleasant one. They didn't talk. He probably couldn't, though he didn't seem to mind. Despite the cabbage soup diet of the past month she was still a big girl. Extra, if not extra, extra large. They stared at each other trying to compute the unexpectedness of what had just happened. Neither came to a conclusion. That's when she thought of the headline. Then she thought, maybe he's thick. The bedclothes had long ago hit the floor, smothering the discarded script, but she felt no need to cover herself. This was a pleasure, being naked without being paid for it. The way it should be. She lolled onto her side. Then, without warning, he slapped her bottom—a resounding thwack.

Oh hello, she thought as she watched her flesh rippling. What do I think of that?

To her it looked just like a draught hitting the surface of scummy bathwater; she made a confused mental note to exfoliate. Nobody had done anything like that to her before. It didn't feel remotely sexy but he seemed to enjoy it and that gave her some sort of pleasure. She liked the fact that he'd surprised her, that she wasn't a step ahead. He did it again—*smack smack smack*—looking straight at her. Bold as you like. Her eyes saucered.

Christ, she thought, I'm being spanked. Me! The things that people get off on. Then she roared laughing, flopped onto her back and just roared.

He propped himself up on one elbow delighted with his handiwork; he'd made her laugh and made her come. Yes and yes again. He nodded and smiled. By now, she had tears in her ears and her laugh had become a dog frequency whine. When she finally wound down to a wheeze, he gave the tip of her nose a jubilant kiss.

'You needed that,' he said, as if it was all in the line of duty, then got up, dressed and left.

Ordinarily she'd have felt like decking him, winding him with a quick One Two. The cheek of him. But she had to admit he did have a point. Boy, did she need it! A good old spring clean.

In the bath she appeared to displace less water. If not noticeably smaller, she certainly seemed less dense. She tried to remember the Archimedes principle of volume and mass. 'A pint a pound the world around,' came back to her from a lost school book but no longer made any sense. Like a ship full of air, the ballast thrown overboard, she bobbed about like a buoy. She would survive.

She was described in the script as The Fat Woman. Every other character had a name. When she introduced herself on that first day of rehearsal, the only other female member of the cast, a ludicrously beautiful girl in her early twenties, said 'I love that name—Lucy.' She wanted to hug her for that, for seeing beyond her weight.

The Fat Woman had to appear naked in the final scene of the play. When her agent warned her of this on the phone, Lucy asked if it was gratuitous.

The agent, a tenacious and wirehaired terrier, barked, 'Listen Lucy, the writer is about eleven years old. A genius, apparently. Probably wants to be smothered by his mother. Of course it's gratuitous. Look, if it's shite, nobody'll see it, and if it's good, well, great, you're… you're brave.'

Brave.

If you knew how I lived, Lucy screamed in her head, loans, overdrafts, unpaid bills. You don't know the meaning of the word. Brave is bothering to wash. Managing to get dressed.

'I told you what money they're offering, didn't I? It'll get you out of a hole.'

Her eyes filled at the very idea of work. In the past year and a half there had been what? Maybe nine scattered days. Being this size, she knew she was ploughing a niche but it wouldn't kill them to give her a name.

'Does she… have dialogue, this gratuitously naked Fat Woman?'

Lucy covered the mouthpiece for almost a minute while her agent searched through the script, the flicking pages like a meat slicer in her ear.

'Ehm… yeeeees. Somewhere.'

'Oh God. Oh no. It's come to this. Indignity squared.'

She watched herself crumple in the mirror by the phone. Sometimes it felt as if she were two Lucys—one doing the feeling and the other, a shadow, checking for emotional truth. She went through the stages— the quivering lip was a cliché the shadow wouldn't brook. Teeth clenched. Breathe through the nose. Swallow like there's a fishbone stuck in your throat. Flare nostrils. Lower the eyes, no, focus middle distance—more truthful. Furrow, then pyramid eyebrows. Oh yes, part lips. A gulp of air. Heartbreaking. Chinese dragon mouth. Hammy but actually quite good with no sound. Her eyes were brimming. She brightened for a second—maybe the Fat Woman has to cry. She can give good tears.

'Lucy… are you still there?'

'How many lines?' Her voice had dropped a full octave.

'Five.'

A noise escaped from her involuntarily, like a hunting horn deep in the woods. The banks of her eyes gave way and her cheeks became a flood plain. She turned away from the mirror. Her tears rolled and rolled.

'So what do you want me to tell them?' her agent asked, clicking a pen.

Broke, Lucy had no option but to be naked and nameless.

She answered. 'Yes.'

There were seven young, male actors in the cast. They skirted around her as if she were a quarry, a gaping hole in the ground, giving her a berth far greater than her size. She thought she saw them clock each other when they did so, winking and chalking it up. Or did she? It was hard to tell. They were good, these young men. The fact that she was going to be naked hung in the air like a plague. So she took to revealing some cleavage, thinking she'd gradually peel back the layers. At the end of Act One she had to kiss Nick, the prettiest of the boys, apparently to great comic effect. First time they rehearsed it—so far just a spoken 'And we kiss' to the side of each other's face—she wrangled him onto a bench, as directed. He squirmed, not at all in character, but much to the amusement of his mates. Determined, she pinned him, her top all askew, exposing much more than intended. A breast actually escaped. The rest of the cast were in convulsions, really in kinks. After several attempts to rein them in, Thea, the director, shouted, 'Oh for Christ's sake. Take a break.' She flung the doors open for some air.

The lads went out to smoke while Lucy went to the toilet to rearrange herself. She could hear them through the window, shuffling and sniggering like kids. Nick had centre stage.

'Man, it was like a car crash. You don't want to look but you can't help it. Fuck. Did you see it? That humungous tit in my face.'

Lucy whipped out to the yard and confronted him.

'Well, you'd better get used to it because there's more to come. I'm warning you, a lot more.'

The boys were sheepish, then someone snorted—there was toilet paper trailing from her shoe.

The cast went for drinks after work that first Friday. Thea bought Lucy a Spritzer and sat down beside her. She wasn't having a drink herself and was watching her cast like a hen. At the table they raised their glasses in unison.

'Lucy, if you don't look people in the eye when you say cheers it means seven years bad sex,' one of the boys warned.

Lucy rolled her eyes and said, 'I wish.'

They laughed like it was the funniest thing ever. She had punctured some hymen of embarrassment. The Fat Woman having sex.

'Fucking hilarious,' Nick roared, slapping her on the back.

She insisted on buying drinks for everybody, applauding them for getting her joke.

At the counter she met an actor she knew from some film job. They'd spent a couple of days together in the movie-world army of waiting for action and being told what to do. They whiled the hours away eating and chatting, retelling the same funny tales. Topping each other and riffing, a lost art among this current crew.

'Ah darlin', been meaning to ring you. Heard you were on this. How's it going? Delighted you got a break.'

'I'm up. I'm out. Being paid.'

'Great. Great. Your man, the writer, read all about him. Good buzz. Sounds fairly edgy.'

'Yeah. I think the word's brave.'

He winked and gave her a thumbs up, then a hug and a kiss on the cheek.

Maybe it was going to be fine.

Because it was set dependent, they wouldn't get to run the final scene properly until the end of week four, when they were already in the theatre. It was a mishmash of choreography, mistaken identity and doors. But then the lighting took way longer than it was supposed to. Thea was marching around like Napoleon.

'Tomorrow night is the preview. Fucking, hello.'

Lucy checked out the green room—microwave, burnt coffee pot and kettle, then brought her make-up to the dressing room. She was old school, and laid it out neatly on a towel. Getting into the theatre was the part she loved most. Yes, the rehearsals. Yes, the company. Yes, the wages. But sitting in a chair, staring in the mirror and thinking your way into somebody else, that was the best bit. The shower stank and had no door. She had treated herself to perfume and squirted some in the air. She undressed and had to stand on a chair to look at her naked self, since there was no full-length mirror. Architects, she thought, give me a break.

'Act Two. Beginners please. Beginners to the stage. We will be running from the start of Act Two straight through to the end,' bellowed a voice over the Tannoy, the tinny speaker way out of reach. Lucy gravely slipped on her dressing gown and went downstairs.

Now that she was finally about to bare all, everybody else had worries of their own. The play was falling apart at the seams. Structural problems were threatening to topple the entire thing. While the playwright stalked like a madman between the upturned seats, Thea corralled them on stage. She looked like she hadn't seen daylight for weeks.

'Right, keep the energy going. Nick, no mugging, please. Remember, it's all about pace. If you get lost shout "line". But whatever happens, don't stop. Keep going. And have fun with it. If you don't, what chance have the audience?'

What chance indeed. The theatre went to blackout and the music and lights slowly began to bleed in. The first few scenes flew by without any mishaps or fluffs.

Lucy was standing by, staring at her bare feet, buttocks clenched. On cue she walked on for her showstopper. It felt more nature table than striptease. The boys didn't seem to bat an eye, more concerned about their own shortcomings being exposed.

They staggered through to the end and Lucy just stood there, starkers, waiting for notes. All in all, the run-through had been a disaster. What had seemed funny in the previous weeks was now shabby, an in-joke. The beautiful girl, Clara, brought Lucy her dressing gown. They hadn't had an opportunity to really get to know one another because they didn't share any scenes. And Clara was always rushing off somewhere or else on her phone.

'Good woman. Fair dues.'

Lucy gripped her. 'Could you see my heart thumping? Was it awful? I'm dizzy from holding in my stomach. That, and no lunch.' She wrapped the dressing gown tightly round herself, closed it right up to her chin.

The house lights came up.

Clara rubbed Lucy's shoulder maternally, though she was probably half her age. Then she withered the playwright with a look, and seethed, 'I mean, please.'

The cast went on a tea break. Nobody said much. They ate biscuits or went outside to smoke. A screaming match erupted in the theatre. Somebody closed the door.

Thea was grim-faced, 'Well done everybody, you got through it.' The playwright hovered behind her, scratching his chest. She referred to her scribbled notes, 'It's too long, guys. Way too long. Gags where there should be wit. Juvenile. Definitely no interval or else the audience will leave in their droves. There will have to be cuts. We'll do them tonight. And Lucy, I'm sorry, we haven't rehearsed that last scene. My fault. We need to break now because they have to finish rigging the lights. I'll text you the call.'

When she got home there was a final delivery failure notice from FedEx. Lucy positioned it next to the kettle as a reminder to herself to phone them in the morning. Her stomach flip-flopped at the idea of the opening on Friday, but at least she would be well dressed post show. At one in the morning a text came through on her mobile. She was to meet Thea at the café across the street from the theatre at eleven. Oh, she thought, that sounds a bit not great.

They sat in a booth down the back. Lucy took out her script and a pencil. Thea was still wearing yesterday's clothes. She had been up most of the night with the writer, filleting the show, saving the day. Now, she had to reassemble the pieces. The final scene was the first thing to go. She apologised for putting Lucy through it; she thought she could make it work, but no. She rubbed her face, the skin moved easily as if it was barely attached.

'Oh,' Lucy said. She felt her organs huddle together. Their coffees arrived. Thea was having a Danish. 'Am I not fat enough?'

'No.'

'Too fat, so.'

'No.'

'Well, what then? To be fair there's not a lot more to her. I gave her as much depth as I could.'

'I mean… it's not about fat. It's not about you. It simply isn't funny. Worse, it's gratuitous. I should have seen that before.' Thea stirred and stirred her coffee. Lucy noticed that she didn't have a script with her. 'And when that scene went, there seemed to be no justification for the character. So, I'm really sorry, Lucy. I'll say what I have to say. The Fat Woman's been cut, for the sake of the play.'

Lucy's lip started to quiver; she tore off a piece of Thea's Danish and ate it in slow motion. Thea went on about the company honouring the contract and of course she'd get full pay. Her name was already on the poster, in the programme, she'd write a—what do you call it—disclaimer, run it by her agent. Lucy continued to eat the pastry, anything to stop that stupid lip.

'You're a better actor than the rest of them—put together. Maybe we'll get a chance to work on something again. Hope so.'

'Are you finished?' asked Lucy, wiping some crumbs from her mouth. Thea blinked in reply.

'I need to collect my stuff from the theatre in a bit. If that's okay?'

Thea followed her out to the street, grabbing her arm. Lucy felt like hitting her, but Thea let go just in time.

'Come to the opening? Promise me, Lucy, please.'

I've been cut. Cut. Cut out completely. Fired. Sacked. Shafted, Lucy thought as she walked away. She wandered the streets, unemployed.

She managed to reach the dressing room without meeting anybody. Rehearsals sounded fraught over the Tannoy, everyone getting confused with the cuts. She gathered her things up quickly, her make-up, her comfy shoes, her dressing gown. Two of the actors passed down the corridor. She didn't hide; she was a ghost already.

'Okay, would you fuck her for five grand?'

'Ten. If you threw in a few tabs.'

'Pills? Man, you'd need chloroform.'

Their roar of laughter ricocheted around the stairwell...

... and around her head as she hid in bed since she'd been axed. As she stepped from the bath with an alien lightness, she concluded that sex must be transformative—since her diet had gone to pot for three days. She tore open her sister's parcel, putting the Good Luck card to one side. The pants looked worryingly small but they fitted like they'd been made for her, right down to the length. Maureen had thrown in a top to go with them. It hit Lucy's best bits and deftly skimmed the rest. Her sister could always divine her fluctuating size. Maybe she was psychic after all. And aquamarine—a colour she'd never have thought of. It made her skin look perfectly poached. Pale and passionate, she fluffed up her hair, and decided that yes. Yes, she would go.

After Benny
Dónal O'Sullivan

LORRAINE REMEMBERED THE FIRST NIGHT. He was standing at the spot where the park curved around the row of terraced houses, the spot that was visible only from her bedroom window. The dim streetlight slanted across his figure, on his indifferent slouch against the railing, the rhythmical, cigarette-to-mouth swing of his arm. His leather training bag was slung across his shoulders. He was still wearing his kit, green jersey with diagonal yellow stripe, socks rolled high up muscled legs. So furtive looked his smoking that it might have been he was concealing his habit from his team-mates.

She watched him from the window. Amber glowed from the lamp on the bedside table behind her. It did not occur to her how clearly visible she must have been to him and how odd her flat-eyed staring must have seemed. At first, he ignored her but then began shifting uneasily. Finally, he turned his head and mouthed the words: 'What are you looking at?'

In the half-light, he looked older than he was. There was dark stubble on his neck and jaw line and his face was neatly balanced and handsome. He stood upright and positioned himself directly in front of the window, foot-rolling the ball on the sodden grass, staring grim-lipped at her, like he was looking at something utterly ordinary. His eyes dropped suddenly and when they rose again he pulled a salacious expression, all pout and deep stare.

She felt her gown undo itself slowly, nervously, as if expecting to be retied. He clapped his hand over an open mouth; a mock expression of surprise. This unexpected act beyond his years forced her to frown then marvel for an instant at his audacity. She quickly scanned the area within eyeshot.

She pulled the curtains and, as if in twisted mockery of the boy, clasped both hands tightly over her mouth. She stood frozen until she heard his steps crunching through the grass, then waited until her heart stopped racing. She knew immediately she'd made a mistake. She ought to have gathered herself in time, and her decision not to reminded her of tidal waves.

That night she explained herself to Benny. She spoke to him nightly, in the stillness as she lay in bed. She knew he'd understand but she asked him to forgive her anyway.

She thought about the routine of their lives. She was never this unsociable when Benny was around, but that was Benny, always the centre of attention, back-slapping and mischievous, smiling as he waved long, open-handed salutes. They used to wonder why he'd picked her, all nebbish and pale, but she knew the reason. Benny had tough days, long shifts spent lifting spirits and shouting instructions; all he wanted in the evenings was peace and quiet. That's why he drove home so fast.

He went off the sloping road in the hills at the time of year those very hills were frozen over.

It continued for a month, at the same time after dusk, once the children were called home and the curtains of the faceless houses pulled. Each evening, she ascended the stairs with nervous pangs in her stomach. She pulled open the curtains of the window. He did not come every night; when he did, they exchanged a look quick and deep enough to be the compression of every single glance exchanged between two people in the world at that moment. Then she simply moved to one side, undressed, put on the dressing gown she kept on the chair by the window and reappeared in front of the glass. Sometimes the straps came undone of their own accord. When they did not, she untied them herself. Mostly he just stood there watching, but every so often his face would break into dark and purposeful expressions that she found extraordinary.

She passed him once on the footpath in the open street. He was with a gang outside the chipper, juggling a ball on his right foot, left foot, keeping it from his buddies, balancing it on his head. All the tricks. She slowed down and passed right by him but he was so focused on controlling the ball that he did not see her. She had hoped to be seen, to swim in the mischief of it, to see him panic and lose the ball then hurriedly defend himself against the taunts, to shower curses on the grimy roadside. But nothing happened. He just kept hopping and heading the ball as his street companions looked on obediently.

She began calling him Little Benny. He looked like Benny, or at least she thought he did. Same thick eyebrows and jagged cheeks and half-shaved head. A young, skinny version, she thought. Benny used to roll the ball like that too. Not full of himself, but massively confident. The confidence to like silent girls.

Even though she saw the other girls watch him and he watch them, she never expected him to leave her. She never bothered to ask him why he liked her. It was the surest way of making him nervous and angry.

He was seventeen when he said: 'We balance each other out.' They were all over one another in the dressing room. He stank of sweat and mud.

'Really?' she asked.

'Are you joking me?' he said and fell silent. 'Plus, you come to all my matches.'

'I like your matches,' she insisted. Then she looped her arms around his waist, saying: 'And I like the way you tell everyone to go fuck themselves.'

He howled with laughter. A kid looked in the doorway then ran away because everyone was scared of Benny.

'You wanna know why I really like you?' he whispered and she knew she could never repeat to anyone what he was about to say.

The only one who kept in contact with her after Benny was Trish. She was married to Benny's brother and she had decided early on that they should be like proper sisters. Their favourite café was pristine inside, with walnut tables and big, enveloping chairs. There were high windows which they liked because, though they never admitted it, the glass made them feel comfortable in each other's company. When silence descended on the table, they could simply look at the street through the window.

Lorraine loved the lift she got from the caffeine. Sometimes they ordered a second cup and made giddy promises and mid-year resolutions. They were meaningful because they were made with excitement and promise and it didn't matter that none of them was ever realised; what mattered was that they were made and, as Trish once said, if you make enough, one will come to pass.

They were staring through the window at people wheeling suitcases on the footpath.

'I need a holiday,' said Trish.

Trish was always saying she needed a holiday. 'And so do you, by the way,' she continued. 'You really should get out more.'

'I prefer staying in.'

'Suit yourself.'

A furious gust struck the window and, moments later, a drizzle descended.

A group of teenagers walked past the window. They were a chaotic rupture in the humdrum of the street: whirling around each other, thumping and chasing and shouting. People hurried to avoid them, tracing wide arcs around them and crossing the street. They stopped at the lights opposite the café. Then she saw Little Benny in the middle of the group, the tallest, the closest to adulthood. She watched him leaning, knee-bent against a shop window, watching the antics of his companions, as if he were rating them.

One boy dragged a traffic cone to the middle of the road. Then a car came around the corner and screeched to a halt in front of the cone. The driver got out of the car and, as he carried the cone back towards the footpath, the boy shouted at him. Hurriedly, self-consciously, the man got back into the car and drove away.

Little Benny looked on, an indifferent smirk across his face. The others laughed but their eyes darted back and forth in his direction. They seemed unnerved by his composure; they did not seem to know how far they could go.

'—You all right there, Lorraine?' she heard Trish say.

'What?'

'I asked you if you were all right. You just blanked out on me.'

'Did I? Sorry.'

Trish frowned suspiciously.

'Go on then,' she said

'Go on what?'

'Tell us.'

'Tell you what?'

'What you were thinking about there?'

'When? Nothing.'

'You're hiding something,' she said playfully.

Lorraine felt her cheeks redden. 'I'm not,' she said.

'Look at you. What is it?'

'Nothing, Trish. Really.'

Her body was tensing.

Trish followed her stare across the street. The boy with the traffic cone was returning to the main group when a patrol car appeared around a corner and slowed down in front of him. The guard in the passenger seat rolled down the window and spoke to the boy. The rest of the gang scattered with exhilarated looks on their faces. Little Benny was first across the street. The rest of the gang followed, looking back and laughing at the plight of their companion, who returned an expression of nervous, suppressed amusement. Then the patrol car crawled towards them and the boys jogged down the street. As they passed the window, he glanced in her direction and their eyes connected. His lips turned into a sly, implicating grin followed by a slow wink.

It was as if her chest, her heart maybe, had suddenly plunged to the pit of her stomach. A faint, nervous smile sped across her face and she glanced at the dark, still liquid at the bottom of her mug. The glare from the window reflected on its surface. She kept her head bowed until, out of the corner of her eye, she saw the group finally depart.

When she looked up again, Trish was staring at her.

'Do you know that boy?' she asked.

'No,' Lorraine said, as if the question were an offence.

'Well, it looked like he recognised you.'

'How would I know him, Trish? How would he know me?'

Trish nodded. 'What has become of this city?' she said.

He came again that evening. She was standing in the kitchen when she heard it from upstairs, a sharp thuk of pebble on glass. The sound became more frequent, each time ringing hollow off the pane. She shut her eyes. 'Go away,' she whispered between clenched teeth.

She considered giving him what he wanted; it was the easiest thing to do. Yet, a kind of conscience, the thing that told her she was wrong to have done it in the first place, kept her rooted to the spot.

He shouted in a voice she did not recognise, the voice of a spoilt child, more high-pitched than before, full of anger. He swore again and again, commanding her to show herself.

The sound of the window shattering crashed through the house. She gasped and felt her chin quiver. She sat down on the kitchen table and, this time, asked Benny to make him go away.

A long time passed before she went upstairs. There was a jagged hole in the window and long cracks across the pane. The rock lay at the foot of the door, dark and mossy. She crawled on her hands and knees towards the window. She was terrified in case he caught her staring. She raised her head as slow as she could above the sill and peered onto the grass below, left and right, then ahead through the drizzle. He was gone.

She decided to confront him if he came again. She would threaten to call the guards. In the dozing moments before sleep, the thought occurred to her that he was probably known to them anyway. Would they even believe him if he told them the truth?

The following evening, the usual time, she heard stealthy steps and mumblings. She came to the window. There was a girl with him this time. They were kissing, groping, hands pressing, eyes closed, slobbering like retrievers, belts and buttons open. The girl looked like she was about to fall into him at any moment, leaving a single creature in the fading light. The girl was letting him handle her; she tried to touch him back but her hands weren't as strong or as daring.

Lorraine was reminded of herself and Benny in the dressing rooms.

She used to give herself to him in the same way.

The boy turned the girl so that her back was to Lorraine. He opened an eye and looked up at her. He stared for a few seconds then stretched out an arm and waved. The girl was too bewitched to notice the gesture, too convinced by him.

Lorraine pulled the curtains.

Then she heard the girl say: 'What's the matter?' Their voices were hurried and frantic. In a dreadful snarl, he shouted the word pervert. The girl began asking a stream of questions. Suddenly, Lorraine heard her scream the words freak and peeping tom bitch. The boy, faking outrage, shouted: 'I wouldn't want to fuck you anyway. I couldn't be arsed looking any more.'

She heard the girl ask him what he meant.

'Nothing,' he said, and told her not to start.

They walked to the front of the house.

Lorraine rushed downstairs, so fast she nearly lost her footing midway through the descent. In the kitchen, she pulled a carving blade from a knife rack on the counter and flung open the front door. She raced outside and saw them squeezing through the little side gate that led to the footpath and the main road. She commanded them to come back and apologise. They looked behind and laughed so she quickened her step and shouted again. They cursed in surprise and began to walk faster before turning into an estate. Lorraine stopped at the gate. She wanted to but she could not stop the terrible words flowing from her mouth. They were the kind of things people only say in their dreams.

The Egg Collector

Breda Wall Ryan

'THIRTY-NINE. She *said*.'

'Plus VAT. Guess again.' The girl from human resources knew everything. 'Still, it was nice of her to invite everyone in the office.'

'The bride's side of the church would be empty, otherwise. Notice how Crazy Clare has no actual friends? He's not half bad, though. For an old guy.'

Six months after they met, Clare married Tom in the wedding she'd dreamed of ever since they'd made her give up her imaginary baby brother. Focus on real life, they'd said, so she'd imagined her wedding in this exact frothy dress, boned bodice, embroidered train and satin opera-gloves; hair in profiterole curls, diamanté tiara. They'd asked about the groom, but she couldn't imagine him, and since she hadn't set her heart on her father or a priest or a pop star, they'd said she was perfectly normal and let her go home.

The whole wedding day stayed fuzzy round the edges for Clare, even the groom seemed blurred but he wore the right costume and stood on her right and let her take centre stage. In his speech he said all the nice things about her she would have made up about herself; she applauded so long that the guests who had stopped began clapping again.

'Did she have champagne?' her mother whispered. 'Did you make her take her pills?' The bridesmaid shook her head.

During the the bridal waltz, Clare stopped mid-swing and stood stock still.

'Look at *me*. I'm married. Married,' she shrieked. 'On to the next thing.' She picked up her meringue skirts and ran up the sweeping stairs to the bridal suite, her groom following like an afterthought.

When Tom peeled off her opera-gloves she told him in a breathy voice something about coming off a swing and flying through a greenhouse.

'My beautiful bride,' he said, kissing his way up the ladder of slash-marks from wrist to breast. 'You have me to take care of you now.'

'I want a baby,' she said. 'Straight away.'

'Two,' she told her mother when they arrived back from honeymoon, the journey in from the airport festive with Halloween bonfires. 'A boy and a girl.'

'Wishful thinking,' her mother said. 'I hope it keeps fine for you. You haven't told him, have you?'

'No. And I'm not going to, so don't *you* go spoiling things.' She pinched the old woman's arms until she promised.

While she colour-washed walls, restored an antique rocking chair, stitched quilts and assembled a cot, Tom sprawled on the couch, a beer balanced on his belly, and begged her to take a break. The nursery waited. Clare waited. False alarm followed false alarm.

At first, Tom tried to make light of it.

'How would you like your eggs?' he asked at breakfast. 'Fertilised?'

'It's not a joke,' Clare trembled. 'Oh, how can anyone *live* with this longing?'

But the months ran on, dominated by her menstrual chart, ending with the bitter purchase of tampons. Clare spent hours in the nursery rocker, a cushion clutched against her yearning belly.

'Any news?' Tom's friends asked, punching his shoulder with the edge of a fist.

'Boys will be boys,' the wives said, turning their mouths down. 'Time enough for babies; you only know each other five minutes.' Clare heard whispers: *infertile, past it.*

'It's *your* fault,' she said, scribbling out the fertile days until the calendar fell asunder. 'I heard they call you Britvic Man—all juice and no seeds.'

Other women fell pregnant at the drop of a trouser, why not her? Tom suggested a check-up; she heard nagging. Her gynaecologist first probed Clare's insides, then the matter of her age, but Clare's faith in her thirty-nine years was set in cement. She passed on the doctor's suggestion that Tom be tested.

'Nothing wrong with my wedding tackle.' He cupped the organ in his palm, like prize fruit. 'Down, boy!' he ordered and preened sideways-on before the mirror, sucking in his belly. Clare didn't smile.

They racked up months of trying; twelve, fifteen. Like a photograph left on a windowsill, Tom's vision of children faded, but Clare refused to let the dream die. She redecorated the nursery three times. Lemon, Robin's Egg, Candy Pink. Arms wrapped tight around her belly after they made love, she pictured Tom's sperm racing towards her egg, the lead sperm butting through the fine membrane, cells multiplying into foetal form. How hard could it be, she wondered, poking a finger through a stretched sheet of clingfilm. Three coats of Primrose it took to cover the pink.

A magazine article caught her attention:

VISUALISE
Achieve Your Dream by Imagining

Here was a message for her from the Great Creator. Speaking through psychologist, Dr Lacey Cloud, He explained how anyone could turn her dream to reality, by removing self-imposed subconscious obstacles. Clare read on. She must bombard her subconscious with images of her dream-come-true. The subconscious never sleeps; it works incessantly to realise our dreams.

'Conception is a question of mind over matter,' Clare repeated hour after hour. 'Tom's sperm is irrelevant.' She slept hardly at all.

'My very own babe,' she whispered to the zygote she imagined clinging to her womb lining. She tended it with sweet words and murmured endearments until it burgeoned into a bean-shaped blob with an oversized forehead that toppled forward under its own weight. The embryo soaked up all her love.

Next, Clare noticed a book title, Open To Channel. She visualised a receiver permanently tuned to the Great Creator, playing at low volume in her subconscious. When the third message appeared, over a feature in the *Evening Herald*, she received it loud and clear:

PARENTS DECIDE
Couples Can Choose the Sex of Their Baby

She gazed inwards at the vein-blue membrane covering her infant's eyes and decided: girl. She named her Mella. Every day she perfected another facet: limbs, internal organs, bones, seedling teeth, pearly fingernails. Bombarded with visualised images and mother-love mantras, Mella reached full term in a fortnight.

The first contraction almost felled Clare. She clamped her lips between her teeth, slid out of bed and crawled to the nursery. There she squatted over her birthing mat, clasped her knees, and rocked back and forth, straining and moaning. From a Channel 4 documentary that had turned Tom queasy, she knew what to expect. When the head burst through, she braced herself for worse, but the body slithered out easily, like wet laundry tipped from a bucket. Thanks to visualisation, she didn't need stitches. She wiped off the waxy birth-grease and massaged her daughter's body. Soon the infant's breathing settled to a steady rhythm. Clare moulded her to the curve of her breast and rocked with her in the pine rocker. When the sky turned pewter, she laid the swaddled baby in her cot and crept under the quilt beside Tom.

'Icy feet!' he hissed. She snatched them away. 'What's up? Cramps again? You should see the doctor, Clare.' He was asleep in seconds. She lay awake, skin tingling, alert for the baby's mewl.

'I suspect you've had an early miscarriage,' the doctor said. 'Pity.'

Clare, sensitised by the surge of post-partum hormones described in her childbirth manual, noticed that the sympathy didn't reach the doctor's eyes, and was glad she hadn't confided about Mella. She was referred to an obstetrician, who ordered a D. and C.

'A good scrape will clean you out, ready for another try,' she said.

I'm not some garden, to be dug over for a new crop, Clare thought. She had the procedure at a clinic and returned to work. Separation from her baby was a physical ache.

*

Clare invented an addiction to lunchtime TV soaps, to explain why she now went home for lunch instead of eating at the canteen. While she fed, changed and settled the baby, she wolfed a sandwich and memorised storylines, then rushed back to work. Her colleagues said nothing; Tom had hinted at a miscarriage.

After Mella's birth, Tom became more concerned about Clare. She had become haggard and slept badly. His friends had stopped calling, he suspected it was because his edgy wife unnerved them.

'I'm too tired,' she explained, when he suggested they go out together.

'For someone who claims to be tired,' Tom grumbled, 'you don't show much enthusiasm for an early night.'

Fortunately, Mella rarely cried. At the slightest snuffle from the nursery, Clare ran upstairs, slammed the bathroom door as she passed and swept Mella up before she could set up a proper din.

'Irritable bowel syndrome,' she said when Tom asked; the word bowel kept him at bay. She coaxed Mella to suck her thumb, so she could soothe herself. She couldn't mislay her thumb.

Back in her armchair opposite Tom (they no longer sat side by side on the couch), she worried that Mella might need orthodontic treatment later, because of her thumb-sucking. She would certainly need a good school, and university fees, and a car for her eighteenth birthday. Clare already felt the pinch of providing the nappies, creams, clothes and toys stockpiled in the nursery. In order to save for Mella's future, she would need Tom's support. She thought about introducing him to Mella.

When Mella was three months old, Claire decided it was time to get pregnant again. This time, she would involve Tom. That night, she slipped her hand under his pyjamas and stroked his belly.

'You're getting as furry as a bear,' she murmured, sinking her fingertip into his navel in the way he used to like. Tom gently lifted her hand.

'Clare,' he said, his voice fuzzy with contentment, 'I'm glad now that we didn't have children. Aren't you?' Not waiting for an answer, he went on, 'I suppose I'm set in my ways; golf at the weekends, a few scoops after work, time to potter in the garden. And there's your routine, too; a child would disrupt everything. Funny how you change your mind, over time.'

He spent a few minutes on what he called twiddling her buttons and practising his follow-through, while Clare clenched her fists and concentrated on the Great Creator's most recent instruction, which had appeared in *My Magazine*.

OPTIMISE YOUR CHANCES
Seven Steps to Becoming Pregnant

Afterwards, she lay on her back with her knees bent and her hips raised, in accordance with step three, while Tom dozed, then woke again and maundered about their lucky escape from domestic chaos.

'Early retirement,' he said. 'Without third-level fees or expensive weddings to fund, I could quit at fifty-five and get in some serious golf.'

'Hmm,' Clare murmured. Tuned to her private channel, she pictured a supersperm arrowing through to the nucleus of the ovum she had mentally released. She juggled chromosomes to create a male, then accelerated the zygote's development.

A month later, Cormac slithered into the world during a television commercial, when Tom thought Clare was making cocoa. Cormac was a dream baby; he never cried when Tom was home, so it was easy for Clare to keep her little family secret.

But when Cormac was a few weeks old and already as advanced as the average six month old, disaster struck.

'We should turn that nursery into a guest-room, Clare,' Tom said. 'Twin beds and a full-size wardrobe are all it needs.' When the furniture arrived, he assembled it himself. Clare wouldn't let him dismantle the cot. Mella could have a grown-up bed, but Cormac was too young.

'I saw this in a magazine, Tom.' She piled the cot with checked blankets and a striped quilt. The cot stayed.

The guests, however, never materialised. Tom's friends preferred to meet him without his jittery wife, and Clare herself never issued invitations; busy mothers didn't have time for guests.

*

In Clare's baby-and-toddler book the Great Creator, under a new pseudonym, advised that even the youngest children respond to reason. She reasoned Mella and Cormac into developing at the rate of a chapter a day, and within a couple of months, Mella reached six, Cormac five. She did her best to teach them the rudiments and they picked up a lot from *Barney* and from re-runs of *Sesame Street*, which they watched in the mornings. Now that Tom had opted to be child-free, she couldn't risk afternoon TV in case he came home early.

'*He mustn't, for God's sake, don't let him, don't let him find out.*'

Tom asked what was wrong. She told him, 'Nothing, nothing, nothing at all.' He made her tea; he didn't know what else to do.

The following evening, while she was dusting his golf trophies, she turned to find Tom eyeing her.

'You're getting a bit of a belly, Clare,' he said. She snatched up a cardigan to shield herself. 'You ought to do sit-ups,' he went on. 'No point in giving in to middle-age spread.'

The realisation hit her like a hammer: it wasn't age larding her hips, blurring her jaw line and leaving dark smudges under her eyes. She hugged the joyless secret to herself; the pregnancy ate at her like acid.

Eventually, Tom realised why Clare's belly was swelling from the bottom up. He drove her to the doctor's.

The doctor confirmed the pregnancy. Clare was miserable. Tom took charge. His home-grown organic produce appeared at every meal; he force-fed her vitamins, minerals and heartburn, and insisted on a brisk twenty-minute walk, morning and evening. He shopped and did the laundry and accompanied her everywhere, arranging that her mother stay while he was at work. On Sundays, he drove her to the seaside, where he strode along the cliff walk while Clare dragged herself in his wake.

'It's too stony,' she complained. 'You're going too fast.' Tom, extra patient, slowed his pace. 'You're driving me crazy. Can't you see I'm going crazy?' she yelled on the cliff-top, and later at home. He held her while she shouted herself hoarse. Later, she rocked and mumbled, mumbled and rocked.

One evening he brought home a walking cane for her, gift-wrapped.

'I take good care of my little woman, with our baby on board!' he beamed. He'd promised the doctor not to let her out of his sight.

'Thanks!' she snapped. She had to explain to Mella and Cormac why she was always worn out and why she took the baby everywhere, while they were confined to their room.

'Don't get under Daddy's feet,' she warned. 'Daddy is under a lot of stress.' They asked if the baby would share their room. Clare couldn't answer. She knew she was snappy; she saw they were frightened.

Tom decided to call the baby Thomas Junior. 'As if,' Clare raged inside, 'a child would choose to be a junior Tom. What child dreams of weekend golf, pottering in the greenhouse and early retirement? The *fiftyness* of it.'

For Tom Junior's sake, Tom quit smoking. He enrolled Clare in yoga and antenatal classes; he even puffed and grunted by her side during breathing practice. Tom Junior would have every advantage.

'I'm just a grow bag for his baby,' Clare muttered. She yanked Tom's tomato plants out by their roots, scattering soil all over the greenhouse. She couldn't bear to watch the fruit swell and ripen under his management. He found them on the compost heap, and shrugged resignedly. Expert on the unpredictability of pregnant women, he even took Clare's habit of talking aloud to herself in the guest room in his stride.

Then Tom decided to turn the guest room back into a nursery.

'Those primrose walls are way too pansy for a son of mine,' he announced. 'I've ordered Manchester United wallpaper and a matching quilt. Wouldn't mind it in my own room. Wait till you see it, Clare, you'll love it.' Clare's teeth ached to bite him.

When the baby was five days overdue, Tom drove to the seaside, as usual. Clare trundled along the cliff path at his heels, blowing like an athlete after a hard sprint. How, she wondered, would she explain to Mella and Cormac why their room was being remodelled, their tastes ignored; why Daddy had become obsessed with Tom Junior, when he never gave his older children a thought? She scanned the newspapers, frantic for guidance, but the Great Creator had gone off-air.

A chunk of cliff-face had tumbled into the sea, leaving a narrow ledge.

'No slacking, Mum. We must keep fit for the labour ahead,' Tom said, ignoring the 'Danger!' signs.

'I'm not your bloody Mum,' Clare muttered, breathless. She gave in to a powerful urge to rid herself of the irritating Tom. Heart pounding with exhilaration, she stuck her cane between his feet and tipped him over the cliff-edge.

There were witnesses, other Sunday strollers. They heard the man scream, they told the Guard, but there wasn't anything the wife could do. He tripped over the walking stick. The wife grabbed for him but her hand clutched at air; he fell like a stone. Lucky he didn't pull her over the edge, too.

Someone wrapped a jacket around Clare and settled her on the heather. Sweat cooled on her forehead. Her mind filtered out the purr of sympathy around her, the ratcheting of the rescue helicopter overhead. She shivered violently, teeth chattering. The rescue crew airlifted her first. She was in labour; Tom's body could wait.

Clare felt revulsion for the tiny infant she gave birth to that afternoon, but she knew what was expected. She bottle-fed and changed Tom Junior, enquired as to the number and quality of his bowel movements, the condition of his umbilicus and the results of his heel test. Three days later, she was discharged from hospital. The taxi-driver said the baby would think the Halloween bonfires were his welcome home. Clare felt like dumping Tom Junior on one of the heaps of flaming tyres and assorted rubbish. She refused the driver's offer to carry her case inside.

She shifted Tom Junior to her left arm and jiggled the lock. At once, she felt something awry, a disturbance of air, as if a door somewhere in the house had shut. She held her breath, listening. The children! She set Tom Junior down on the rug, ran to the nursery and swung the door wide, her chest heaving.

'Mella? Cormac?' The room was empty. The window yawned wide, the beds were dishevelled. She peered down into the garden, fear thumping her ribs. The grass was undisturbed, there was no evidence of a fall. Clare fumbled downstairs on jelly legs. Tom Junior's wail sounded as distant as the past.

She stopped at the living-room door, sobbing. Had her children crept away during the three days she had been gone? She turned the handle.

Mella and Cormac sat on the couch, on either side of Tom.

'You should have told me, Clare,' Tom said reproachfully. 'Children need their father.'

'Daddy is reading to us,' Cormac tapped the open book on Tom's knee, beaming into his father's face.

'You never said our Daddy is nice, Mummy,' Mella added. 'We like Daddy.' She cozied closer to him. 'We like him better than *you*. We don't have to stay out of his way, we can go wherever we like; Daddy said so. He took us to the park.'

'Now, Mella, be nice,' Tom told her. He smirked at Clare.

He can't take them over, Clare thought. They're *mine*. Frantic, she ordered, 'Go to your room, children. Now.'

Tom's arms tightened around the children's shoulders, making them bold.

'We're not your prisoners,' Mella sneered, safe behind the tweed barrier of Tom's arm.

'No!' Cormac pouted his lip, wriggling tighter to Tom.

'I'll take over now, Clare. We have a lot of time to make up, my children and I.'

'But they're *mine*,' Clare wailed. 'My children. *I* gave birth to them, *I* brought them up. They're nothing to do with you.' She screamed at the children. 'After all I've done... how *dare* you... your mother... break my heart.'

Tom escorted the children to the stairs, urged them on with an affectionate pat. They ran lightly up, giggling, sure of his protection. Their Daddy.

'Let's try to calm down, Clare,' Tom said. She wanted to race after the children and shake sense into them. Instead, she had to listen to Tom saying she had wronged him by keeping Mella and Cormac from him; by keeping them as her playthings. He was ready to make it up to them. 'And I want you to know I forgive you for the accident,' he added, drawing invisible quotation marks in that annoying way he had. Shouldn't she attend to Tom Junior now? It was irresponsible to leave a newborn on the floor in a draught.

Clare held the baby away from her body and followed Tom meekly to their bedroom. She placed the infant on the bed. He had stopped crying and was asleep. Tom lay beside him, cradling him in his arms, while Clare paced. He should have stayed dead, she thought, instead of coming back to spoil Mella and Cormac with his daddying.

She crept from the room and locked the door. She locked the children's door, too. Then she fetched Tom's toolkit and drilled guide holes in planks before offering them up to the door frames and driving the screws home. Tom didn't wake until the last plank was secured. He pounded on the door then, pleading that they could parent the children together.

'Please, Clare,' he wheedled. 'It's Halloween. It's just one night.' The baby set up a thin wail.

'No,' Clare retorted. 'You can't have Mella and Cormac; they're mine. Take the brat, he's all yours.'

She hardened her heart against the children's whimpers. The nailed door wiped out six virtual years of mothering. If they had called for Mummy, Clare would have levered out the nails, hugged her children and forgiven their betrayal. But they cried only for their Daddy. The wailing got on her nerves. She went downstairs, shut out the voices and made up for the sleep disturbance of pregnancy. She drifted in and out, while milkbottles multiplied on the doorstep.

When the health visitor called, a bleary Clare offered instant coffee. No, she assured her, she had no baby blues. She unlocked the room where Tom Junior had been asleep with his daddy ever since she got home. The health visitor used her mobile phone. She spoke calmly, so as not to alarm Clare.

A year passes. Clare has learned to interpret the psychiatrist's questions and to give answers that will secure her release. He has signed the papers; tomorrow she is going home.

She settles in one of the hospital's tall windows, cocooned in her quilt and wipes a circle clear of condensation. Below, the long drive disappears behind a shrubbery; she picks out the city's floodlit churches, idly working out the location of her own home.

'All better now, Clare, isn't that grand?' a passing nurse asks in the sing-song voice she puts on for patients. 'Wearing our own tracksuit instead of the ol' gown, and our own trainers. And we're getting our laces back tomorrow.' Clare ignores her.

Visualisation, she now knows, is a flawed technique. The message in *The Examiner* is unambiguous: *Scientists predict human babies will be cloned to order in Petri dishes in the near future.* Under the quilt, she picks up the boning knife she stole from the kitchen. On Monday, she will get out. The city is filled with young women, women with ovaries full to bursting with millions of eggs, ripe and semi-ripe; more than they could ever use. She knows where to find them, in Lover's Lane and on park benches and the back seats of parked cars, and where to locate their ovaries. Meanwhile, she must harvest her own eggs, opting for multiple births. She'll have a Petri dish brim full of embryonic sisters: dozens of miniature Clares. The photograph on the front of the newspaper, of a hospital ward full of tiny bundled infants in transparent cots, makes her smile.

She takes a deep breath, plunges the blade to the hilt. Twists. Scoops. The pain is astonishing.

Almost a Fairy Tale

Ingo Schulze
translated from the German by John E. Woods

THREE DAYS AGO I SAW MARGARETE SCHNEIDER AGAIN—in the old cemetery in Dresden Klotzsche, where I was visiting my grandparents' grave on the way to attending my class reunion. She wasn't alone, but in the company of a young, elegant man with almond eyes. What I know about the two of them I know from my old classmates. But it's just a provisional sort of knowledge. At least I hope so, because I would love to learn more about Margarete Schneider.

Ever since the class reunion I've been trying to imagine what it would be like if I were still living where I grew up. Would I see things differently if the streets where I walked to school, or the streetcar stop, or the cemetery were still as familiar to me now as they were thirty years ago when I saw Margarete Schneider again for the first time? Tall and slender, walking between her parents along Haupt Strasse. I was riding my bike to Moritzburg and passed them in the very same moment that the three of them turned left to climb the little hill to the church.

Margarete Schneider had been my kindergarten teacher.

Fräulein Schneider, as she was properly called back then—it must have been in 1968 or early 1969—had said her goodbyes to us children. She had moved, I had no idea why or where to. Not to my regret at the time. She had seldom, almost never smiled, let alone laughed, and when she did her sheeplike face—a broad nose spread peculiarly across it—was all wrinkles. She had hard hands, bony and sturdy is how I'd put it today. At least it always hurt when she grabbed hold of me to drag me into a different row of kids. Fräulein Schneider's successor was Frau Böhme, and we all loved Frau Böhme.

Not only was I surprised that my former kindergarten teacher was a churchgoer, but it was also the first time I experienced what it's like for someone to suddenly resurface after eight or nine years. Along with an awareness of the past—and with it a sense of sovereignty— that rushed through me, I was equally struck by how old Margarete Schneider looked that first time I saw her again. Although I gave her just a quick nod—a greeting that received no response—I can recall perfectly how sympathy and dismay were blended in the glance I cast down at her. In the years that followed, every time I would see Margarete Schneider, either walking with a group of kindergartners in the heath or on the way back from there, I had a definite sense, or so I thought, that this woman's life was without joy or happiness, even if she did live in a huge old villa whose immense backyard opened on to the Dresden Heath. She attended church on Sundays with her parents, sat way up front at Christmas, as close as possible to the pastor in his pulpit, and loudly sang 'Lo, how a Rose e'er blooming.' At the end she passed the collection bag down the rows, with a pole so long it looked like it would be good for picking apples from the top of the tree.

Once I left for the army and then university, I no longer saw Margarete Schneider. I was seldom at home. On Christmas we chose a long walk rather than church. That was also because of our guests, foreign colleagues of my mother, who would otherwise have sat alone in their dormitories. One year it was two young doctors from Benin, who spoke perfect Saxon dialect and had a great interest in cancer surgery and none at all in obstetrics. Another year our visitor was a Syrian who, upon his return home with a friend or colleague, hoped to take a second wife. Ho from Vietnam must have joined us in 1985 or 1986. My sister, who was a docent in the Gemäldegalerie (I no longer know whether this came before or during her application for an exit visa), explained for Ho the connection between Bacchus and Zeus, likewise between Jesus and Titian's *Tribute Money*. As was not the case with our other Christmas guests, I ran into Ho several times afterwards. During the short February break between semesters I tried to find him a 26-inch Tourenrad, which turned out not to be all that easy. With the help of a fellow student I finally located one in Weixdorf, near the end of streetcar line 7. When I showed Ho the bike, however, he just shook his head and, despite our questions, finally left the shop with a smile, but with no explanation.

Yesterday I phoned my mother and asked her if she could recall how it was that Ho and Margarete Schneider became acquainted. "Probably because she was one of my patients," she said. Margarete Schneider owned a treadle sewing machine that she no longer used and gave to Ho as a gift. Ho was absolutely overjoyed. Now he could finally get married. His wife would have work.

The last time we met I accompanied Ho to his streetcar stop. In those ten or fifteen minutes he told me about the war. All I remember is one fragmentary episode. His unit had been given special rations, and then ordered to swim with a mine out to a ship. I don't know if I've got the story exactly right; I haven't thought about it for a long time. As he told it he seemed out of breath and laughed a lot, then moved on to another story.

When it finally all came out—Margarete Schneider had looked especially pale during her walks to church on Sunday, with rings under her eyes and an even more sheeplike face, whereas her belly was huge and almost came to a point—my sister confessed that Ho had also asked her if she wanted to sleep with him. She had tried at great length to explain that her refusal had nothing to do with his stature. That was not the reason. But he hadn't believed her.

Margarete Schneider brought a boy into this world, Sebastian Ho Schneider.

After the wall came down and as early as the first local elections in May 1990, Margarete Schneider was a candidate of the Christian Democrats for the Dresden city parliament. Happy to attract anyone who had not been a member of their pre-1989 party, Christian Democrat campaign strategists found their darling in Margarete Schneider. At least so my mother claimed. Margarete Schneider took some training classes and discovered her talent for speeches, which always sounded a little like sermons, but people found her credible. One newspaper article attributed her believability to the way she talked about her own bitter experiences. She spoke about unremitting paternalism, about the suppression of Christians, and about the ghastly regimentation to which teachers and instructors had been subjected in the kindergartens and schools of the GDR. Her campaign posters showed her smiling, with just two small wrinkles, left and right, at the corners of her mouth. She became the deputy to the alderman responsible for education and professional training.

What most surprised the people of Klotzsche—who assumed they knew just about everything—was that the Schneiders not only owned their villa, but also a half dozen of the finest houses along the edge of the woods. During the 1930s Margarete's grandfather had received various patents that made a rich man of him. Margarete Schneider was suddenly a millionaire.

But she fell to the charms of no man, nor did she fail to attend Sunday services. She would walk to church with her parents and Sebastian Ho, who, if he was not dressed in a dark suit, at least wore a white shirt. Now that everyone knew the Schneiders, so my mother said, they had no choice but to respond to a barrage of greetings.

By 1990 Margarete's father had sold one or two houses at a good profit, restored the others to their earlier nobility, and likewise proved he had a gift for acquiring real estate at forced auctions. Two years ago, at any rate, he placed Schneider & Schneider Realty with its twenty employees in the hands of Sebastian Ho, the young man with the almond eyes whom I saw at Margarete Schneider's side three days ago.

As Margarete and Sebastian Ho passed under the old entry arch and walked towards me that day, I knew nothing about their monetary windfall. They were simply a delight to look at. To be honest, to me they appeared downright majestic. Sebastian Ho is as tall as his mother, who had linked her arm in his. Time had softened the sheeplike qualities of her face—indeed someone who did not know her from before might find that term totally inappropriate. I stopped to let mother and son pass me on the narrow path. For a moment I thought that Margarete Schneider of all people had managed to send time in another direction, to turn the clock backwards. She returned my greeting without recognising me. Sebastian Ho likewise gave me a nod.

I was uncertain if I should strike up a conversation and inquire about Ho. My classmates knew nothing about Ho, they didn't even mention that Margarete Schneider is now a representative in the Saxon state parliament. They were merely puzzled that I was interested in no one as much as in Margarete Schneider.

A Hare's Nest

Helena Nolan

THEY HAD BEEN DRIVING ALL DAY in the heat wave, stopping for only half an hour in each village to hand out the flyers. Even so, by the time they reached the final stop on the peninsula, it was already too late and the last of the market traders were packing up their stalls. Mick went to park the van and find a cheap B&B. She walked down to the harbour in search of something wide open to look at.

It was a small working port, cluttered with the debris of fishermen and their weary craft. In the late evening heat, the smell of fish blood and motor oil seeped out of the cobbles as she stood at the top of the slipway. The air was like warm breath. Everyone seemed to have packed up for the day here too, gone for a well-deserved drink. She was about to turn away when a man stood up in one of the small boats, silhouetted against the setting sun like a knife-edge. Then he stepped out. For a moment she expected him to walk across the water like another Christ but he sank like a stone.

Before she had time to move or speak, his head emerged, sleek as a seal, and he began to walk towards her, out of the water, more and more of him emerging as he reached the pier. He stepped onto the slipway and walked up to her. The situation appeared to demand some conversation.

'Don't worry,' he told her, 'I do that sometimes, after a long day, it clears my head, it's not as deep as it looks at this time of the evening.' He was dripping, great drops of water running off him. He wiped his face with his wet hands.

'I wasn't worried,' she replied. 'I was thinking about something else.'

He looked at her then as he might have studied a painting or a sculpture in another time or place. Except that this statue stared back. She saw that he was as much a man as any she had met. She saw him overall, but as to whether he had blue or black eyes, dark hair or slightly grey, was very tall or too thin, she could not have said. Only that he was masculine and smelled of the water, of the sea.

'Come with me,' he said and she followed him to his truck. She got in while he dried himself off with a rough towel, which he threw over the driver's seat. He took off his sodden shoes, flung them in the back and drove barefoot.

As they chugged back up through the town, she thought she saw their van parked near a pub with a B&B sign swinging above it. They usually slept in the van but sometimes, after a really long day, they took a room, just for the luxury of being able to walk around in it. She needed something more than that on this night, more than just space—respite. Mick was probably taking a shower. He wouldn't be worried, not yet. She began to build a dam in her brain, brick by brick, keeping back the thoughts that were trying to seep through. The fisherman pulled the truck over at a small shop with petrol pumps; he filled the tank and returned with two large chocolate bars and a bottle of whiskey, laying them in her lap. She held the bottle as the truck swung out and then soon after turned down a side road to his house.

She could not have known that he lived here with his brother, who might have returned at any time, if he failed to score in the pub. She knew nothing, not even his name. But when he picked up the whiskey and chocolate, she got out of the truck and followed him inside. It was still light enough not to need the lamps on. She could just make out the blurred shapes of furniture in a shabby room. The heat of the day hung in the house like a thin fog. He put the stuff down and closed the door, bringing a greyer edge to everything.

Then, without speaking, he kissed her mouth, moving her backwards through the room. She thought of asking him to slow down, of telling him that she hadn't been close to anyone since Tom left; she wouldn't let Mick near her and no other man had even appeared visible to her until this evening, but it was already too late and they were in the bedroom and he was inside her quickly, inside her and holding her down like water; she could hear it roaring in her head.

Afterwards he lent her a thin jumper and made coffee, which they drank sitting at the small kitchen table, the sharp edges of the room still softened by twilight. She began to speak, slowly at first, as a tap left unused for a long time begins once again to release water when turned. Soon the words were pouring from her, no space between them for interruption or response. As she spoke, it got darker and darker but he left the light off until soon she was only a voice.

'It was their thing,' she said. 'Tom always went out river fishing with Mick, he loved it, soon as he was old enough, he was gone. But this time I said no, he'd had a cough and I didn't want him out in the damp again so soon. We went to bed, Mick left before dawn with his gear, I didn't even hear him go. But when I went in to call Tom for breakfast the bed was empty, just the hump of the duvet pushed back and the hollow where he always snuggled down to sleep.' She swallowed. Her voice dipped then picked up again, a wavering transmission in the gloom.

'I was so cross at first but then I laughed at the cheek of him; he was growing up, shaking off his mother's fuss and worries. It was only when Mick came back alone and looked at me blankly when I asked—where's Tom, is he unpacking the car?

'We called the police. They suspected that Tom had tried to follow Mick, got lost or been in an accident.'

She stopped here for a second time and this time it seemed as if she would not continue; she was sick of the people who told her to talk about it, talk about it, but his silence gave her strength and so she went on.

'We organised search parties, phoned the hospitals, police divers trawled the rivers, all the local newspapers wrote about it but—nothing. The house was always full of people. Then one day everyone went home. They left us there to accept it, that he was gone, or dead, or worse.'

Now she continued in a rush, as if she had to race to the finish. 'We couldn't do it, stay in that house with all its empty places and missing noise. We couldn't look at each other. Oh, we blamed each other, for being too careful, for not being careful enough, but worse than that, we saw him in each other's faces. So, I wrote out the flyers, added the photographs, Mick had them all printed up. Now we travel in the van, handing them out in the streets, mostly on market and fair days, we know the dates, the routine.'

Before he could ask, she answered into the pitch black, 'It's been two years.'

'Two years?'

'Yes, haven't you heard about it? We were on the national news at the beginning and they picked it up again on local radio last year, on the anniversary, but it's hard to hold their interest. So many children go missing, I never knew how many.'

'I don't have a TV, just the radio.' He nodded towards it in the darkness. 'And I really only use that for the weather reports to be honest, that's all I need to know.'

She shrugged, accepting this.

'Where did it happen?' he asked.

'We're from the northeast,' she said. 'A long way from here.'

'Yes,' he agreed, 'a long way.'

He got up and switched on a lamp then; moving slowly and carefully he prepared a bath for her and afterwards took her back to bed, still damp, her long dark hair in mermaid curls across the pillow. This time they were slower and she cried large silent tears, which he only noticed as they pooled on his shoulder.

'Well, that's a first.' He looked at her, smiling. 'Like the song.'

'Get over it,' she said and they both laughed and knew for the first time the rare benediction of laughter in bed.

The hours passed in this way like a dream, sometimes talking, sometimes coffee, the laughter and the sex, the intervals of sleep, no requirement to finish anything; it didn't seem to matter. At some point they ate all the chocolate. The whiskey remained unopened.

'Stay,' he said, sometime before dawn. 'Stay here with me.'

'Isn't there someone else?' she asked.

'None that worked out, none that lasted.'

They both heard the key in the lock and the heavy thump of a bag on the floor. He went out to his brother.

'Where were you? Jesus, you missed a wild night in The Arms, some fella buying drink for everyone, cryin' about how he lost his only son and now he's lost his wife too, he was quiet for a bit but then he went cracked altogether, started smashin' the place up, pullin' people up out of their seats to go searchin' with him. Cops came and took him off; don't know if it was down to a cell for the night or the mental in town.'

His brother was pulling off his boots and his shirt as he spoke and rooting in the kitchen for a square of bread, shaking the kettle and filling it. He didn't appear to notice the close companionship of the two kitchen chairs, the two used mugs on the draining board. And, of course, he was speaking at the top of his voice, still a bit high from the drink and his latest conquest. The walls of the bungalow were like cardboard.

No real surprise then to find the bedroom empty, the weak morning sunlight pouring through the open window into the hollow where she had lain; a hollow like a hare's nest, still warm from her body. He curled into it, arms wrapped across his belly; as he knew she must have done, once, in another bed, in another place, so far away.

Writer-in-Residence

Michael J. Farrell

THINK OF THIS AS A WORK OF FICTION. Any resemblance to real people, therefore, is purely coincidental. Otherwise they might sue. They live in a town everyone knows. It has a Tesco and Spar, Toyota and Ford and Fiat dealerships, flower shops and hairdressers with quaint names. There is a river and crumbling ruins and a round tower out the road. The locals play Gaelic and soccer but seldom win, due, it seems, to some vague lack of determination. Children, meanwhile, loiter around sweet shops at the end of each school day. The place nearly won the Tidy Towns on several recent occasions. In short, a fictional town.

Clarence arrived there on the train on a dark December night.

May met him at the station. She was big and buxom, there's one of her in every town, the conscience and instigator, keeping citizens on their toes. Christmas decorations conferred on the town a glitter daylight wouldn't even recognise. Strings of blinking bulbs reached from the Bank of Ireland across the street to the AIB in admirable harmony. A choir of three, possessed of a guitar but no drum, sang 'The Little Drummer Boy,' *pa rum pum pum pum*. Shoppers lugged shopping bags from Dunnes or Easons, unaware that Clarence had come among them.

'Years from now,' May was saying, 'we'll be able to boast that we gave you your start.' She was chair of the sub-committee set up by the county council to choose a writer-in-residence from the four applicants on her shortlist. 'That is, if we do give you your start.' Driving recklessly with one fat hand, adorned with four rings, on the wheel of her Audi, she pointed out the church, the farmers' market, a chip shop where a drug dealer killed another drug dealer the previous week. She double parked outside the hotel and strode ahead of Clarence to the De Valera Room on the second floor where the three other sub-committee members waited amid an assortment of bottles. A tree in a pot in the corner was visibly wilting.

There was a pattern to civilisation. Once prosperity bought people their immediate needs and wants, minds turned to speculation: what now? This loose, unruly question always perplexed thinkers with time on their hands. The unexamined life was old as the Greeks but the examined life was older. A tentative solution to this search for psychic ballast has, for some time, been writers-in-residence: unusual people invited someplace they don't belong to accept money to write about the locals or the Zeitgeist or about nothing at all. Once only a trend, this procedure has become the rage. Cities and towns boast writers-in-residence; cultural institutions likewise, from academic groves to the local creamery.

'It's not just writing,' said a maneen called Mylie, seventy or more, with a pointy chin just above where his chin should be. 'It's thinking things out.'

'No, that's philosophy,' said Mr Kerb, a grey eminence from his hair to his shoes, a building magnate whose houses would sell better in a town known to cherish culture. 'Consider the high kings of Ireland,' he said to Clarence, 'who always made room for a poet at the top table.'

'Poet my arse,' said Mylie, 'unless the poet in question was a sexually disposed female, and scantily clad at that, with, let me tell you, attributes. High kings didn't become high kings by being stupid.'

'What do you think yourself?' May asked Clarence, who was drinking a sober lemonade.

'There are thousands of towns, from Ur of the Chaldees to the stones and dead bones in your own county, buried in oblivion for one reason and one reason only—there was no writer-in-residence in place to immortalise whatever it was.' Clarence had found this in a book and learned it by heart.

The fourth member was a shy girl, Virginia, who asked: 'Are you more at home with fiction or non-fiction?'

'Oh fiction, for sure.'

His great misfortune was to be left the farm by his father.

'I'm not cut out for farming,' he announced when he turned seventeen.

'Nor for much else,' his father looked up from the boiled egg. His mother put his clothes in a small suitcase with a view to England.

'Come home whenever you want,' the father said with what sounded like remorse. Clarence would text messages home, and the mother would text back. Their topic was the old man pining away.

'Come home or he'll die.'

'If I come home he'll die,' Clarence replied. But he came. And the father died.

'If you're going to stay, you'd better find a wife,' the mother, a realist, said. This led to marriage to Brona, whom he met in the Mace market, a quiet girl, small. The father would have vetted her up and down and decided she'd be a poor breeder.

The mother died to make room for the new woman. If they were going to have children, Brona announced, they'd need to extend the house, make it over with big windows and curtains and an all-electric kitchen.

'It's an odd way to go about having children.' Clarence was droll. No one at school told him what irony was, but he saw it everywhere: a little cloud of humour floating about and pointing at people, who were, without exception, ridiculous.

Brona conceived the night after the new refrigerator was delivered. That's ironic for sure, Clarence's funny bone whispered in his ear. A beautiful daughter was followed a year later by another. Ambitious Brona transformed the old farmhouse. Under the plaster she discovered fine stone walls. Isn't that just like life, she would say to Clarence.

Gradually he found himself unable to get up in the mornings. He was physically fine. He was still a good eater, and Brona's cooking put his mother's memory in the shade. What was lacking was motivation, a word as vague as irony but when you came across it you knew it. Why? That was the issue. What was the point? It dawned on him that people must have been asking this question since the beginning of thinking, but the answers remained unclear. It surprised Clarence that people nevertheless carried on, looking the other way when it came to motivation. He found himself unable to do it.

Every morning, after hating himself for a while, he would read. Though his sojourn in England had been otherwise unproductive, it brought him into contact with second-hand books. At first he didn't discriminate—his reading was dictated by the price of the book. He always knew about libraries but not until he was thirty-two did he venture in. All those novels were strumpets to seduce him.

He loved Brona. When the girls arrived he loved them too. When Brona eventually confronted him he was full of remorse.

'I wasn't cut out for farming.'

'It's late in the day to find that out.'

'Come on to the pictures,' he'd say to soften her.

'After you move the cattle to the high field,' she would relent.

Cattle farming was lucrative as long as you fed the cattle. Clarence's cattle found themselves on a diminishing diet in a European Union where animals were coddled like children. Associated with the cattle coddling was endless work designed to keep the farm looking spiffy.

'Clarence,' she would whisper in the early days. Then the whispering turned to badgering. She talked less to Clarence, more to the two girls. Until, one morning, she had gone back to her mother, the note said. She did not ask for anything. She did not sound angry. He would have welcomed anger. Not that he thought he deserved it. He knew from his reading that his case was not unique. There were rotten scoundrels who abandoned nearest and dearest, but there were also decent people who did it. The more he read, the more he realised that writing was a tyrant. All artists were ruthless predators.

Not that Clarence was an artist. He was down to earth like a farmer. Six feet with, as the song said, some inches to spare; the big round shoulders and hairy arms seemed wasted in front of a book. There was a jut to his jaw that belied the lack of ferocity with which he confronted life. But once all that reading got a grip in any household, the traditional way of life was history. Imagination began to outweigh common sense. Yet there was something hectic and even heroic about it. Above all, it was inevitable, a calling that took no prisoners.

He sold all the cattle. Then sent the money to Brona. Wrote remorseful letters. He never asked them to come back home—he could not promise them he'd get up in the mornings. He was sure Brona did not hate him. 'But if you do, a divorce is your best bet,' he wrote her. 'Your best years are ahead of you, and I, it seems, am behind you.'

The shine went off the electricals in the kitchen. It was hard to believe so much dust could gather in a house, coming, it seemed, out of nowhere. He read that most of the earth's dust was the discarded, pulverised dead skin of humans. He started making notes of such things. When he would get up, sometimes toward evening, his head would be full of the ideas he had read all day. To the notes he started adding new thoughts of his own, original ideas that had never before existed. He would survey the words and sentences, would rearrange them; he was rewriting before he even decided to write.

One cruel irony, he thought, was to look like a farmer without being one. This had worked for Patrick Kavanagh, but times had changed. He thought: denim, head to toe. He thought: a floppy hat, but with a plastic band under the chin, because he intended, when he got on his feet, to walk the fields. The denims required money. He sold the high field, which lay alone beyond the river, an orphan. Clarence remained on good terms with the neighbours, who never mentioned the empty fields that would be knee-deep in grass come spring. Once one slowed down and allowed irony to penetrate, a more reasonable world came into focus. The spring would take care of itself, even tomorrow would. He had news for naysayers should he come across any: each life needed a fresh story and no one else could write yours for you.

Facts of life heretofore ignored became important. One was the writers' group that met once a week in the snug at Gilligan's. He wandered in on a Monday evening.

'Have you taken up the pen, Clarence?'

'Aye, I was thinking about it.'

'Good man, good man.' He liked the way they encouraged him and each other. One read a short story; another a chapter of what she called creative non-fiction; several read poems. Clarence, enthused, joined in the low-octane critique.

'Have you anything yourself?' they then asked.

'I'm working up to it.' Their offerings ranged from serious to depressing. He might, for a change, let irony creep in through the cracks.

The next morning was an eye-opener. Sleep abandoned him. The sun came up fresh and demanding. Clarence reached for a yellow pencil. Writing was easy. All you needed was words, and no need for jawbreakers or showing off. Get the important things down. Emotions and that. There would be decisions to make. Punctuation would be a killer: he was never good at commas.

He was up by noon, hours ahead of himself. He couldn't wait to make sentences, as if he hadn't been doing it all his life. He had bought a computer when he sold the field. It whirred all day and into the night.

The next day, he was up with the sun. Life had a purpose.

The following Wednesday he read a long piece about the South Pole and the intrepid explorers who risked everything to go there.

'Good man yourself,' the others were enthusiastic, a dozen of them, mostly women, getting their pensions now. No one said he was ready for the Nobel Prize, but no one said he wasn't. 'You should write about what you know,' one said bluntly. 'Write about yourself.' He didn't tell them he knew the South Pole better than he knew himself. That was where the irony came in.

Once destiny gets started, it doesn't know when to stop. Clarence saw, in the arty page of the local paper, that a certain town far away needed a writer-in-residence. The farther away the better, he thought. He was not surprised eventually to find himself on the shortlist because a logical inevitability was coming to pass.

Experts can tell you there is a bureaucracy for running things since art became lucrative and sculptors and scribblers came out of obscurity to limn the soul of a new, improved nation. This process is complicated and has been accused of strangling imagination. The Muse, they say, now has a degree in art management instead of art.

Since this is fiction, though, the local committee, instead of bringing an expert down from the city, opted to make up its own mind. It embarked on another bottle of wine.

'Fiction is fine,' Mylie was in his shirtsleeves and the red tie askew like a hangman's knot, 'but between you and me, fiction is no match for what actually happened.' He was the local historian, he said several times.

'But what actually happened?' Clarence asked innocently. 'That's the thing.'

'I know it's the thing,' Mylie conceded. 'Did you ever hear about the UFO that came our way, back in fifty-eight, or was it fifty-seven, no, what am I saying, it was fifty-eight?'

'A UFO from outer space, do you mean?'

'Where else would it come from?'

'And where did it land?'

'Land? Are you out of your mind? No now, it came motoring down. There are only a few of us left who remember that historic day. Towards evening, it was. Around milking time—I can still remember the mournful lowing of the cows, as well as the thrushes, do you see, like they knew something was afoot, it was that class of an evening. Not a cloud in the sky, as if they had been cleared out in advance of the thing—some of us thought the pilot might have been blinded by the sun. What a noise. What a catastrophe.' The De Valera Room fell silent.

'And did you see them?'

'Who?'

'The little fellows in the UFO?' Nothing in his background had prepared Clarence to frame the question. 'The extraterrestrials?'

'All we ever saw was a hole in the ground. The smart money said they kept on going and came out on the other side, down by Australia, it would be no bother to them with their amazing brand of technology.' Mylie looked from face to face. The others were running out of awe, but that did not make the story less true. He would drink half the pint at a time, Mylie, with a gurgling sound as the porter passed his adam's apple. Yet he never once went to the toilet, which in its own quiet way was as big a wonder as the UFO.

At approximately this time, Clarence, while he was away on a visit to the loo, was appointed writer-in-residence by unanimous vote after a quick confab. In any genre but fiction there would be awkward questions to answer here. Such as what happened to the other three writers on the shortlist. Or why the sub-committee entrusted to such an untried rustic the reputation of a contemporary town.

The truth is, fiction is quite like reality, which is hard-nosed and wants to get on with things. Mr Kerb, May said to Clarence when he returned from the toilet, would be funding the venture in lieu of the county council or anyone else who might insist on strings attached. The stipend, furthermore, would be doubled, enough to pay the piper for a whole year.

'What do you want me to write?' Clarence was unsure how any of this worked. Would he be paid by the page? He'd prefer a day rate because his best words didn't come to him until late in the day.

'Write whatever you want,' Kerb combined the self-assurance of the filthy rich with the benevolence of medieval monarchs eager to elevate impoverished minds struggling out of the dark ages. 'We hope you'll leave our town a better place, that's all.'

'I will, I will,' Clarence said earnestly.

'You'll need to get out and talk to people,' May admonished. 'Get their life stories, their hopes, their bunions,' she had taken on a lot of red wine. 'You'll find they're mostly hypocrites. Thieves, half of them. The dirt. Get the dirt. Oh, I envy you, Clarence.'

'And don't forget that murder in the quarry,' Mylie added. 'In 1939, or was it 1938?'

'It must have been 1939 because Hitler was at—it must have been the big war he was at. Would you try a whiskey, Clarence? You'll think better.'

'Aye, and write better.'

'Cox, it was,' Mylie wagged his feisty little chin. 'Felled his neighbour, Wallace, with a hatchet. Or was it Wallace felled Cox?'

'I think it was vice versa,' May said with a hiccup.

'What was it about?' Though unsure how to be writer-in-residence, Clarence knew he needed some demeanour, an attitude. He needed to be quizzical yet aloof. He thought of Graham Greene in his trench coat—though it wasn't the coat, it was something more psychological, formidable yet devil-may-care. There were never any gods on Mount Olympus; people had put gods there so that they could then look up to them to keep themselves in perspective. Despite being ridiculous, people were smart. He realised there was a lot of thinking to be done. Sophistication, if he could harness it, would come in handy. He might ultimately need to try whiskey.

'About?' May was saying. 'It was about a woman. Whatever about Cox, Wallace killed for love.'

'And vice versa,' Mylie was sinking slowly into a historical fog in which ancestors were ghosts inspired by mythical causes. 'Along these country roads there isn't a mile in any direction where someone didn't die for Ireland.' He had turned to drinking water. 'For the kidneys,' he explained.

Bashful Virginia, auburn hair reaching far down her back, sat upright with her orange drink. She's here because she's the future, Clarence decided; she'll require special attention like the high kings gave the naked poets.

'A few words about my new development wouldn't hurt,' Kerb stood tall and important in front of the gas fire.

'Oh aye,' Mylie confirmed, 'and don't forget Mr Kerb's mall. Grander than a cathedral, that place. We're richer now, Clarence, than the saints and scholars ever suspected we'd be.' It sounded like praise but there was an undertone—it might be sarcasm. Clarence would need to watch for undertones. New buildings would vie with old ones for his attention, but buildings were the easy part. They didn't connive like people. If he could sort out people he'd be on the pig's back.

'Then there's the castle,' May announced. 'You'll be sleeping in the same bed as the Earl of—what was that earl, Mylie?'

'Now there's some dispute about that earl.'

'Ah fuckit, Mylie, don't start that again.'

'It's your castle, Mr Kerb, no two ways about it.'

'Exactly. Here,' Kerb handed over a monumental, rusty key. 'Treat that national treasure with respect. There are memories of dead people there, though they're too long gone to be ghosts.' Clarence felt euphoric when he realised there was so much more to Irish capitalism than dog-eat-dog.

'There never was a poorer poorhouse than ours,' Mylie was still talking to the night after the others had left. Virginia was detailed to take Clarence to his castle. A moon floated above the Christmas decorations. The choir had gone home but the melody lingered.

In the small hours of the morning, the castle walls made sinister shapes. Water from a lake sulked in the black shadows. Clarence, still cold sober, saw the Earl at an upper window.

'It's only rubble,' Virginia said.

'It's first class rubble. There's no roof, or am I imagining it?'

'Kerb is going to make a luxury hotel.' One room, however, had already been refurbished. 'The scriptorium,' she called it. There was a bed and refrigerator and a microwave, 'and in there is the place when you need, you know, to go.'

He waved goodbye to Virginia, an understated wave like the Earl's. He lit a fire in the sprawling fireplace of the scriptorium, then fell asleep on black bricks the long-dead ancestors had put there. Clarence saw them at it. He had arrived at a place where the real and imagined blended, and this epiphany derived, he knew, from being writer-in-residence. The ancestors he saw had bad teeth and one had only one eye, and fights would break out, which was how the one eye came about. Yet, slowly, they put the brick floor in place, a practically everlasting floor if left undisturbed by the barbarian Kerb.

In the pocket of his country topcoat was a fat envelope deposited by May, including a wad of money from Kerb, and a contract specifying that he needn't write if he didn't want to. I won't let them down, Clarence said to himself before falling asleep. He had stumbled on an outlandish stroke of luck. Including dodging miles of red tape. The bureaucrats would have made him do the writing first to prove he deserved the money to do the writing.

By broad daylight not much had changed. There were people everywhere, all dead. The castle was full of souls, as were the gardens and fields. He saw children playing and women working. It wasn't all harmony. A body with outflung limbs was thrown from a high window into the lake. A writer-in-residence had many options. He could romanticise it all; he could praise the good and make excuses for the dubious in a hodgepodge of ethical stirabout; he could pack up and go home.

He had no idea what other writers-in-residence did. Some got away with nonsense about the lark in the clear air. It was a problem being oneself, in his case an ignorant farmer. He had learned lots of things from books but there would always be a lack. A lack of common sense, for one thing. Moments when he wasn't exuberant, he would remember the homestead deserted and the family dispersed. He would write to Brona. He didn't say he loved her because any day now she might file for divorce and he didn't wish to complicate her life. He would then write to the darling daughters and say, yes, he loved them fiercely.

The castle had a toaster. The Earl would have killed for a toaster. Or for the imported marmalade with foreign descriptions in three languages. Breakfast was followed by a bowel movement in the gleaming toilet. He was not the least embarrassed—even poets laureate did it—but he wouldn't write about shite as some writers loved to do. He circled the town, getting the lie of the land. When he ran out of roads and boreens, he took to the fields, crossing walls of loose stones waiting to break his leg, crawling under electric fences, saying an odd word to farm animals in a language that was neither his nor theirs.

'God bless the work,' he greeted a farmer stringing up barbed wire.

'Are you lost or something?' the farmer asked.

'No loss on me.' A laughing dog stood by the farmer, a dog that could bite your behind in a minute because dogs were suspiciously like people.

Eventually the walking took him into town, up and down every street in search of the unpredictable. He stopped in a sandwich place for a snack. People were naturally curious. A soft talker for a big man, he replied modestly that writing was his calling and he would like to ask them about the town, including themselves.

'Why would we bother?' was the frequent reaction.

'For posterity, I suppose. That way you won't have lived without being noticed.'

'You'll write it down?'

'Oh for sure.' This alarmed some and pleased others. Several invited him into pubs for a pint. 'All right, so.' Lemonade would never get the job done. Millions had been drinking porter for centuries, people and porter were a match, each a boon to the other.

By dusk he was drunk as a lord. My first day on the job and look at the change in me, he said to the locals with a lisp he had never noticed before. Life is ironic, he told them in reply to every awkward question, 'and when I sober up I'll write about ye all.' A dozen of them surrounded him on wooden benches, hanging on his words, and he fleetingly regretted all the days he had wasted sleeping.

'What can ye tell me about the UFO beyond?'

So they went out the road in vans, soon after midnight, in search of the legendary aliens. Each one remembered the thing in a different field or down a different lane. Squabbles arose. A farmer appeared out of the darkness with a spade and threatened to decapitate anyone who stepped on his grass. The story was already forming in Clarence's head. It wouldn't be fiction; it would be epic fiction.

Days passed. Clarence climbed to the turret of his castle each morning and observed old battles won and lost. He observed evictions, and long-dead blue-bloods chasing maidens through thickets and into cow byres whence shrieks of passion would soon emanate.

Virginia arrived in her small car wearing what looked like a see-through dress. 'You're looking well,' he told her.

'If I can be of any help?'

'It's a good thing this is fiction,' Clarence said. 'Otherwise I wouldn't know what to do.'

'Well now you know.'

When they finally awoke in Clarence's narrow bed, it seemed to be twilight. Birds were singing.

'Do you know what I think?' Clarence said. 'I think this is not how the writer-in-residence thing works. This is the twenty-first century, and everyone is sophisticated and has gone to see the world in Prague or New York or at least Cork, and people with laptops keep track of the whole caboodle, they'd know better than to let loose a moron like me to chronicle the living never mind the dead of this town. They'd want people with degrees and diplomas, extroverts and social networkers and cool dressers.'

'If there was a formula for writers-in-residence,' she said, 'that would defeat the whole purpose.'

'Would you like to see the castle?'

'They were all mad, all the earls. Those were the days when the

English sent their mentally handicapped over here to keep an eye on the Irish.'

Soon after Virginia left, Mr Kerb drove up in his Land Rover.

'Don't let the past beguile you,' he admonished. 'Look unflinchingly at the future. Then tell me how do you see this heap of stones in, say, another thousand years?'

In response Clarence told him how he had deposited his stipend for safe keeping behind a loose stone in the castle wall. But there were so many loose stones he could no longer locate the money.

No letter came back from Brona, not even a phone call.

'The more I yearn, the more I don't know what for,' he confided to May—the entire sub-committee was keeping an eye on its investment.

'Tell us about her,' May, kind for a curmudgeon, encouraged him.

'You have me now. I never paid much attention, and when she was gone it was too late.'

'What colour was her hair?'

'Hard to say. She was a toe short on her left foot, I remember that.' But he couldn't see her face, not plainly. She had gone leaving no photos behind, neither of herself nor the children. And anyway, last year's faces would be different now.

'Would you say she was pretty?'

'Oh she was. Pretty alright.' He searched his memory. She must have laughed when she still loved him. She surely had a small soft hand before the farm hardened it. He remembered her wide backside, unless it was someone else's. In the days that followed he would sometimes glimpse her face, then it would be gone wherever memory hid it. She was pretty, surely—he would look up at the battlements and feel he had made a monumental mistake.

The townspeople brought bags of turf when they learned what Clarence was up to, namely art. Not since the Earl succumbed had such fires flourished, making shadows on pillars and lumpy walls. When it rained, the drip dripped into his room leaving puddles. He sat on a wooden stool and wrote codswallop.

Write what you know, they used to say at the writers' group. But how was a writer to know what he knew? He wrote about the UFO until it became unreal and no longer existed. Mylie told him yarns about a dead hangman between the wars and about the shenanigans of the LDF during the Emergency. He wrote about a local saint who had a stained glass window in the church in Church Street, until Mylie informed him the saint had been discontinued in a Vatican purge. That's ironic for sure, Clarence mused, but not a bit funny. Each time he ran out of ideas he would hear the drummer boy, *pa rum pum pum pum* on his drum. It's not memory remembers, he'd then say to himself, it's imagination.

He arose every morning at dawn. He wrote to Brona that getting up was no longer a problem.

Clarence read in a book that what you look at hard enough will look back at you. The more he wrote about Brona, the more she looked back at him. Gradually he brought her to life until she eventually talked to him—she and the babies, whose names were Una and Ebana, were gone a year and more.

Then a letter came. It was battered and smudged front and back with post office stamps and scribbles—try such a place, the scribbles said as the letter travelled throughout Ireland in search of Clarence. He left it sitting behind a stone in the castle wall for two days while he prepared his mind for what it might say. He walked the streets. When will his report be ready, people would ask, eager for an outside appraisal of themselves. He walked the fields, overwhelmed by all he didn't know, especially people's secrets. He climbed the little dunghill of a mountain for perspective, a God's eye view. The town remained unclear as the misty weather.

'Did you read the letter?' the postman asked, because the town knew more about Clarence than he knew about the town.

'First thing tomorrow, I'll do it.'

Brona's was a short letter. 'In case you never receive it,' she explained. 'The little girls are fine, and so am I.'

How could they be fine? Hadn't the babies' father taken to sleeping all day? When it came to letters, so much was written between the lines. The more he read, the more pain he found there: loneliness and hopelessness. This was never blurted out because that wouldn't be Brona, who was gentle, not a mean bone in her body. Clarence found himself slipping into a hell where the memories were pitchforks torturing him.

He talked to his mentors: May and Mylie and Virginia and Mr Kerb. They had great power, he reminded them. When they provided opportunities for writers, they would need to be careful. Art was fierce wild, it didn't obey rules, it didn't show mercy, didn't do favours.

'Sure all we did was give you money,' Mylie's eyebrows refused to sit still.

'That's not all,' May corrected. 'We gave him ideas. Especially about himself.'

'I'll write to her,' Clarence promised, and the emergency meeting broke up.

'I remember you well,' he wrote to Brona. 'I remember you on the tractor and around the house hanging curtains and frying rashers and black pudding. You were always jolly and you singing Elvis Presley songs.'

'I never sang E. Presley songs,' she wrote back, 'and as for curtains, you wouldn't let me have the money.'

Fiction was easier. It didn't talk back.

He wrote to her about the babies once so small he held one in the palm of each hand. 'You fitted into this world better than me,' he wrote. 'I was always a misfit.' Yet he didn't give in to her on everything. 'Don't think it's easy lying in bed when you don't know what else to do. Don't think there's no pain.'

He would eat potatoes baked in the castle microwave and lathered with butter. Sometimes Virginia would visit him with vegetables and ice cream.

He looked up delirious in the dictionary. It was as he suspected, neither all bad nor all good.

When December came around, May drove him to the train station. He was sad leaving that mysterious town. People waved to him and he waved back. He had been the only writer-in-residence they had ever known. He had spied on them, chatted and confided, eating and drinking with them and hoping for something to turn up. He had done them favours they didn't realise, such as an embellished history and brighter prospects coming soon. In some small way he had lifted them up, given them hope. He had discovered Mylie's UFO under a bush. He had found blue skies for the town, and a taller, more purple mountain, so that people bought Kerb's houses each of which had gold fixtures inside and cuckoos outside. The Earl made a comeback, nobler than before, no more rack rent but pomp and processions for tourists.

In the square the little shivering choir was back singing:

> I played my best for Him,
> Then He smiled at me,
> Me and my drum.

'It's a pity you didn't get the dirt on half of them,' May was saying, 'especially the liars and fornicators. This town is full of them.'

'Love is better than the other,' Clarence replied. 'Come rain or shine, love is nimble and your best bet.' Since buying the dictionary he had learned a way with words. May, won over, smiled, pa rum pum pum pum.

The train took him within walking distance of the old homestead. He walked under outstretched bare branches of ancient ash and sycamore. Fields by the road were waiting for new cattle. The house needed work. Weeds had been thriving and were resting for the winter. Windowpanes had been broken by local yokels. Clarence, too excited to sleep, worked day and night until the house was a marvel. The transformation was finished just in time for Brona and the girls arriving happy and waving.

All this was in the novel.

The Meaning of Missing

Evelyn Conlon

I THINK OF THE FEELING around a person being missing as being a narrow thing. It has to be, in order to get into so many places. I told my husband this once and he laughed at me.

'Well if you can think of heartbreak as a thin piercing agony,' I began again.

He said that the turnips needed thinning and that he was away out to the garden. He didn't like talking about heartbreak because he had once caused it to me by going off with his old girlfriend for three months. It obviously didn't work out because he turned up on my doorstep on Thursday the sixth of June, twenty years ago. At ten past eight. Evening. He wasn't contrite, just chastened. He has been here since, but he never talks about that time. I don't mind too much because I never admitted that I had cried crossing every bridge in Dublin, the only way to get to know a city I was told by someone, who was clearly trying to get me away from her doorstep. Nor did I admit to what I'd done as soon as the crying had dried up and all the bridges had been crossed. I didn't have to, and he couldn't really ask me or hold me accountable.

Thinning turnips, hah! You'd think we had an acre out the back, and that he was going to have to tie old hot water bottles around his knees because the length of time on the ground was going to be so hard on them. We have one drill of turnips, a half of cabbage and a half of broad beans. Although it's not strictly an economical use of the space, I insist on the broad beans, because of the feel of the inside fur. Only two drills. They could have waited. Of course he didn't like me talking about missing, either. It's about my sister.

'She's not missing,' my husband insisted, 'you've just not heard from her.'

I often replay my conversations with him as if he is standing right beside me. I bet I'll be able to do that if he dies before me.

'For a year!'

'Yes, for a year. But you know how time goes when you're away.'

I don't actually. I've never been away for a year. Nor for three months.

When my sister said that she was going to Australia there was a moment's silence between us, during which time a little lump came out of my heart and thumped into my stomach. We were having our second glass of Heineken. In deference to the scared part of our youth, when we were afraid to be too adventurous, she always drank Heineken when out with me. She didn't want to hold the predictability of my life up to the light. I know that she had gone through ten different favourite drinks since those days, none of them Heineken.

'Australia!' I squealed.

I coughed my voice down.

'Australia?' I said, a second time, in a more harmonious tone. Curious how the same word can mean two different things when the pitch is changed. *Béarla* as Chinese. I must have hit the right note, curious but not panicked, because she smiled and said yes. Not only was she going, she had everything ready, tickets bought, visa got. She may even have started packing for all I know. It was the secret preparation that rankled most. How could she have done those things without telling me? If we were going to Waterford for a winter break I'd tell her weeks in advance.

The day she left was beautifully frosty. She stayed with us the night before, and after I had gone to bed I could hear her and my husband surfing for hours on a swell of mumbling and laughing. Apparently she was too excited to go to sleep, and he decided to get in on the act, not often having an excited woman to lead him into the small hours. The morning radio news said that if there was an earthquake in the Canaries, Ireland might only have two hours to prepare for a tsunami. Brilliant, another thing to worry about. And us just after buying a house in Skerries. At the airport, my emotions spluttered, faded, then surged again, like a fire of Polish coal going out. The effort involved in not crying stiffened my face, and yet it twitched, as if palsy had overcome every square inch from my forehead to my chin. But I was determined. I would keep my dignity, even if the effort was going to paralyse me. It would be an essential thing to have, now that I was not going to have a sister. My husband touched my shoulder as we got back into the car, because he can do that sometimes, the right thing.

In the months that followed I mourned her in places that I had never noticed before, and in moods that I had not known existed.

First there is presence and then it has to grow into absence. There are all sorts of ways for it to do that, gently, unnoticeably, becoming a quiet rounded cloud that compliments the sun with its dashing about, making harmless shadows. Or the other way, darkly with thunder.

'It's not as if you saw her all the time,' my husband said, unhelpfully.

'I did.'

'What are you talking about, you only met every few months.'

'But she was there.'

She wrote well, often referring to the minutiae of her journey over. But no matter how often she talked about cramped legs or the heat in Singapore, and despite the fact that I'd seen her off at the airport myself, I still imagined her queuing for a ship at Southampton, sailing the seas for a month, having dinner in pre-arranged sittings at the sound of a bell, because that's the way I would have done it.

And then she stopped writing, fell out of touch, off the world. My letters went unanswered, her telephone was cut off. I'm afraid that because my pride was so riled, the trail was completely cold by the time I took her real missing seriously. And still my husband insisted that there was nothing wrong with her, just absentmindedness.

*

I was in bed sick the day she rang. I love the trimmings of being sick, mainly the television at the bottom of the bed, although after two days I was getting a little TVed out. I had just seen John Stalker, a former chief of English police, advertising garden awnings. I was puzzled as to why they gave his full title. Did the police thing have anything to do with awnings? Was there a pun there, hidden from me? I didn't like being confused by advertisements. If I'd had a remote control device I could have switched the volume down occasionally and lip read the modern world. Then *Countdown* came on. Making up the words made me feel useful. I had seen the mathematician wearing that dress before. It was during the conundrum that the phone rang; it wasn't a crucial conundrum, because one of the fellows was streets ahead of the other, even I had beaten him hands down, and I had a temperature of 100 degrees rising.

'Hello.'

And there was her voice, brazen as all hell got up. I straightened myself against the headboard and thought, 'it's the temperature.' I straightened myself more and my heart thumped very hard. It sounded like someone rapping a door. I thought it would cut off my breathing.

'Hi,' she said.

'Hello,' I said, as best as I could manage.

'Oh my God, it's been soooo long.'

The sentence sounded ridiculous.

'And I'm really sorry about that. But I'll make up for it. I'm on my way back for a couple of months. I'll be arriving on Saturday morning.'

Back. Not home. Well, Saturday didn't suit me, and even if it had done so up until this moment, it suddenly wasn't going to. I was speechless, truly. But my mind was working overtime dealing with silent words tumbling about. I could almost hear them cranking up, scurrying around looking for their place in the open. What would be the best way to get revenge?

She must have finally noticed because she asked, 'Are you there?'

'Oh yes,' I said.

Short as that, 'Oh yes.'

I don't think I said more than ten words before limping to a satisfactorily oblique fade out.

'See you. Then.'

I put the phone down, my hand shaking. How many people had I told about my worry? And would I have to tell them all that she was no longer missing? And had I also told them about my husband's view? And was he now right? If a person turns up have they ever been missing? How could I possibly remember what conversations I had set up or slipped into casually, over the past year? I hoped that my sister would have a horrible flight, bumpy, stormy, crowded, delayed. But that's as far as my bile could flower.

My husband went to the airport. He would, having no sense of the insult of missing. He fitted the journey in around the bits and pieces of a Saturday, not wanting me to see him set out, not wanting to leave the house under the glare of my disapproval.

By evening I had mellowed a little because I had to. It was seeing her, the shape of her, the stance of her at doorways, the expressions of her. My sister had never giggled, even in the years that are set aside for that. She had always been too wry. Getting ready for her life, no doubt. On the third evening, by the time the ice in my chest had begun to melt, the three of us went out to our local.

'What's Wollongong like?' I asked.

'Just a normal Australian town,' she shrugged.

And she mercilessly changed the subject. I had thought it would have jacaranda trees in bloom all year, birds calling so busily that it would be the first thing a person would mention, sun flitting continuously on the sparkling windows of every house. A town rampant with light. I had thought it a place for rumination, with colour bouncing unforgettably off the congregation of gum trees.

'Are you sure it's just a normal town. Have you been there?'

'Yes, totally normal. Of course I've been there.'

I didn't believe her for one second.

'Why do you particularly want to know what Wollongong is like?'

'The name,' my husband said, as if he was my ventriloquist. But something in my demeanour made him hesitate, and he looked at me as if he had made some mistake.

'It's just that I met someone from there,' I said.

'When?' they both asked. Normally my sister and my husband have a murmuring familiarity between them, born presumptuously of their relationship with me. But they were both suddenly quiet, each afraid to admit that they did not know when I, I of the dried up life, would have met someone from Wollongong. Was it during her year or his three months? Damn, they would be thinking, now they each knew that the other didn't know. And me sitting there smiling away to myself. Smug, they would have been surmising. But it wasn't smug. I admit to a moment of glee but I was mostly thinking of Wollongong, and I swallowed the sliver of triumph because I am known for my capacity to forgive.

However, I didn't answer their question and went to the bar to buy my round, feeling like a racehorse, unexpectedly out in front, showing the rest of the field a clear set of hooves.

Brown Brick

James Lawless

THE STREET LIGHTS ARE COMING ON as Mr Washington, hatted, coated, gloved and sporting his goatee, marches towards me whistling, with my brown brick under his left oxter. His right arm swings a brolly, giving a rhythm to his walk. What is that tune of his fading, on the tip of my tongue? Concentrate, I say to myself, on what is in hand, or rather what is in head, which is the thudding remembrancer of the near death experience of the night before. 'Don't mix your drinks,' Heno had said (how many times had he warned me?). 'You get so fucking blotto.' My thoughts come slow now like sludge oozing out of my mind. I don't socialise. I'm a homebird, a non-recovering alcoholic. I don't need to mix, except for my drinks of course, not when I have Heno. He needs to get out from the house every now and then. I don't mind. I understand. In affairs of the heart, one has to play along with the whim of the other.

That's why I'm out in the air now, getting in a walk after the evening meal, seeing Mr Washington. That went well between Heno and me, the candlelight, the wine, the lamb cooked to his satisfaction, and not overspiced as had been done before. And then the holding, the afterwards. The most pleasurable part of an intimate meal has to be the dessert.

I wheel around, a compulsive I always was (the brick coming to the forefront of my mind). The dark mass is moving some hundred yards in front of me. I take a left out of the cul-de-sac where my house is and shorten the distance between Mr Washington and me. I'm on the opposite side of the street, getting a lateral view. He walks briskly for an elderly man—who is young any more? I'm in the middle era, balding, spectacled with the paunch, the ultimate legacy of all good drinkers.

I lose him for a moment as he turns a corner, but I can follow the whistle ringing through the night air. But what is that tune? It is specific, unlike those infuriating tuneless whistles Heno engages in from time to time to cover things up, to hide his annoyance with me or with the world. I follow quickening my pace, cross the street, bringing Mr Washington's rounded shoulders back into view. The drooping walk (Heno, a boy who was never told to straighten his shoulders?). Looking at Mr Washington, he belongs to the past, a gentleman in his cloth, the long grey coat, the fur lapels, the black brimmed fedora. Who wears such hats nowadays? Heno wears a woollen Nike which he pulls down over his ears when he goes out on the streets.

Mr Washington stops at his broken garden wall, the scene of that night quarrel. He reaches over and spikes his brolly into the lawn. He dips into his coat pocket and takes out a trowel from the covering of a lemon silk handkerchief. He whistles loudly. Not a tune this time but a solitary note: a signal. Mrs Washington shuffles, like a rat in the darkness, out of the house carrying a bucket. Without looking at her (the signal received), he dips his trowel into the bucket which, with effort, she holds up for him by its handle, and by the light of the street lamp, he applies the mortar to the brick. He places the brick—*my* brick—on a line in a broken part of the wall. My arm rises to stop him, but no words come, and my arm just hangs there in the wind like the branches of the denuded cherry blossom under which I am standing. All the time Mrs Washington says nothing. Her head is bowed like a woman defeated. She waits patiently, her bony arm (like Heno's), bearing the weight of the bucket in a light tearaway tulle. Mr Washington resumes his tune, indifferent to her. All his concentration is on getting the brick straight and into place along a cord pulled taut on a rusting nail.

The whistle is low and satisfied now. A job well done. She slinks away back into the house. The door creaks. There is no light coming through the curtained windows. A house without a son.

I'm used to it now: the evenings, the same time, him, marching towards my house. It's a short journey through the suburban streets, two turns to the left, one to the right. The silent twilight retribution.

He works in flitting light and shadows, disjointed images like in a silent black and white movie, scratching with the trowel, the grey mortar, its ashlike powder filtering down like a death.

The brick drops solid into his waiting palm. He wipes the trowel carefully on the lemon coloured cloth, slides it smoothly into the flapped pocket of his coat. He ensconces the brick, as is his custom now, under his left oxter, lifts his brolly like a sword, looks towards the sky (for what? For rain, for inspiration, for challenge?). He proceeds to walk, whistling that tune.

Mocking condoms and 'what of it?' Heno says. 'What if?' I say. 'You give out to me for mixing my drinks. But you... what cocktails do you mix?' The nightclub called SIN. Often wondered about the word, whether it was in the indicative or imperative mood. Heno goes there. The pink disco. The porno videos. The sauna. The cubicles. The soft white towel he stole.

'He's breaking up the garden wall.'

'Let him fucking break up the garden wall.'

Mr Washington sees me on the third (or is it the fourth?) evening. He had seen me all along, no doubt, but this time his eyes momentarily catch mine in an involuntary collision. The whistling stops. He gives me a look of such unmitigated hatred that I freeze. He returns his concentration to the wall and concludes his trowel work. He walks past me with my brick as if I am not there. As if I am a ghost. For a moment, the way his mouth opens, I think he is going to speak, to unleash some dreadful imprecation, but it is just the O of the whistle forming, and he marches on. It is a march, the tune, I recognise that now, like a summoning, a rounding up, slowing down sometimes and then livening up. *Adagio. Grave. Presto.* Funny that, the terms sticking with me more than the music I studied long ago. I can see his embroidered shirt peeping through his coat. No mere suburban dweller he, with my brick under his arm. The whistling grows louder. *Con brio.* I begin to wonder. His action is a diurnal doing, like a jogger out for a jog, a therapeutic act, an aristocratic gesture to manual labour, by the sweat of one's brow, to achieve a sated self at the end of the day.

Not like revenge at all.

I approach my house. My front garden wall, with its cavities like teeth missing, still manages to stand. He attacked the centre. The pillars are still secure.

My wall has disappeared. It is winter now and the garden has become an open space for dogs to defecate on the lawn and around the stricken roses.

Ah yes, the garden. Heno sought refuge in it soon after we first met, when he used to come around to take a breather from the war on the homefront. He would sit in the sun on a summer's evening on my front window ledge and look out, at what I couldn't say for sure: people passing on the street, the white trail of a jetplane in the sky. Certainly his gaze was not on my roses, for he was never horticultural. He would sit there stripped to the waist taking the sun on his milk-white torso. I would pretend to busy myself with the lawn, clipping the edges with my longhandled shears, stealing furtive glances at the staring blue eyes, the pigmented aureoles of his pectorals, the concavity of his chest as he inhaled on his cigarette, the strap of his trouser belt hanging free from a loop.

He is reluctant to talk about himself or his family. He was an only child. His father was a civil servant who was *meant* to be a judge; a man of reduced gentility in his own eyes, not like the riffraff that live around here. He had great plans for his son, like fathers who want a second chance on the merry-go-round of life, riding on the back of their offspring. The son that disappointed. That quarrel, the breaking down of the wall and now the rebuilding. And I, the catalyst. 'That fucker,' Heno says, 'I don't want to talk about that fucker.' I coaxed him, calmed him as I usually do when he gets a bit hyper, and when he was feeling okay again, relaxed after his fix, he said what he did was done in a rage, because his father threw him out when he found out about me. Heno went to the wall with a hammer. Why he should have chosen the front garden wall on which to vent his anger, I do not know. He will not, or perhaps more plausibly, cannot tell me. He went at it with a fury, the way he does most things, chipped and broke off the bricks from their moorings until his father came out roaring, 'Faggot.'

I don't know where Heno goes sometimes apart from the nightclub or the public lavatory in the park. He takes off when the fancy seizes him. He could be gone for a whole day or even days on end. He worked at bits of jobs—the last one as a packer in a supermarket from which he was sacked when he was caught shooting up. His accent varies. It is rural broad-vowelled when he is high. He disciplines it most of the time with a clipped vulgarity, disguising it in a near monosyllabic accent-proof simplicity to blend with the argot of the street. 'Wherever the bollix you're from,' he says, 'does it matter for people like us?' The Nike comes down almost covering his eyes. He wears a tracksuit with a zebra stripe and tennis shoes. He wants to look like the boys who hang around the public lavatory.

I thought that was the end of it when Mr Washington took the garden wall: the gesture was made, retribution secured. How wrong I was. It was snowing the night he went to the brown bricks (matching the wall) on the facade of my house. Holding a strong-beamed torch, he started scraping the mortar with his trowel, as thick feathers of snow stuck to his hat. He freed the bricks in the same way as he had done with the wall and, tantalisingly as always, took away just one brick at a time.

The weather fails to thaw. The night temperatures are subzero. Heno complains of the cold. I am not doing enough to keep the heat in us. The cold is coming through the walls. The radiators burn to the touch, there is a blazing fire in the hearth, extra blankets on the bed; but they are not enough to keep the warmth in my lover. I massage his joints with heated oil.

The brown bricks have gone from the facade of the house like fruit picked by birds in the bleak winter scene. I walk through the park pulping dead leaves under my feet.

Mr Washington appears at the turning on of the street lamps as if they are his cue. Never an evening goes by now when I do not hear that maddening whistle as he makes his way towards my house. A syringe on the footpath he kicks aside with his polished leather shoe.

There was a storm last night that brought hail and snow and trees down. The grey walls of my house shifted, shook a little, their brown brick dressing removed. Poorly mortared, not meant to be seen, drydripped over the grey eight by fours like frozen tears. The living room window frame rattles loose.

Heno is growing thin. How can one *grow* thin? Becoming thin. His formerly chubby cheeks are gaunt and bony now. His buttocks have a wasted look inside the shapeless tracksuit bottoms. He does not eat a full meal. He drinks the wine. He smokes. I know for sure he is not well when he doesn't taunt me any more about the mixing of my drinks. He doesn't care whether I asphyxiate or not in the dead hour of night. I can't help myself there, the short and the chaser like fox and hound, the kick is not there otherwise, like Heno with his lovers, but I keep saying to myself it's not as bad as the needles. I hate the sight of them.

The storm outlived the night. There was the sound of squad cars at some unearthly hour. They woke me. Perhaps they saved my life. The morning shows debris and a window frame on the street. I go to the living room and witness the gaping hollow where the curtains flap in the wind, and my drinking glasses on the hearth make a music.

The park holds ice pockets and light snow drifts among its bare sycamores. Stalactites hang like frozen snot on the public lavatory gate. Two boys with glazed eyes are sitting on the icy ground, sharing a needle. They roll up each other's sleeves tenderly. The crinkled sleeve of the tracksuit top of one is stained with dried blood. The other boy, shivering in a hooded parka, proffers a veiny arm, the end of his tightened tube suspended like a worm. He looks up. 'Mister.' The pleading sound. 'Any spare...' The seraphic face.

I see Heno lurking near the urinals. He doesn't see me. His gaze is elsewhere.

We are growing apart. That word again. I was his first, his initiator to the subtle ways, not like the uncouth ways of the street. He came willingly from that oppressive family. There was no enticing needed. Just that holiday in Italy. I gave him a place, a security, a home. I was his mentor for a long time, but now he is drifting from me, seeking youth, always seeking the earliest blooms as if... as if he can ever be sated. Like a premonition, each *petite mort*, like a flower spreading its seed before its final expiration.

There is no sound from Mr Washington's house. His brown brick wall is sturdy now. No sign of the slinking woman. A temptation to ring the luminous doorbell I resist. The side entrance has my window frame stacked against its gable wall.

The ridge tile has fallen from my roof, loosened no doubt by the storm. It smashed on the side concrete. The other tiles follow in their course. The house shudders in its underfelt.

Heno has sores from the needle jabs, big suppurating blisters. The evening is too cold for loitering. He seeks the warmth of the hearth. But there is no heat. Nothing. 'The streets are better than this,' he declares, refusing to sit on any seat. He shivers in a corner of the living room, crouched down in the manner of the boys outside the public lavatory, sucking in the cigarette smoke with his hollowed cheeks. The bristle on his chin is the colour of mortar.

The snow has turned to rain. Winds are blowing from a different direction bringing thunder and forked lightning. Holding a tinkling short in one hand and a beer chaser in the other, I watch the night flashes from my bedroom window. The flash is like a match being struck in the darkness (Heno lighting a cigarette), the ssshh, so beguilingly quiet, illuminating the window, taking a snapshot of me, capturing my negative on the pane.

At dinner this evening, Heno pushed his plate aside. 'Try the dessert at least,' I said. I had made an apple crumble which he normally likes. He rose, I thought, to fetch the bowls from the worktop (he helps me sometimes, not often; he will dry a dish or make the coffee if the mood seizes him). He stretched to his full six foot two, sighed. Suddenly he grabbed the back of the pine chair, doddered for a moment. 'Are you all right?' I said. He fell, a straight stuntman fall, facing up.

I visit him in the hospital. He lies collapsed in the pillows. He does not reck me. He has a cold unblinking stare which he directs at the ceiling. A rosy-cheeked nurse looks in, smiles.

I walk—not without some trepidation—towards my own house or rather the remains of my own house. The ground carries an inch of snow. The night is starry with a frosty moon. My house is reduced to a frame. There is no felt on the roof now, just the rafters and joists in their geometric form. The stairs have gone. There is no way up.

A pong permeates the house despite all the aeration. It clings to the spot like ground fog.

The boys from the public lavatory are crouched on the wool carpet in a corner of my living room, sharing syringes. They don't even notice me. Their bodies, their hoods and needles and blood and my floor, are all coagulated into one amorphous mass. My house. The shell of a being, an existence, the smashed up marble fireplace, dreams of Sorrento and gondolas from Venice.

I walk. I pass by the public lavatory in the park where an old ex-lover stands looking forlorn.

I hear Mr Washington in the distance whistling a slow march, as he makes his way towards his house. He is carrying just his black brolly now, its ferrule marking time on the path.

I visit Heno. He is in a sweat; he rambles, words I pick up, he speaks of the home he left, was driven out of.

'Where is he?' he says. 'That pox-classed father, have you seen him?' Saliva drools from his mouth. I dab his lips with a soft white towel. A smile, a moment of recognition, of clarity.

'What was it,' I say, half-knowing the answer, 'between you and him?'

'An impropriety.'

'What?'

'That's what he called it.'

Heno delights in vagueness. Words are games, to prevent commitment to anything, to anyone, to me.

'Sent me for sessions,' he says.

'Sessions?'

'Yeah,' he says, 'he sought the doctor's cure for me.'

His breaths race. A moment of panic.

'What is it, Heno?'

'My mother,' he says, 'I've lost her, her image. I can no longer remember what she looks like.'

I'm beginning to suffocate in the ward with its sealed windows, and the heating up high. I feel something rising in my gullet. I drink water from a glass at his bedside, afraid to go out, to abandon him for the air that I crave. I am getting tired, too old for the way of life that beckons, to start a new search on those lonely streets: the hostels, the wandering, the sleeping rough, all that stuff again. He has won, Mr Washington. When I met Heno I had begun to believe in a continuation, a fond wish of never ending.

He tosses in his bed, keeps shaking his head on the pillows from side to side, like a denial, a negation, like he is trying to expel all that is inside, tormenting him. He turns towards me with a sickly smile.

'He wanted me to change,' he says. 'I changed. See how I've changed.'

He is crying. I try to console him. I lift his head from the pillows. I cradle him. I run my fingers through the spiky pins of his hair. He furrows into me, his head finding that crook in my shoulder, that familiar secure place. He is diminishing before my eyes, the sunken orbs, the flesh falling from his face, his wrists, his fingers, showing the bones.

The rosy-cheeked nurse wheels in a trolley. Smiles, when I recoil, as she holds the needle ready.

'Now Heno,' she says.

'What's in it?' I say. 'I mean is it… is it safe?'

'Safe as houses,' she says.

Perfection Comes Too Late

William Wall

I KEEP GETTING THIS EMAIL. It may be something I have signed up for, but I suspect not. Sometimes it comes with a return address that turns out to be fake. Here is the text:

> Even if you have no erectin problems SOFT CIAzLIS would help you to make BETTER SE X MORE OFTEN! and to bring unimagnable plesure to her. Just disolve half a pil under your tongue and get ready for action in 15 minutes. The tests showed that the majority of men after taking this medic ation were able to have PERFECT ER ECTI ON during 36 hours!

Who is sending me this message? How do they know where I am? It worries me. Another aspect that worries me is the way certain words are broken. ER ECTI ON. So far as I know, these words, with the exception of the last, exist independently in no living language. They may be a code, or they may be typos. Simple, to dissolve a pill under the tongue (I'm translating here), and bring unimaginable pleasure to her, fifteen minutes to action, and it has been tested on the majority of men, which is reassuring.

The thing is, I have not clicked on the link provided.

Partly because I'm not sure what I'd do with a thirty-six hour erection.

Also because I'm always so uncertain as to the outcome. Some men approach women from a position of certainty. There is some arcane sign, some feral perfume, that tells them that the object of their actions is ready to capitulate. Whereas I have never been in a position to be certain, even during coitus, that the woman I was with was having a good time. This is linked to persistent self-doubts that have troubled me ever since I was an adolescent; however, I detest those writers who, at the first opportunity, work back into a comfortable childhood setting, and blame, usually, their parents, or their upbringing (Catholic, for example), or some central figure in their past like a priest, for what, let's face it, is an adult failing. Children are supposed to be uncertain, but as adults they should learn to be happy.

Happy men certainly are more attractive to women. If I were a radio talk show psychologist this is the first principle I would lay down. Be happy and secure and you will pull women. Whereas what radio talk shows usually say is something like, Learn to love yourself. Which used to be called onanism.

Er ecti on sounds like the beginning of an alphabet though. *Alpha, beta, kappa; er, ecti, on.* I sometimes think that an alphabet exists in which my strange state of existence is perfectly described. Given that we shape reality through language, perhaps even create it, perhaps there should be a personalised alphabet for everybody. I'm surprised that a guru hasn't worked this one out.

So the email arrived again. My wife heard the ping while I was in the bathroom, and since we were expecting news from our daughter in Australia (a boy, seven pounds one ounce, Mark William) she read it. The title gave nothing away, it was just a random piece of text that happened to contain the word babble.

So, she said, why have you been making these enquiries?

It's just spam, I said, I get spam all the time. Then I made a mistake. I said, They're idiots.

My wife assumed that this addition implied some kind of personal relationship. It's a reasonable reading of the expression.

So, she said, have you bought other stuff from them? How did they get you on their list?

Everyone is on their list, I said.

She folded her arms and looked at me. My wife is an American. This is a classic American gesture that I first saw on the Jack Benny Show.

Jack Benny always accompanied the gesture with a slight turn of his head and the words, Do you believe this? Something like that anyway.

So after that she found my MSN records. I've been saving them in order to fine-tune my responses, although, as it happens, I haven't gotten around to actually re-reading them. I don't think she read them in full either. MSN records are virtually unreadable. LOL and NBD and all that stuff. It took me a long time to learn the code. Fortunately I found a useful site with an alphabetised list that went something like this:

Acronym	Meaning
AFAIK	As far as I know
AFK	Away from computer keyboard (for wireless users)
AIM	AOL Instant Messenger
A/S/L	Age/Sex/Location
ATM	At the moment

Most of which I never came across anyway.
So she said to me, Who are these people? What does RUOK mean?
It means Are you okay.
Is this you asking this girl are you okay?
That's me. Or at least that's the me on MSN.
What the hell are you talking about?
What you're reading.
Are you okay implies that whatever came before this was something that might upset her. She says, What? Then you type RUOK and then you type this (::[]::). What is that? Where is the question you asked her? It's not in this file.
I don't know.
What does that symbol mean?
It's a Band-Aid.
What?
It's what they call an emoticon. It means I'm offering support.
You're offering this girl support.
Assuming she is a girl.

My wife walked out of the room. Then she walked back in again. What is going on, she said.

I said, Sit down, you're making me nervous.

So, my wife said, you pretended to be a psychologist.

I do have some experience…

Oh yes, thanks to me.

She looked at me a little longer. Her father, Jeff, was an engineer who worked on hydroelectric projects. He was a tall man with a slight stoop. He served in the Navy during the war. He didn't talk about it. Her mother was a doctor who never practised. When they visit us they exude a kind of generosity and warmth that after a few days is overwhelming and makes me want to hit one of them.

And what has happened?

Nothing. They tell me their stories. Or the stories they want to tell me. And I console them.

She laughed. You console them?

Yes. I'm an older wiser man who has seen a lot of life.

She laughed again.

And I give them words of wisdom.

Now she stared at me intensely. So, what did you say to this girl here. Level with me now.

I told her she should sleep with her boyfriend.

What?

I said chances like that may not come twice.

For a long while my wife said nothing. She looked at me and looked away several times. She folded her arms and unfolded them. I said, You'd need to know her. Things are bad for her.

My wife got up and went to the kitchen sink. She ran the cold tap and stood watching the flow for a few moments with her hand still on the lever. It's a stainless steel lever, a Franke, and Jeff wanted to take the tap apart last time he was over—to see how the valve worked. The stream comes out milky-looking because of some filter in the pipe. It's milky because it's full of turbulence and air bubbles.

You think five or six sessions with a shrink makes you an expert?

I said I didn't think there was a lot to it. I said I thought most psychologists were paid to dispense common sense and it was only the fact that they were paid that gave it any authority.

Level with me, do you want to fuck these girls?

I don't even know that they are girls. This is the internet. They could be fifty-year-old married men.

Have you ever met any of them?

I looked at my wife. One thing I would like to have done at that moment was change the balance of power. I thought about what would happen if I said yes. I imagined describing the meeting, the girl, what we said, how I seduced her, her eagerness. But I also thought my wife would immediately recognise it as some kind of weak fantasy.

No.

Would you like to?

No.

So you get your kicks out of this remote control relationship where you're the wise old owl and she's the frail adolescent. Didn't you get enough of frail adolescence with Maya? Remember when she went to that disco and she came home in bits. You passed her on to me like a hot coal. You didn't want to console her. You wanted to get rid of her. You went into the den and turned on the TV while she was crying. And when I asked you to visit with his parents you said you couldn't face it. I had to do it myself. Imagine how that made me feel, a woman, going about a thing like that? At least they were nice about it. At least they took Maya's side.

I remember.

Well what is it? What's driving you to this.

I'm not being driven. I just like doing it that's all. I'm their agony aunt.

Is it me?

Aw fuck, I said, it's always you.

Ever since you had that little problem, she said.

My wife is still beautiful. She was beautiful in that American way when I met her and she still is. She buys her clothes from the Sears & Roebuck catalogue. She wears Classic Elements Pull-on Twill Pants and Covington Twill. She wears an Apostrophe Three Quarters Sleeve

Sateen Blouse. I know because it is one of our rituals, browsing through the S&R catalogue and choosing that season's look, which has turned out to be, over twenty-seven or so seasons, the same look every year. It's a kind of beauty that wears thin. She has perfect teeth and wears her hair short. She took creative writing at Colombia and when I met her used to describe herself as an author.

I told one of the girls that I specialised in adolescent psychology. I said I hoped she didn't mind being called an adolescent. She said she couldn't even spell it. I also said I had medical training, which is true. I told another that I wrote a syndicated agony-aunt column for newspapers in the United States. Do they syndicate agony aunts? She asked me if I just made up the answers. I was touched by the simplicity of the question.

After she found my MSN records, my wife tried to get me to make love to her. She thought if she used what she called my fantasy thoughts about these girls.

I said, Look, I like helping them. I think I can make their lives better. I like them telling me their stories. It helps them.

She said, You should go back to the doctor.

I said, I don't have any problems to talk to him about. I'm a happy man.

So while I was away at a conference I checked out the link. It looked shabby like a scam, a bit garish, tacky, some of the buttons didn't work—which is exactly what I expected, but even so, I felt cheated. I was away from home and I was ready for something. I didn't know what. Who buys drugs on the internet anyway? Who would be that crazy? So instead I had a few at the hotel bar and tried to initiate a conversation with a woman who had a laptop beside her. I told her about the email and we laughed over it together. I was implying that thirty-six hours of sex was not beyond the bounds of possibility. She was at the same conference and had similar interests. She was thin and tall. She had intense blue eyes. After about an hour I became terrified of their blueness. She had unbuttoned her jacket and was complaining that she had eaten too much and that her slacks were too tight. She loosened her belt even. We were talking about young people and saying that one of the great joys of our profession was being able to help them. Then we were joined by other people. They were interested in a club that ran in the basement at the back of the hotel. You had to walk out onto the street and around the corner. Everyone at the conference had a free pass, they said. It was in our conference folder. I said I would follow them over. But instead, when I got to my room, I powered up the laptop and took another look at that site. I wondered if having a thirty-six hour erection would be empowering. It could easily be painful. I ordered some anyway, and paid by credit card. I had them send it to my home address and I put my wife's name on it and asked them to giftwrap the package.

LOL, I would have written if I were on MSN.

I'm laughing out loud.

I am in fact an orthodontist. I used to be a dentist but after a couple of years extracting and filling teeth, cleaning teeth and prescribing things for gingivitis and so on, dentistry becomes a little like a kind of antique restoration. Orthodontics offer some opportunity for artistic expression. I believe the mouth is the focal organ for the entire personality. Orthodontic manipulation has all of the characteristics of drama: the longed-for perfection, the purgative suffering, the adjustment, the epiphany, catharsis. There was once this beautiful girl who came to me with a terrible mouth; overcrowding was turning her into a kind of large-beaked bird. I extracted some teeth and set up a brace system. I'm going to put a beautiful smile in your face, I told her. I fitted Hawley retainers. I didn't say that teeth move throughout life; that if she wanted everything to stay the way it should be she would have to wear retainers every day from then on. By the time she was twenty I was finished the reconstructive phase. Then she didn't turn up and I found out she'd died. I see in those steel wires a metaphor for inexorable time. Perfection comes too late, as always.

Daragh Maguire and the Black Blood

D. Gleeson

THE DAY AFTER THEY PUT HIS BROTHER JOHN in the ground, Daragh
Maguire climbed the Carraigdubh rock and he made a wish.

Daragh had entered Kilcoole graveyard that afternoon, surprised by
the summer sun and the sounds of the birds singing. The gravel path
through the headstones crunched under his feet as he forced himself
to the back corner where they had put his brother. He saw the black
shapes of old women kneeling against the flowers of the grave. The
hum of the rosary droned towards him. The women nodded to him,
and at first he knelt with them and rattled off the sorrowful mysteries.
But his head grew full, and his tongue grew thick and the stone that
had lodged in his belly since the day his brother died seemed heavier
than ever and he found that he could not speak. He rested back on his
ankles and his head dropped low.

Finally he felt a craggy hand on his shoulder and the women left
him. He raised his head and looked at the grave. The bright blooms
that had been laid on it covered his brother entirely. He felt his anger
rise beside his pain. He took the flowers and flung them from him.

The bulge of earth beneath the wreaths lay revealed to him. His
heart was breaking at the mound and the thing that made the mound
and he was undone.

He pushed his hands into the swell of the earth until his fingers
vanished into the clay and he felt like his body might follow. Daragh
was suddenly afraid of his grief and of himself. He pulled his brown
hands from the earth and he sat back on his heels again.

It was there that Fionnuala found him, still as a stone, staring at the soil that had wrapped itself around his fingers and wormed its way under his nails. She saw the holes in the mound where his hands had been and the child she carried leapt inside her.

'Jesus, Daragh, what are you doing?' she said and pulled him up by the elbow.

He looked up and saw her shock of red hair and freckled skin and whitest teeth. She thrust a handkerchief at him.

'Clean your hands, love,' she said.

She piled the wreaths back on the grave as he dragged the traces of earth from his fingers with the cloth. She led him out of the graveyard and up the chapel hill, where the oak trees crowded in the road and choked the light with their cover. Daragh rested his head on her shoulder as they walked.

When they reached the crossroads at the top of the hill, he said, 'I'd like to climb the rock today.'

So they turned left at the cross and walked towards the gate of Lacey's field. And Fionnuala thought about how Daragh's fingers had been in the grave of his brother, but she forced herself to take his hand and guide it to her belly.

'He is kicking today,' she said.

Daragh did not hear her.

'Your son is kicking today,' and she willed him to feel the foot of the child inside her. But Daragh only thought of how John would never marry now, or feel the swell of a child in his woman's belly, or see his own sons.

The sun was blocked by the mass of rock at the top of the field. Its face looked old and forbidding in the shade.

The going was easy at first. Years of wind and rain had slashed ridges into the stone. Fionnuala climbed ahead despite her bulk, her hands finding the well-worn hollows and pulling her upwards. Daragh felt a burn in his heart to overtake her and reach the top first, but he remembered the glint in John's eye the morning that he died, when Daragh had goaded him to race across the Kilcoole river. He slowed his pace.

*

Daragh looked down from the rock and saw the entire village of Kilcoole beneath him. The lights winked already in Devine's where Davey Considine would be telling jokes and playing his fiddle. John would not be there tonight to play with him. May Murphy's shop was closing—with only her scratchedy cat to keep her company that evening. Beyond the shop he looked at the bend in the road where John said he had seen a ghost once. His eyes wandered onwards past the turn to Clonbeara towards the river where the chunky brown bullrushes lined the ditches. The river snaked the length of the village separating the back of Kilcoole from the Clare hills on the other side and Killybrack where Fionnuala's family were from. But Daragh could not look at the river now and his eyes shifted back to Clonbeara and his own house that glowed orange in the evening light. He knew every brick and piece of glass, every hole in the yard and every turn of every hoof of every cow in his fields. He saw John in all of them. His face, his hands were soaked into every stone and blade of grass in the place.

'Do you remember the time we all mitched from school with John and we hid up here?' Daragh said.

'I do,' said Fionnuala, and she laughed, 'John was a never a great one for schooling.'

'Do you remember the time we saw who could steal the most apples from Ryans and we ate them all and we were sick?' Daragh said.

The sun's light was failing now and it began to dip behind the hills across the river.

'Shall we make tracks home?' Fionnuala asked.

'You go on, Fin, I'm just going to wait here for a little while,' Daragh said.

He waved to her as she picked her way down the field to the road. Only when he could no longer see the figure tramping down the hill to the village, did he allow the tears to come.

The air was cooler now and he shivered, pulling his knees up to his chest, shaking, so his feet rat-tatted off the rock, sending messages by morse into the heart of the stone. He thought about the fishing trip they would not take this summer. He thought about the sons that John would never see racing through the fields and stealing apples and growing into men or the pints of porter that he and John would not drink together as old men, chewing on their gums and baking their old bones in the sun.

The river glowed in the fading light like a living thing. He looked at the mass of her water, but he saw only John's body in it. He saw the stones that were John's eyes when he had pulled him from the current. He felt again the meaty weight of him as he had dragged him back along the Clonbeara road to the village, and how he did not rouse and how the life was gone out of him entirely.

He turned his eyes from the river and the black hills on the other side and he looked up at the evening star that hung alone in the sky. His feet tapped his cold message into the rock and he said to the star, 'I wish—I wish that the pain would go away.' His tears fell from him sinking deep into the cracked heart of the rock.

And the evening star heard Daragh Maguire's plea.

The house was dead with night when Daragh returned. He could hear only the sound of the clock ticking as he pushed the door open. Fionnuala had left a plate of bread and cheese for him, but he did not eat it. He pushed himself closer to the fire, but he could not warm the coldness in his bones and the lead in his belly. He watched the flames dying in the hearth and he thought about going to bed. Instead he pulled his father's old coat down from the hook by the door and he covered himself with it.

He woke with a crick in his neck and a shiver from the cold. The fire had fallen into ash, but the room was bright as if the moon had taken the night sky. A silver light streamed in the window, bleaching the walls of the kitchen and blinding Daragh in his chair. Daragh felt cold hands tightening around his chest. He took the poker from the fireplace, swung the door open and stepped into the yard.

A woman in white stood against the wall of the turf shed in front of him. The light flowed directly from her head and body. She was tall and slender and her fingers spread like white branches from her robe. As she moved, the colours in her dress shifted and shimmered. Her hair gleamed silver, but her face was not lined at all. Her eyes were grey and she had the whitest skin that Daragh had ever seen.

The woman started to move towards him.

Daragh's poker clattered on the cobblestones as he fell to his knees. 'Please don't kill me,' he said.

'I will not hurt you,' the woman said. 'I am here to help you. You summoned me here.'

She put her hand on his shoulder and he felt the coldness of her shoot down his arm.

'Get up, Daragh,' the woman said, 'I have something to help your pain. I ask only for a small thing in return—a lock of your hair.'

'Why would you want a lock of my hair?' he asked.

'In return for what I give you, you must give me something—it is an exchange,' she said.

'And this can take away the pain in me for John?' he asked. He rose from the ground and looked at her face.

The woman nodded, and as she smiled he saw the sharpness of her small yellow teeth like an animal's.

She put one of her long fingers in her mouth and bit on it. A black bubble of blood welled up at the tip of her finger.

'Daragh, take this. This will help you to feel better. Take it,' she said.

Daragh looked at the slate in her eye and the whiteness of her face and the teeth knocked like stones in his head from the fear. But he thought about John and the lead weight in him and he took her finger. He closed his eyes and he opened his mouth and received the blood of the woman. Each sour drop curled in the back of his throat. The hairs stood up on the back of his hands and he felt a coldness in him, but for the first time since John died, the heaviness in his belly went away and the sickness in his heart began to fade.

The woman said 'Daragh, I will come again once three days and three nights have passed to take payment for what I have given you.'

Suddenly he felt tired and his head felt light. He stumbled in the doorway to the house catching his foot on the step. He turned twice in the kitchen and lurched into the chair by the fire. Within seconds he was sleeping.

Daragh woke the next morning as the sun was blazing in through the room. His limbs felt light and his head was clear. He sat up in the chair. He recalled his dream of the woman in white from the night before. He stood and looked out the window. The poker was still lying in the yard.

Fionnuala stood by the table with her back to him. Daragh crept up to her and spun her around as if they were dancing. He kissed her. She returned his kiss and her heart smiled, for he seemed returned to her.

'How're you feeling today, my love?' she asked.

'I feel fine,' Daragh said and he smiled.

Daragh thought about John and he felt a small sadness that his brother was no longer living, but it was a wispy regret that fled when he looked at it directly.

'I think I'll go back to the grave this morning,' Daragh said as he chewed on an egg. 'I would like to look at it again,' he said.

'I'll come with you,' Fionnuala said.

'If you like, my love,' he said and continued to eat.

They walked down the road past Devine's and beyond the shop where a few of the neighbouring women stood chatting. The women saluted them. Daragh raised his hand in a jaunty wave and smiled.

'Drop your hand!' Fionnuala hissed.

'Why?' asked Daragh.

'They do not expect you to be so... happy,' Fionnuala said. She dropped her hand from his and shuffled ahead around the bend in the road past Dwyer's fields and the long meadow beside the church.

Daragh pondered what she had said. He thought about the heavy, hot weight of pain that had sat on him and he thought about the coolness that filled him now and he did not feel guilt in him. For did he not love John just as much as he had before?

They turned up the road at the chapel and walked halfway up the hill until the graveyard. Fionnuala drew her coat around herself.

Daragh looked at the headstone and the earth and he knelt beside the mound. He forced himself to think of John. But he only recalled how John had not shared the cigarettes he had stolen from old Mick Fanning when they were kids, and his dirty tackles on the hurling field and he thought of his quick temper and his lack of patience and consideration. He wondered why he had been so upset, now that he had a bit of distance from the whole thing.

Daragh looked again at the blooms on the grave. He reached out towards a wreath and Fionnuala stiffened, but his finger curled around the head of the flower and he pulled it off and kept it in his hand as he stood again and walked out of the graveyard.

Fionnuala was filled with unease, but she ran after him and she prayed they would not meet anyone on the road home. She suggested they go up the back road, past Carraigdubh rock with the view of the river through the trees. He hummed as he strolled along the back road, but Fionnuala saw that if he looked at the river he was silent, until he would turn away and begin to sing again.

That night Daragh slept like the dead. He did not stir and he hardly dreamed at all, except for one dream where he was walking around the village and there was nobody there. All the buildings were empty and the roads were empty and even the fields themselves were empty of every animal. But this did not bother Daragh in his dream.

Jamesie Farrell was already turning the lines of hay with his pitchfork when Daragh arrived in the meadow the next morning. Jamesie stopped his work and came to him, clasping both his hands around Daragh's.

'Daragh, you're great to come—thanks,' he said.

'Sure why wouldn't I?' said Daragh and he smiled.

Jamesie's own smile stuttered a bit on his face, but he nodded his head and he said, 'Myself and Dadda were down this morning, checking the hay. It's dry enough to build the cocks today.'

Daragh saw that Jamesie's father Tommy had set up the wide wooden tumble-rake behind their horse at the far end of the field. Tommy had coiled the leather reins around his shoulder and the horse began to move down the lanes raking the long lines of hay they had mown the week before.

Daragh and Jamesie worked side by side pulling the hay that the tumble-rake had missed and Jamesie began to sweat freely in the growing morning heat. But Daragh's face and arms were cool and he did not feel any heat from the work.

They worked together on the first cock, twisting hay into the base of it, then building it high on the outside and forking in more hay that tumbled down the inside as the haycock rose.

'Jesus, Daragh—I'm wrecked,' panted Jamesie, 'let's rest for a minute.' And Jamesie collapsed on the ground, wincing as his backside hit the hard stubble in the meadow.

But Daragh did not join him and he said, 'You take a rest, I'll push on for another bit.' He kept forking until the haycock was large above his head with a sloping point at the top for the rain to run off. Each lift of his fork was as smooth as his first pitch that morning and Jamesie could see no shake in his arms or a bit of sweat on him. Jamesie pulled himself up and forced the fork into his hand. He examined the cock that Daragh had finished but it was not at all poorly made for the speed of it. It was as sturdy as a house.

And so it went for the morning, Daragh blazed ahead and Jamesie struggled behind him. Jamesie took off his jacket, his cap and finally his sweat-soaked shirt. The water ran down his face and he could tell by the burn on his hands that there would be blisters the next day. But Daragh kept up his work. When Mairéad came with bread and butter, and bottles of tea with milk, Daragh stopped only for a sip of tea.

'I don't know what's gotten into Daragh,' Jamesie said to his father as they ate their bread.

'God knows,' Tommy said.

'Whatever it is, it's good for us,' Jamesie said, and he pointed at the field.

'I wonder if it is…' said Tommy, but he would not say any more.

That evening as the sun was setting, they found they had done two days' work in the time of one, and Jamesie said to Daragh, 'Come on home with us now Daragh—Mairéad has a full pot of bacon and potatoes for us waiting.' The water ran in Jamesie's mouth as he thought about it. But Daragh shook his head and would not come back to Farrell's for food. So they left each other on the road, and Tommy and Jamesie went home with an uneasiness in them instead of a pleasure for the work that had been done.

Daragh found himself watching the hours and when the time drew near for the woman to come again, he thought about the blood he had taken and the feel of its trickle and its tickle on his throat. As the day's light dimmed and the clop clop of the cows on the evening roads faded into the stillness of night, he felt restless. An itch came into him and he thought about his brother again. He remembered how he used to tease John as a child and chase him around their kitchen table, and the mitching they did from the school and the summers making hay. The memories flooded into him and his gut shifted in his body. He felt himself growing heavy with the sorrow again. He sat beside the hearth, but he did not look at the turf that glowed and cracked in the fire, he looked instead at the wall and waited for the shine of her light on it.

When it came, he took no poker with him. She stood there glowing even brighter than before. Her hair glistened and sparkled. Daragh felt a hunger rise within him that he could not contain, and his mouth was filled with water.

'I want more blood,' he said.

The woman spoke, her voice softer than he remembered. 'Daragh, you must first pay for the blood you have taken.'

He reached for the hair at the top of his head and he pulled and pulled until a clump came off in his hand and his blood spurted out the top of him and ran down the back of his neck. But he was looking at the woman and he did not pay heed to the loss of his own blood.

She took his hair and put it in a small bag that she held in a belt at her hip.

'Now, may I have more?' and he tried to keep his voice from trembling and the shake from his knee for fear she would say no.

'I will give you more, in return for a nail from one of your fingers,' the woman said. 'Do you promise me that?'

'Yes,' Daragh said, 'I promise.'

She raised her hand out to him.

He did not wait, but sank his teeth into her wrist like an animal, and he was surprised at the strength of his teeth cutting through her flesh and at himself for the biting he was doing, but all was forgotten as the dark blood from her poured into him and down his throat and all around his body until he felt a glow in him and the sick sadness that threatened him was gone, and the stinging in his head was gone and he felt a tingle in every part of him. And still he drank and sucked at her hand, until finally she said to him, 'Enough.' And she pulled her hand away and hid it in her sleeve, so he could not see the wound he had made.

'Daragh—I will return again to you after three days and three nights to claim payment from you for what you have taken from me,' the woman said. But Daragh lay on his back and looked at the sky, and the stars were a blur to him and the wind was a song and the gravelly stones beneath his back were soft as the feather of a bird to him.

The morning dawn was grey and the sun struggled in the sky casting watery light on the yard. Daragh felt a sickness in him when he woke and at first he could not recall why he was sleeping outside. But then he remembered. He stole into the house and crawled into the bed, shivering at the stony coldness of the sheets he had not slept in.

He woke again with the sun blazing in on top of him. A brown clump of his own hair sat on the pale pillow beside him. A further shower of hair fell from him when he touched his head. He ran to the mirror and he saw the reflection of his head and a stretch of pale skin where his hair used to be. Another lock of hair came away in his hand.

Daragh felt a panic rise in him and his breath was short and came in gasps. He pulled at his scalp and the hair flew from him under the frenzy of his hands, until it was mostly skin that he could see on his head and mostly hair on the floor.

But some of his hair remained and would not budge and clung onto him in curly strands. He thought about the woman and the hair he had given her and he was afraid of what he had started.

When Fionnuala saw him she dropped the pan she was holding and she ran to him.

'What happened to you?' she said.

He looked at her and he felt his shame burn the bare flesh on him. He dropped his head and did not meet her eye.

She looked at him for a minute, but then she fetched the scissors and a blade and a bowl of warm water. She leaned into him and she whispered, 'I will shave your head so no one will see where the hair is left and where it is not.'

The shears felt stiff as she closed them on the first lock of his hair. She caught the curl in her palm as it fell, a little poem of a thing, but it felt like a hook in her hand. She remembered the first time she kissed Daragh Maguire, the bristle of the hair on his chin and the soft twist of the hair on his head. Fionnuala felt her sorrow sharp inside her, but she saw the shake in Daragh's knee as he sat there, so she bade her mind be still and her hand be steady.

She put the lock in the pocket of her apron, and she made a wish for Daragh as she did so. She held each lock that she cut in her hand and she thought about letting it fall on the floor. But she put each one into her pocket until it swelled with his hair. And with each lock that she put in her pocket she made a wish for Daragh or for herself, or for their son that she carried inside her.

Then she dipped the blade in the water and she traced its edge along the curve and dip of his head. Her hand shook but she left no mark on him, nor did she draw any blood from him.

Daragh felt the heat from her hands, and the heart cracked inside him. He saw the bulge in her pocket and he felt the shake in her body. He stood and turned to her and he held her, although he was shaking himself. And neither moved for a long time.

Daragh went to see to the cattle. Every few minutes he lifted his cap up and he passed his hand over his head and then he would look at his hands and wonder what would happen to him if he did not give the woman the nail.

After the cows were milked and brought back to the top field, Daragh said to Fionnuala, 'I'm going back to finish the hay with Tommy and Jamesie for we did not get it all saved yesterday.'

He walked down towards Clonbeara past the meadow where Jamesie and Tommy were working and he lifted his hat and saluted them as he walked by them. Jamesie raised his hand and waved. But Tommy saw the gleam on Daragh's head. He leaned on his pitchfork watching him walk by and he did not salute him.

Daragh was halfway down the road to the river, but already he felt the weight of the water looming behind its banks. And he found that the hunger he had to face his fear of the river was going off him. All he could think of now was the nail.

He hurried back into the village and onto the chapel hill, but he did not turn into the graveyard. Instead he went into the church grounds, through the doors and far, far up the church, right to the altar. Daragh knelt and looked at the cool plaster on the face of the statue and he tried to pray. But when he joined his hands and fingers together, all he thought about was how much longer he would have the use of them.

And so he left the church and wandered back into the village, and went into Devine's. He passed through the narrow shop in the front nodding at the women there and went on through the door into the public house behind.

Daragh took off his cap and he ordered a pint. Matty Devine looked at him and the shine on his head that lit the inside of the gloomy pub. He did not say anything, but he did pull him a pint.

Daragh saw that the same men who had shouted him pints of porter at the wake were now not meeting his eye, but were staring into their own drinks or at the floor. He replaced his cap and sat in the corner. He drank his pint. And then another. And another. At the fourth he added a whisky to each order.

When Matty offered to get his son to help him home, the sun still blazed outside. Though the legs were buckling under him and the tongue lolled around his mouth, the bright light of terror still burned in Daragh's eyes.

Fionnuala took him at the door and thanked the boy. She helped her husband into the bed and she pulled off his boots. And then she went up to the top field and brought down the cattle and milked them herself. She thought about the pain that dug into her back and she tried not to think about her husband. But later that night as she sat at the fire, she stared for a long time at the flames and she wondered what was happening to the man that she had married.

On the second day Daragh's head was thick from the drink he had poured into himself the day before.

And Fionnuala said to him 'What is happening, Daragh?'

'Nothing,' he said, and he ate his breakfast and then he fled the house. Daragh worked like a thousand men that day. He built fences that needed fixing. He restacked the turf that had fallen in the shed since the spring. He turned the hay in half of the low field on his own.

But for all his work, his body stayed dry and no sweat fell from his brow. He thought about the woman and he resolved that he would not take the blood any more. He looked at his hand and he thought that even if all of the nails were to fall out of him he would still have the use of the hand. He continued to work.

The hail of tea leaves hitting the metal on the weighing scales in Murphy's shop stopped as Fionnuala walked in the door. She felt the narrow shelving would topple in on her and she hugged her arms to her chest.

Chrissy Dwyer heaved herself up from the counter where she had been leaning. Her eyes gleamed like a bird's, and, moving quickly for her size, she sprang at Fionnuala.

Chrissy dragged Fionnuala by the arm to the counter, where May Murphy stood frozen, the bag of tea forgotten in her hand.

'We were just saying, May, weren't we...' Chrissy smiled and looked at her companion.

'Oh yes,' May said, 'wasn't it a terrible tragedy about poor John?'

They waited.

Fionnuala ducked her head and nodded.

'Wasn't I saying to Pat the other night though, that Daragh's looking fierce well for all that's happened. He has a glow about him. A fierce glow,' Chrissy said.

'Fierce, fierce,' May nodded.

Fionnuala looked at May until the older woman's eyes finally dropped and she clutched the bag of tea.

'Of course he's not right in himself after it all,' Chrissy blessed herself. 'But still he's looking very well, wouldn't you say?' she persisted.

'Yes, I suppose he is, Chrissy. Now I'd better be getting on back home, I just wanted a few candles and some soap,' Fionnuala said, and she forced a thin smile.

She pushed Chrissy's arm from hers and put the coins on the counter and waited.

'Of course, if you're in a rush... Chrissy, you don't mind?' May huffed, and left the bag of tea on the counter. She pulled the candles out and the soap and wrapped them tightly in brown paper and handed them over to Fionnuala.

The twittering of the women followed her down the street and up the hill and in her own door. That night she could still smell the staleness of their words on her clothes and on her hair and it clouded her mind. So she forgot to take the meat from the pot and it burned tough and black on the outside. Her husband chewed on that meat as if it was the finest cut, cooked to perfection. His head was turning with the promise of a nail. As the last of the sun burnt in the window, Fionnuala fancied she did see a glow on his cheek and a glitter in his eye she had not seen before. She stuck her fingernails into her palms until they made little white half-moons in her reddened flesh and she did not speak.

Although his arms and legs were worn out and his body was bruised and tired, Daragh lay in the bed and he could not sleep, for the fear gnawed away at him. He rose from the bed and went out to the yard. He stood there and stared at the stars and the moon and the black shadows of the hills behind him, and he rued his wish that day on the rock. And he told himself he would not take the blood again.

Fionnuala woke and saw that there was a space in their bed. She went to the window and she saw Daragh standing solitary out in the yard, but she did not go to him. She watched his stillness and the way he clutched his arms to himself and she moved back to the bed only when she saw him turn towards the door.

When Daragh woke on the third day his fear hung heavy in him, but he was eaten also with a dull ache in his belly and a stirring hunger inside himself that was not satisfied by bread or meat. And when he thought about the woman and her blood, his mouth filled with water.

So he went to the shed as dusk fell and he took the pliers in his hand. He put the nail of his little finger between the nose of it and he pulled as hard as he could. He screamed with the pain as the nail was torn from him, and he wrapped his finger up tight to stop the bleeding.

And then he waited for the woman to come.

She stood again by the whitewashed wall of the shed. Her face glowed at him and he stared anew at her light.

'Daragh, I have come to claim the nail that you owe me.'

He fumbled in his shirt and pulled out the nail that he had torn from his little finger.

The woman took the nail from him and weighed it in her hand, feeling the shape and the heft of it.

Daragh's gut twisted inside him, trying to push its way out of his body to take more of the blood.

She said, 'I accept this nail in payment for what you took from me.'

He nodded, and held out his hand for more.

'I will give you more of my blood. But I will claim something in return. In three days and three nights, you will give me a tooth from the head of your wife Fionnuala.'

Daragh's arm dropped to his side. He looked back at the small black window of their bedroom.

Inside the room Fionnuala woke suddenly. She had thrashed the bedclothes around in a nightmare, but she could not remember any of it.

'I will give you a tooth from my own head—is that not enough?' Daragh said. His voice sounded weak and though his heart felt heavy as a stone in his chest, his gut continued to writhe and jump up in him demanding to be fed.

The eyes of the woman flashed dark and her skin turned a shade of grey.

'It is not yours to determine the payment for what I give to you. I will have the tooth of your wife.'

Inside the bedroom Fionnuala looked around. The other side of the bed was empty. Then she saw the light outside the window.

Daragh fell to his knees in the yard and reached out his hands to the woman. 'I will give you a tooth from my head and another nail from my hand. Please.'

The face of the woman darkened and he could see white veins popping in her cheeks amidst the grey.

'Daragh Maguire, this is not your price to name,' she said.

She lowered her head and folded her arms in front of her. Her light began to fade and Daragh could see the whitewashed bricks of the wall through her body.

Fionnuala clutched the bedclothes around her and inched her way towards the window.

'Wait!' Daragh called, crawling towards the woman on his knees, 'wait—I'll do it…'

The words ran from his mouth like beetles and he wept.

'Do you give me your word, that you will present to me the tooth of your wife in three days and three nights?' the woman asked.

'I… I promise,' said Daragh and he hung his head.

'Then you may take of my blood,' she said and she bared the shiny whiteness of her neck to him.

Fionnuala stood at the window and watched her husband.

Daragh leapt at the woman, grabbing her shoulders and clawing at her neck with his fingers and his teeth until her blackness ran down his throat and into his belly and into his gut and the gut calmed itself and his blood carried hers around his body. And still he drank more, and his body sighed and groaned with pleasure. But the shame rose in him like a bubble in his chest. The greater the bubble grew, the more savage he became, and he sucked on her until she began to shake and she pushed him away.

'Enough. I will return and claim my payment,' she said.

Daragh fell back on the ground and his fingers and feet twitched, but he could not feel the twitch and the tears rolled down his face and he did not see the form of the woman fade in the night.

Fionnuala stumbled to the bed as the shroud of darkness returned to the room. She lay very still until sleep finally claimed her.

Finally Daragh struggled off the ground and into the house. He wrapped his cold arms around Fionnuala as she slept but he felt no comfort in it.

As Daragh woke the next morning, he was warmed by the blood that the woman had given him but heated also by the promise he had made.

When he pulled his hand out from under the bed covers, he saw that the fingers were bloated black on his left hand and there was no movement in his fingers as if they were made of stone. He touched his dead hand. The nails from each finger fell from him onto the cover of the bed. He felt that his throat was closing in on him and that he could not breathe.

Fionnuala stirred and woke and she saw his dead hand and the nails on the covers and she was filled with visions from the night before. She leapt from the bed and stood back against the wall.

'Daragh, what has happened to your hand?' she asked.

He looked at the blackened meat of his fingers and the face on his wife as white as the teeth in her head. And he opened his mouth to tell her about the woman, but he remembered he had promised that which was not his to give, and he was filled with shame and a fear for Fionnuala and for himself. So he said instead, 'I caught my hand in the back door coming in last night.'

Fionnuala's hand flew to her mouth as she saw the lie slide across her husband's face.

Daragh said, 'Will you bandage my hand for me?'

But Fionnuala did not hear him, for she felt a dizziness rise in her and the legs go from under her and she sank to the floor. Daragh came to her and he helped her back into the bed. She felt the room close in around her but not before she clutched the nails that had fallen from Daragh's hand in her fist.

Daragh went into the back room where Fionnuala kept the linen and he took an old sheet and the scissors. He wrapped a length of cloth around and around his hand, binding the fingers together from the tip to the wrist, and he had no feeling in them as he bound them tight. Once he had covered the hand entirely, he tied the ends in a knot pulling one end with his right hand and the other end sharply with his teeth.

The milking took him twice as long as it normally did. He struggled too getting the horse tethered to the trap, but she was old so she waited while he fumbled with the harness. He tilted the back end of the trap under the full tankard of milk and tried to wedge it underneath, but the tankard slipped under the sheet around his finger. It lurched and he thought that the milk from the morning and the night before would surely be lost. But he jumped and managed to catch it before it fell over onto the ground.

Jamesie Farrell passed on his trap on his way to the creamery and he saw Daragh's struggle with the tankard. At first he drove on but he thought better of it. He went back into the yard and helped lift the tankard onto Daragh's trap and led the horse out to the road. He saw the cloth on Daragh's hand, but he did not ask him about it.

When he went to her, Fionnuala's eyes had purple shadows under them and she could not get out of bed. She said, 'Daragh, will you ask Jamesie if you can take his boat out and bring me over to my mother to care for me. I feel so poorly.'

Daragh felt a heat in his body when he thought about the river.

'I suppose we could go by the road. I hear the river is flooded now—it's dangerous to go on it.'

'She lives right by the river on the other side—it'll take us two days to get to Killybrack on the road.'

'I'll take care of you,' he said, 'what need have you of your mother?' An anger and a shame and a fear flushed in his cheeks. In his head he heard himself say to John, 'You won't beat me to the Clare banks.'

But Fionnuala was saying, 'I'd row myself over, pregnant or not, if I wasn't sick.'

'You won't be going on any river,' he said, and he felt cold inside.

'I could do it I think,' she said and made to get up.

'Stay there—I'll ask Mairéad to come in and help you. I'll be back soon.'

Daragh slammed the door as he walked out and he tried to calm his breath as he passed through the black gates where Jamesie Farrell lived. Daragh walked through the yard to the house and knocked on the front door.

Mairéad heard the knock and she called to her sister Noreen. They looked out the window of the parlour at the man outside.

'That Daragh has a strange look on him—look at the shine on his bald head,' Noreen said.

'It glows bright like the moon,' Mairéad agreed.

Daragh saw the twitch of the curtain and he listened for the sound of steps to the door, but none came. He felt an anger in him that they were hiding from him, but then he looked at himself in the front window and he pulled his hat down further on his head and dragged up the collar of his jacket and he turned away from the picture of himself in the glass.

So he brought Fionnuala water and tea himself and he made her soup. But all the time the fear gnawed in his gut and he wondered what he would do.

Daragh dreamt that night that he was down by the river again and he was getting ready to race. John was not there to race him, it was Fionnuala and her belly was bigger, as if she was about to give birth. Every single one of her white teeth was gone from her head and her gums were black and shiny. 'Let's race,' she said, 'you want to race.' And he fought with her to change her mind, but she went into the water and was taken from him.

The next day Fionnuala tried to get out of the bed but her legs felt like water under her. So she called for her husband and she asked him to help her into the back room where she did her sewing.

Daragh shook as he helped her, but he knew not if it was from the fear of the promise, or the fear of what he would do to keep his promise.

He wondered if he could wait until Fionnuala was sleeping and if he could take a tooth from her then. But he saw how his own teeth clung firmly to his head and he knew she would wake. And he thought that if he gave her a feed of drink, then she surely would sleep and not rouse no matter how many teeth he took. And he walked into the parlour and he stood at the press and he looked at the golden gleam of the bottles within, but he could not do it and he felt a burn in him for the thoughts he was having. So he put on the kettle and he brought her tea into the back room where she sat mending a coat. When she looked up at him her face was pale and tight, but she saw the tea and she half-smiled at him. He still felt small and dark and he found that he could not linger in the room with her.

Daragh wondered if she had kept any of the teeth that had rotted and that she had lost before. So he searched the dresser in the kitchen and he searched the drawers in the bedroom but all he found was a lock of his own hair between the pages of her prayer book. He sat on the bed and the tears ran down his face and he felt a hot shame in him for thinking of taking a tooth from his wife.

Fionnuala sat in the room and heard the clatter in the kitchen and the bedroom. She forced herself not to think about what he was looking for, and to think only about how she could get herself across the river.

That night he could hardly sleep with the terror of what the woman would do to him if he had no tooth for her. He thrashed and he turned, for he dreamed that Fionnuala had borne him a thousand sons and that the faerie woman had taken them down to the river and had drowned them one by one.

On the morning of the third day Daragh woke with a churn in his belly and a heavy sickness in him. But Fionnuala felt a slight strength return to her and she was able to make her way into the kitchen unaided.

At the table Daragh's cup rattled off his saucer for he could hardly hold it steady in his hand. Fionnuala looked up at the noise he was making but she did not say anything and she continued to eat her breakfast.

Daragh finally told her a story:

'I met a beggar man walking the roads yesterday. O'Meara was his name. He was blind and he carried his home on his back,' Daragh reached for his tea and drank an enormous swallow. 'And he asked me for a tooth—of a woman.' He loosed the top button on his collar for it had tightened around him.

The lump of bread in Fionnuala's mouth grew large and threatened to fill her throat entirely. She felt a flush in her face and a heat in her veins.

'And who would have any value in a tooth, unless it was in his own head?' she asked.

'That's true,' Daragh said, 'but this man O'Meara has more value in a tooth than in a drink or a woman or a coin or a prayer.'

'Well, it's crazy he is then,' said Fionnuala and her anger grew in her so that she felt she could no longer sit at the table and suddenly her legs had strength and they held her as she stood up and began to clear her plate away although the food was still piled on it.

'Indeed, but he is a good man, and in need of help,' Daragh said and his face glowed red and the sweat rolled down him as he twisted in his seat.

Fionnuala stopped the clearing. She came around the table to Daragh and she put her face close to his and she hissed at him, 'If you are so fond of this man O'Meara, then maybe it is your own tooth you should be giving him?'

She turned away from him and the din she made clearing the table and washing the delph would have woken the dead themselves.

So Daragh walked out to the shed and he sat there in the dark and he tried to still his mind. But his mind jumped and bucked in his head and so he left the shed and walked down the road towards Ballyowen Cross.

Chrissy Dwyer saw him coming towards her with the eyes wild in his head and she turned off the road into Ryan's house although she had no business there, because she was afraid to cross him. And Daragh spent the day walking the roads, kicking the stones in front of him into the ditch. But each stone was a tooth in his mind and it brought him no peace.

Finally as the sky was filled with the redness of the dying sun, he went back to the shed and he got some twine from the bale and he tied one end around the latch on the door and he tied the other end around a tooth in the back of his head.

He kicked the door closed with all of the pain and anger and fear in him and the tug on his tooth loosed it from his mouth and the blood came too and he shouted with the pain. But he scrambled on the ground to find the tooth, so he would not lose it in the gloom of the shed.

He wrapped an old coat around himself and he went out to the yard where he sat with the tooth wrapped in a handkerchief and waited for the woman to come.

He felt a familiar fluttering in his chest and a roaring in his ears. He thought then of the body of his brother rotting in his grave, not a half a mile away and he felt a blackness fall in front of his eyes so that he could not see. A small voice inside his head said to him, 'Be still' and he tried to tell himself it was the black blood inside him that made him think these thoughts. But still he shook.

The woman appeared shining white and gleaming in the night. His heart and body shook and his hand closed in around the handkerchief. He felt the hunger in him again and he was weak with it. The thought of no blood filled him with fear, but he saw too the price he had paid and would pay for it, and he felt he would surely drown in the blackness that covered him.

He stood and faced her. 'Here is the tooth,' he said and handed her the cloth.

The woman clasped the tooth to her and she weighed it in her hand and she felt the heft of it.

Her face grew dark until her cheeks were slate, and her eyes grew large and black. She held the tooth in front of him and crushed it to dust between her thumb and forefinger.

The woman's hair flew around her head and she roared at him, 'Do not attempt to trick me, Daragh Maguire! You shall pay three times for this. I shall claim this tooth and all the others in your head!'

Daragh opened his mouth with the pain that struck him and each of his teeth fell from his head and pelted like hailstones off the gravel.

'For the second: you shall not see me again, although you will cry out for me and covet my blood and although your body will scream for it. I shall not return,' the woman continued.

The gut jumped in Daragh's body and he felt it in his flesh and blood and bone and muscle, and his body twisted and turned, for it loved the black blood she had given him.

She said, 'The third is that your son and all of his sons and their sons to follow shall be–'

But the woman did not finish, because Fionnuala came out from the shadows of the door of the house. Daragh saw her and his heart fell and he said to her, 'Stay away from this woman, she is no good, go back inside.'

Fionnuala felt a shake in her but she came towards the woman and she thrust her hand in her left pocket and she pulled out a fistful of hair. And she put her hand in her right pocket and she pulled out the nails from her husband's hand and she waved them at the woman and she said to her, 'I have hair and nails from my husband too, and they were freely given with nothing asked for in return. You have taken enough from this house. Now be on your way.'

The woman's face blackened and she said, 'I have no value in these things,' and she blew a breath from her mouth. And the breath grew to a wind that blew the hair and nails from Fionnuala's hands.

The woman said, 'Your husband promised me something which he did not bring to me. And so he must pay in another way.' The woman bared her yellow teeth.

'Here is the payment that you wanted,' Fionnuala moved forward again and she opened her hand and held out a tooth, which was smaller than the one that Daragh had given.

The woman took the tooth and she felt the heft of it in her hand.

Fionnuala felt the pain in her mouth, as the woman claimed her tooth, but she said, 'You have been given what you asked for. You have no claim to ask for more than that.'

The woman nodded and she put the tooth in the bag she carried at her hip. Her light began to fade and her form vanished in the night.

Daragh stuttered and stammered to her but Fionnuala did not heed his speech. She walked down the road to the river and she pulled Jamesie Farrell's boat free from its mooring, and she rowed across the water to the house of her parents as she had promised.

And Daragh Maguire lived out his days in the shell of the house that his wife had left, with only the collection of his own teeth in a jar on the dresser for company.

Notes on the Authors

Ragnar Almqvist was born in Dublin. He is a graduate of University College Dublin and Trinity College, where he was awarded an M. Phil in Creative Writing. He has been published in the literary anthology *Incorrigibly Plural* and was longlisted for the People's College Short Story Competition.

Evelyn Conlon is the author of three novels, her most recent being *Skin of Dreams* (Brandon, 2003). Her latest collection of short stories, *Telling: New and Selected Stories*, was published by Blackstaff. She has compiled and edited four other books and her work has been widely anthologised and translated. She is presently completing a fourth novel.

Danny Denton is originally from Cork and completed an MA in Writing at NUI Galway. He has published work in *The Stinging Fly*, *Southword*, *The Sharp Review*, and *The Galway Historical and Archaeological Society Journal*, and is currently working on his first novel, *The Golden Road*.

Damien Doorley was born in Galway and grew up in England. He lives in London, and is working on a collection of short stories. His piece 'North Circular' appeared in *The Dublin Review*, Spring 2008.

Michael J. Farrell grew up in the Irish midlands. One of his careers was a quarter century of journalism in the USA. His novel *Papabile* won the Thorpe Menn Award in 1998. His stories have appeared here and there, for example, in *The Faber Book of Best New Irish Short Stories 2006-2007*. A collection will be published by The Stinging Fly Press early next year.

Mia Gallagher's acclaimed debut novel *HellFire* (Penguin Ireland, 2006) received the Irish Tatler Women of the Year Literature Award and is being translated into Portuguese and Italian. Her short stories have been published in Ireland, the UK and the USA and she has also written for theatre and TV.

D. Gleeson lives in Dublin. This is her first published work. Thanks to Sean O'Reilly and all in the Stinging Fly fiction workshop, and to Holly and the Skywriters for workshopping parts of this story.

Rosemary Jenkinson is from Belfast. A collection of her short stories, *Contemporary Problems Nos. 53 & 54* was published by Lagan Press. Her plays include 'The Bonefire,' winner of the Stewart Parker BBC Radio Award 2007, which was produced by Rough Magic and 'The Winners' by Ransom Productions.

James Lawless was born in Dublin and now lives in Kildare. His story, 'Jolt', was selected by Zadie Smith for the anthology *New Short Stories 1* (Willesden Herald, 2007). His first novel, *Peeling Oranges*, was published in 2007 by Killynon House Books.

Colm Liddy lives in Clare with a kind-hearted wife and several rascally children. His stories have been rejected by many periodicals and never been shortlisted for a prize. Then one day, he met a leprechaun who made him a deal. 'The Bride is Crying..." is from his forthcoming book *40 Fights between Husband & Wife* to be published by Penguin Ireland in Spring 2009.

Viv McDade was born in Northern Ireland, grew up in Zimbabwe and lived in Cape Town and Amsterdam before moving back to Ireland. She is currently studying for an M. Phil in Creative Writing at Trinity College. Viv lives in Dublin where she is working on a collection of stories.

Emer Martin is from Dublin. Having lived in Paris, London, the Middle East, and various places in the USA, she now lives in the jungles of County Meath. She is the author of three novels: *Breakfast in Babylon* (1996), *More Bread Or I'll Appear* (1999) and *Baby Zero* (2007).

Gina Moxley is a performer and playwright. Two of her plays have been published by Faber. Her radio play 'Marrying Dad' will be broadcast by RTE this autumn. She graduated from Trinity's M. Phil in Creative Writing in 2007.

Helena Nolan is a member of Yvonne Cullen's Writing Group (dublinwriters. net). Her poems have been published in the anthology *All Good Things Begin* and in *The Stinging Fly* (Featured Poet, Winter 2007) and short-listed for the FISH Prize, 2006 & 2007. She is currently completing a Masters in Creative Writing at UCD. This is her first published short story.

Jim O'Donoghue grew up in Nottingham and lives in Brighton, UK. His poem 'Unmarried brunette on the London train' was included in the Arvon International Poetry Prize anthology for 2006. 'Carson's Trail' is his first published fiction.

Dónal O'Sullivan is a native of Ardfield, West Cork. After completing a Master's Degree in French at UCC in 1997, he lived and worked abroad for several years. He works as a freelance writer and is also writing a novel.

Breda Wall Ryan has an M. Phil in Creative Writing. Her stories appear in *The New Hennessy Book of Irish Fiction, The Faber Book of Best New Irish Short Stories 2006-2007,* and other publications. She was shortlisted for a Hennessy Literary Award for Fiction, The Davy Byrnes Irish Writing Award and The Francis MacManus Short Story Award.

Ingo Schulze was born in Dresden in 1962, studied classical philology at the University of Jena, worked in Altenburg as a dramaturge and newspaper editor. He was awarded the aspekte Literary Prize for his first book, *33 Moments of Happiness* (1998). For *Simple Stories* (2000), he received the Berlin Prize for Literature. His major novel, *New Lives* (2005) will be published this autumn by Alfred A. Knopf. In 2007 he was awarded the Leipzig Book Fair Prize. His books have been translated into 27 languages. [**John E. Woods** is the translator of the three Ingo Schulze titles listed above and many other books, most notably: Arno Schmidt's *Evening Edged in Gold*; Patrick Süskind's *Perfume*; Christoph Ransmayr's *Terrors of Ice and Darkness, The Last World,* and *The Dog King*; Thomas Mann's *Buddenbrooks, The Magic Mountain, Doctor Faustus,* and *Joseph and His Brothers*. He lives in Berlin.]

Tom Tierney lives in Skerries in County Dublin and works as a teacher. He has written a Physics text book and his stories have been published in *The Stinging Fly* and in *Mr. Beller's Neighborhood*. He is currently working on a novel.

William Wall is the author of four novels, one of which, *This Is The Country,* was longlisted for the 2005 Man Booker prize, two volumes of poetry, and most recently, a collection of short fiction entitled *No Paradiso* (Brandon, 2006). He lives in Cork.

Acknowledgements

The editor would like to thank Emily Firetog, Caroline Key, Paul Leyden, Louise McCaul, Brendan Mac Evilly and Kevin Power for helping him read through and shortlist the original submissions. Emily Firetog assisted in copy editing the selected stories while Ailbhe Darcy and Sarah O'Connor took on the task of proofreading the manuscript. Thanks also to Philip Ó Ceallaigh for kick-starting the introduction, and to Maria Behan for helping to beat it into shape.

Fergal Condon is the man who makes our book covers look as good as they do. Thanks are due to him and to Peadar O'Donoghue for the photography.

The book's title and epigraph come from Mr Leonard Cohen and Ms Sharon Robinson. Long may they reign! Thanks to them for their songs and for allowing us to borrow their words. The lyrics are reprinted with kind permission of Leonard Cohen (Sony/ATV Publishing) and Sharon Robinson (Sharon Robinson Songs (ASCAP), Sharonrobinsonmusic.com).

The Stinging Fly would like to express its gratitude to the various individuals and organisations, who continue to support our endeavours by offering us their time, energy, goodwill and financial assistance.

Also available from the Stinging Fly Press

Watermark
by Sean O'Reilly
First published May 2005
152pp €10.00 ISBN 978-09550152-1-2

A tale of one woman's obsession and longing, *Watermark* is the stark, powerful fourth book from the acclaimed Derry-born author whose other titles include *Love and Sleep* and *The Swing of Things*.

'a devotee of innovative and complex prose who is simultaneously one of our least condescending writers... Read and reread and reach for your superlatives: in all senses, *Watermark* is a sheer physical experience.'
—*The Irish Times*

'People who think poetry or poetically-charged prose should be all positive thoughts will have a rollercoaster ride of it here. But poetry this certainly is, and not despite but because of its earthiness, its earthedness, its refusal to look away. This short, uncomfortable, sometimes brutal, hugely important book is a triumph.'
—*The Irish Independent*

visit www.stingingfly.org

These Are Our Lives
Declan Meade (editor)
First published July 2006
203pp €12.00 ISBN 978-0-9550152-2-9

The first anthology from the Stinging fly Press offers twenty-two short stories from an exciting mix of Irish and international authors. Writers include David Albahari, Kevin Barry, Claire Keegan, Toby Litt, Martin Malone, Nuala Ní Chonchúir and Philip Ó Ceallaigh, alongside a host of the finest new writing talent.

'...elegant, attractively packaged collection... it offers superior value and grittier, more modern fare than Picador's recently published *Shots* collection.'
—*Village Magazine*

'Certainly the editor of this collection is aware of the short story's endless possibilities in the contemporary moment... a celebration of new voices in fiction, sprinkled, too, with some more established names... a collection worth having.'
—*The Irish Times*

visit www.stingingfly.org

There Are Little Kingdoms
Stories by Kevin Barry
Winner of the 2007 Rooney Prize for Irish Literature
First published March 2007
154pp €9.99 ISBN 978-09550152-9-8

Fast girls cool their heels on a slow night in a small town; a bewildered
man steps off a country bus in search of his identity; lonesome
hillwalkers take to the high reaches in hope of a saving embrace. These
are just three of the scenarios played out in Kevin Barry's wonderfully
imagined and riotously entertaining short stories.

'Kevin Barry's immensely entertaining debut collection of stories
is filled with compelling characters, each of them fleshed out by
his pungent power of description.'
—*The Sunday Business Post*

'a collection of vibrant, original, and intelligent short stories…'
—*The Irish Times*

*All Stinging Fly Press titles, including the magazine, can be purchased online from
our website. They can also be ordered in any bookshop within Ireland and the UK
by quoting the title and the ISBN. Our titles are distributed to the trade by
Columba Mercier Distribution. If you experience any difficulty in finding our
books, please email us at stingingfly@gmail.com.*